THE TWICEBORN QUEEN

MARINA FINLAYSON

FINESSE SOLUTIONS

Cover design by Karri Klawiter
Formatting by Polgarus Studio

Published by Finesse Solutions Pty Ltd
2017/12

Author's note: This book was written and produced in Australia and uses British/Australian spelling conventions, such as "colour" instead of "color", and "-ise" endings instead of "-ize" on words like "realise"

National Library of Australia Cataloguing-in-Publication entry:

Finlayson, Marina, author.
The twiceborn queen / Marina Finlayson.
ISBN 978-0-9942391-1-2 (paperback)
Finlayson, Marina. Proving; Book 2
Paranormal fiction, Australian.
A823.4

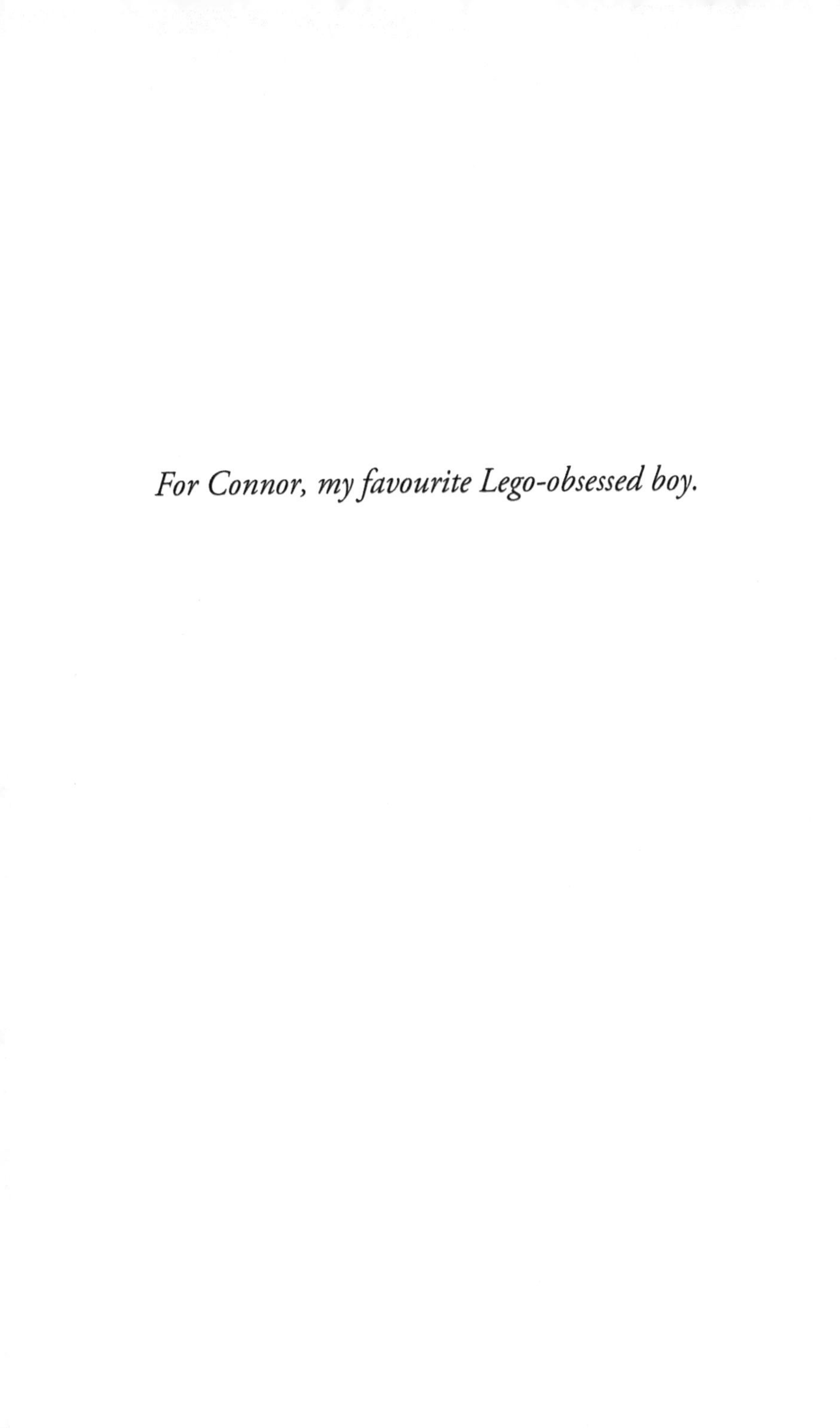

For Connor, my favourite Lego-obsessed boy.

CHAPTER ONE

They say hindsight is 20:20 vision, but still I can't help that niggling feeling, the one that whispers that I should have known. Mothers are supposed to have ESP, right? Or at least eyes in the backs of their heads. There must have been some sign that things weren't right, some little clue to tip me off, if only I'd been paying more attention. But I was still high on happiness, my world one giant bubble of joy, and the only thing I was paying much attention to was how good my son's hot little head felt nestled under my chin.

I was so happy I'd forgotten bubbles always burst.

The chief reason for my happiness sat on my lap, his attention riveted by the small TV that hung from the ceiling. His sweaty curls tickled my chin as we squished together into the visitor chair by the side of the bed. Like hospital rooms everywhere, this one was cramped and smelled of disinfectant and sick people.

The window showed a grey day outside, with a light summer rain falling. Other wings of the hospital stretched off to the left and right, with the multi-storey car park hulking in all its concrete glory in the distance. Not a view to lift anyone's spirits, but mine were in no need of lifting.

I hugged Lachie a little tighter and he wriggled in protest—though he didn't take his eyes off the TV. Typical. Screens of any sort have a magnetic attraction for ten-year-old boys. After seven months of believing him dead, I had my boy back. I'd been to his funeral, spent months in a hell no mother should ever have to go through, all courtesy of his father's scheming—and now, here he was, alive after all. Talk about a miracle. The parting of the Red Sea had nothing on it. Not even the thought of my ex and the pain he'd caused me could dent my bright new happiness.

The other reason for my smiles lay in the hospital bed asleep, looking like a Greek god with his curly dark hair and chiselled jaw. I shifted one hand to cover his big one where it rested on the crisp white sheet. Ben had suffered nearly as much from Jason's scheming as I had, knowing that Lachie was alive but unable to tell me. Jason had promised to kill Ben's own nieces if he gave me even a hint that I was grieving for nothing.

Dragons. Such a class act.

"Hey, look, Mum!" Lachie's bony little elbow nudged me. "It's you again."

"Uh-huh."

The TV replayed the footage from New Year's Eve. Like half the population of the planet, I'd seen this footage at least a dozen times in the last few days, but I watched again, fascinated by the sinuous curves of dragon necks and tails, the power of those golden wings as the two fantastic creatures swooped and soared over Sydney Harbour in their deadly battle.

Seeing yourself like that was strange—especially when you hadn't even known dragons existed a week ago.

And now I was one.

"I'm glad you killed her," Lachie said as the dragons on the TV dived into that last fatal plunge toward the water.

That had been one terrifying moment. Valeria was bigger and stronger than me, but I'd been fighting not only for my own life but Lachie's too. I'd only just discovered Lachie was still alive, and I was damned if I was going to lose him again.

I put everything I had into protecting him. And when I say everything, I mean *everything*. A few days earlier, Valeria's sister Leandra had managed to colonise my body in a last-ditch attempt to cheat death. She'd been fighting me for control ever since. But when I realised only her strength could save Lachie, I'd let her win, never expecting to be me again.

God knows why I was still here—whoever "I" was now.

"Me too," I said as the dragons on the screen disappeared into the harbour in a gigantic fountaining of water. Was I a dragon or a human now? Did I have one soul or two? I still felt like Kate—but I felt like Leandra too. I had two sets of memories, but only one purpose: do whatever it took to keep Lachie safe.

Maybe that had unified us. I couldn't feel Leandra as a separate presence any more. That had been one crazy week as we fought for control of the body. Poor Garth had never quite known who he was talking to.

The big werewolf was another reason to smile—he'd been a true friend at a time when friends were pretty thin on the ground. Strange how quickly things could change. The first time we met he'd been trying to kill me. Now he was waiting at home, probably watching the clock, too. The guy fussed over me more than I did over Lachie.

Ben's fingers twitched under mine, then turned to clasp my hand.

I leaned in for a kiss. "Hey, sleepyhead."

"Hey, yourself." His dark eyes warmed with a smile.

"How are you feeling?"

"Why don't you feel for yourself?"

I rolled my eyes. "I prefer my men with slightly fewer bandages."

"Can't blame a bloke for trying." He shrugged, then tried to hide the resulting wince.

His arm was swathed in heavy bandaging. Jason had done his best to take it right off in the fighting at Valeria's mansion on New Year's Eve. In fact he'd meant to kill me, as I lay defenceless and half-dead on the ground, but Ben had leapt between us and taken the blow instead. The doctors weren't sure whether Ben would ever regain full use of the arm, but frankly he was lucky even to be alive.

He sat up, his tanned skin dark against the bleached white of the hospital sheets, and I propped pillows behind his back.

"How's my main man?" he asked Lachie.

"Good."

"Look at Uncle Ben when he's talking to you."

He dragged his gaze from the TV and made an effort to remember his manners.

"Good, thanks. Is your arm feeling better?"

"Much better." Liar. "Are you looking after your mum for me?"

"She's got Garth for that."

Ben frowned but said nothing. He was having trouble adjusting to the changes in my life and the new people in it. Sometimes I thought he didn't believe I'd actually turned into a dragon on New Year's Eve. After all, he'd been a bleeding mess on the ground when it happened, so you could understand him being kind of distracted. Yet there was the evidence, in glorious technicolour on his TV screen, replayed at least once an hour. January was a slow news time of year, and news stories didn't get much bigger than this.

TV, newspapers, magazines, the Internet—*especially* the Internet—had exploded with speculation. *Dragons are real! Giant hoax over Sydney Harbour! Secret government experiments! Supernatural wars threaten civilisation!* The headline writers would wear out their exclamation mark keys if they weren't careful. And that was before we even got started on the mounting speculation as to what other types of supernatural creatures might turn out to be real or, my personal favourite, whether little green aliens were about to invade.

As far as I knew, little green aliens were off the menu, but just about everything else was fair game—perhaps even more than the wildest speculations. No one mentioned goblins, for instance, and I'd seen plenty of those. Or at least Leandra had.

Having someone else's memories that seemed as real to you as your own could get confusing.

Vampires and werewolves were the main object of fascination, and they were certainly both real. My new best friend Garth was a werewolf. He was alternately revolted and amused by the speculation about his kind. Some people would have jumped his hunky werewolf bones at the first hint of his shifter nature. Others were too busy sharpening the pitchforks and axes. On the whole I think he preferred Option B. You didn't want to mention *Twilight* around him.

Some talking head on the TV was calling for the establishment of a centre for paranormal research, "to enhance our understanding of the weird and wonderful creatures living among us". Right. God knows how he thought that would work—we "paranormal creatures" didn't tend to leave evidence of our presence lying around for humans to find. Navy divers had been all over the harbour in the last few days, searching in vain for any sign of the giant dragon corpse that should have been lurking in its depths. But of course they found nothing. Valeria had returned to her human form in death, and there was no reason, other than coincidental timing, for the police to link the body of the naked woman they'd pulled from the water with the death of the dragon.

"Elizabeth must be beside herself," Ben said, one eye on the TV.

I was pretty sure "beside herself" wouldn't even begin to cover my dear mother's emotions. The shifter world had been hidden from humans for centuries, and that was just the way she liked it. As one of the eight dragon queens who divided the world between them, she was accustomed to having things arranged to suit herself. I'd heard nothing directly from her, but the waiting was killing me. If the other shoe dropped, it was going to make a hell of a noise. She'd killed shifters before, for breaking the great taboo against taking trueshape where humans might see. And that was just for isolated incidents. It didn't get much more public than what Valeria and I had done. The shifter world had its arse well and truly hanging out. Valeria was dead and beyond her reach, but what she might do to me had me tossing and turning at night. She wouldn't give a damn that Valeria had instigated the whole thing.

Ben turned his full attention to me. "Have you got somewhere safe to stay?"

"We're at my old place in The Rocks. Leandra's old place." God, this was doing my head in. I/me, she/we: I had to find a way to keep it all straight in my mind. "Garth rounded up a handful of … *her* old thralls, enough to keep the place secure."

I hadn't enthralled them again, though. I'd had some personal experience with the terrible foggy state of mind being enthralled produced. Sure, you got unquestioning loyalty. Thralls could follow orders like champions, but thinking for themselves wasn't part of the deal. With everything in such a state of flux, a certain liveliness in the wits department seemed like a better option.

And besides, enslaving people didn't sit as easily with me as it used to when I was Leandra.

"You should find somewhere less obvious." His face was drawn, whether with pain or worry, I couldn't tell. Probably a bit of both. "Everyone knows where she lived."

Ben, at least, had no difficulty speaking of Leandra as separate and dead. He glanced at Lachie, as if he would have liked to say more, but didn't want to alarm him. Ben didn't have kids of his own, or he would have known: we could have planned a detailed moon landing, or the assassination of the Pope. As long as the TV was on, Lachie wouldn't take the slightest bit of notice.

"You worry too much. If Elizabeth hasn't acted by now, she's probably just going to let the proving run its course, and hope Alicia does the job for her." Maybe if I said it with enough conviction it'd turn out to be true.

I glanced sidelong at Lachie. Yep, Pope-assassination time. Even if he'd been paying attention, I doubt he knew what the proving was. I sure wasn't planning on telling him. He didn't need to know his mum was one of the last two players left standing in a fight to the death to see who would be the next queen of Oceania after Elizabeth died.

"Don't underestimate her. God, I can't wait to get out of here. I feel so useless lying in this bed."

I leaned in and cupped his stubbly cheek in my hand. "Didn't the doctor say you'd be out by Monday? Just a couple more days. You'll be back in the shop in no time."

"Fu—forget the shop!" He caught himself with a guilty glance at Lachie and lowered his voice. "I don't give a rat's arse about the stupid shop. It's you I'm worried about."

"Well, you should be worried about it. You can't exactly be a herald any more, can you?"

Heralds were the couriers of the shifter world, running messages between sometimes warring parties with guaranteed neutrality and dedication to the task. Now Ben had thrown in his lot with me, no one would trust him to be neutral for a second. There went most of his income.

And I certainly wouldn't let any man of mine walk willingly into enemy territory. Valeria had already proved that some shifters had absolutely no respect for the rules when it came to the safety of heralds. Ben may as well have painted a target on his back when he hopped into my bed.

Although, to be fair, it had been more me jumping him than the other way around. Not that he'd been exactly reluctant, mind you.

"No, I can't." He shut his eyes for a moment, long enough for me to admire the long sweep of lashes against his cheek. He still looked good enough to eat, despite the bandages. He couldn't get well soon enough for me. "I spoke to Mel today."

"Oh? How is she?"

He turned an intense gaze on me. "I told her to take the girls and leave town."

"Surely that's not necessary?"

Jason had forced Ben to keep Lachie's survival secret by threatening the lives of his sister Mel's two little girls. But not even Jason, wherever he was, would be concerned that the secret was out now. He had way bigger things to worry about.

"Just taking precautions. Elizabeth can't be very pleased with me. Who knows what she'll do?"

"Probably nothing." Leandra's memories of her mother weren't very complimentary. Like most dragons, the woman was bone lazy, with a sense of entitlement bigger than Sydney Harbour. True, she did take a dim view of certain things, like threats to the queen's peace—it made more work for her—or shifters taking trueshape in front of humans—ditto—but my guess was she'd see Ben's defection from the ranks of the heralds as a move in the proving. Queens rarely interfered in that traditional battle between their royal offspring. They had no maternal feelings at all, and were happy to sit back as their daughters died, waiting to see who proved the strongest. "It would be out of character for her to use Mel as a means to get revenge on you."

"But not impossible. Better to be safe than sorry. The situation at the moment is pretty volatile."

You could say that again. And dragons could be unpredictable. I wouldn't put it past Elizabeth to decide to punish me through Ben. I had Garth or one of the thralls—ex-thralls—stationed in the hallway outside Ben's room most times when I wasn't visiting, just in case. Not that I told Ben that. "I'll be glad when we can get you out of here."

"It'll be nice to sleep in my own bed again."

"You mean my bed." I grinned at him. The thought had a certain appeal. "I need you somewhere I can keep an eye on you."

He didn't smile back. "I can look after myself."

He sounded like Lachie in a sulk.

"With one arm in a sling?"

"I only need one arm to use a gun." His mouth set in a mulish line.

Lachie looked our way. Must have been an ad break. "Are you two fighting?"

Maybe I had raised my voice a little. "Of course not, Monster. Just discussing things."

Clearly I wasn't convincing. Or maybe the scowl on Ben's face gave it away. He turned a serious gaze on Ben. "You shouldn't argue with Mum, Uncle Ben. She always wins."

Damn right, kid. God, I loved that boy.

Ben didn't crack a smile. His good hand picked at the sheet in a frustrated motion. "I hate hospitals."

That was when the nurse bustled in, rushed off her feet as they always seemed to be. Her name was Amy, or Amanda, or something. She was one of the regulars who'd been looking after Ben, a slight, dark-haired woman who somehow seemed to find the muscle to manhandle him with no trouble.

"How's your pain?" In typical nurse fashion she gave him no chance to answer before giving her thermometer a professional flick and shoving it under his tongue.

"Goob," he mumbled.

She consulted the chart hanging on the end of his bed. "It's four hours since your last painkillers. You can have another dose if you need it."

"I'b fine," he insisted, still with that mulish look on his face. Probably wouldn't admit to any discomfort unless his arm was about to fall off.

She bustled about, and rattled the blood pressure machine closer to the bed. I set Lachie on his feet and squeezed past her to give her some room to move.

She smiled. "Thanks. Oops!"

My handbag hit the floor as she brushed past. It had been hanging on the back of the chair. She scooped it up and handed it to me, then whipped the thermometer out of Ben's mouth, all in one fluid move.

"Come on, Lachie." It was getting late. "Uncle Ben looks tired."

And grumpy. He made a bad patient—one of those annoying people who never get sick. Probably last time he'd been in hospital was the day he was born, and he wasn't dealing well with the whole confined-to-bed-being-weak-and-helpless thing.

I kissed him goodnight and hustled Lachie out into the hall while the nurse was still making notes on the chart. We marched down the sterile corridor, Lachie's small hand warm in mine.

Once we left the air-conditioned hospital the heat hit us in the face like a wet sock. Beautiful Sydney, so humid in summer it was like walking round inside a sauna some days. The earlier rain had cleared, leaving the evening air hot and sticky as we trudged to the multi-storey car park.

I'd got as far as the ticket machine and started scrabbling around in my purse for change to pay for parking when I realised that something else was missing.

"Where the hell are my car keys?"

I stared at Lachie as if I expected him to pull them out of his ear.

"Did you drop them?"

Maybe. My bag had hit the floor, and Amy or Amanda or whatever her name was had snatched it up so fast half my belongings could have been left behind. The keys were probably still under the bed.

"Come on. Let's go back."

The lift seemed to take ages to arrive, and then we had to wait for an old lady on a walking frame to stagger her way in and dither over which button to push. I forced myself to breathe deeply and smile at her. I seemed much more impatient since Leandra and I had merged—or whatever had happened. Clearly she hadn't been the kind to suffer fools gladly. I had to make a conscious effort not to let her attitudes colour my view on life.

We hurried down the corridor on Ben's level, my heels tapping an impatient rhythm on the vinyl floor. His door was shut, and I threw it open without knocking.

Amy/Amanda stood there, holding a pillow over Ben's face.

For one astonished moment I stared, unmoving. Ben thrashed wildly, his feet drumming against the mattress, the sheet tangled around his legs. The nurse stared back at me, her face showing no emotion. She might have been still taking his temperature instead of trying to kill him.

Then I spun, shoving Lachie out into the corridor. "Nurses' station! Quick, get help!"

I slammed the door on him and dived straight across the bed, hands outstretched for the woman's throat. She sidestepped with a single-minded focus on the job that chilled me to the bone. Ben's struggles were growing weaker. He made surprisingly little noise. No one passing in the corridor would guess a man was fighting for his life in here.

"Get off him, you bitch!" I snarled, rolling off the bed.

I threw a punch that would have taken her head off if she hadn't dodged it, still without releasing the pillow. Desperate,

I swept the water jug off the rolling portable table and slammed it into her face. That knocked her aside at last, and I snatched the pillow and threw it into the corner of the room.

Ben lurched up off the bed and heaved in desperate breaths, his face bright red. I only had time for a quick glance before the nurse scrambled upright and launched herself at me. A knife appeared in her hand as if by magic, and I sidestepped just in time. Neat party trick. I guess we were lucky she'd gone the pillow route first, or Ben would be dead already. Probably trying to make it look more natural. Hacking someone up with a knife did tend to raise a few questions.

I kicked out, catching her in the knee—always a good strategy in a fight. It's hard to run with a busted kneecap.

She was strong, though, and it barely slowed her. Behind me Ben half-staggered, half-fell off the bed, and I heard the ding of the nurse-call button. Wouldn't want to be the poor nurse answering that call. You expect a request for a bedpan and you walk in on a knife fight.

She bared her teeth in a savage grin and circled round, trying to get between me and the door. Closer to Ben.

"Who the hell are you?" Not just Amy/Amanda the nurse, obviously. But she wasn't a shifter, or I would have been able to see her aura. One of the perks of being a dragon—only we could see the coloured glow that surrounded each shifter. I backed away. As far as I could anyway. The room was barely big enough for visiting in, much less staging hand-to-hand combat. She must be on somebody's payroll. "Who sent you?"

She said nothing. I watched her eyes and backed up as far as I was willing to go, watching for her next move, trying to plan my own. I could feel Ben right behind me. I hunched over a little, trying to look non-threatening, maybe a little scared—though if she knew who I was that probably wasn't going to fly. Worth a try, though.

She feinted with the knife and I flinched back, waiting for the real move. I opened myself to the other, felt the familiar welcoming tug of trueshape. My breast warmed as the channel stone inside me flared with the magic of transformation. Only a little, though. This room wasn't big enough to hold a full-sized dragon even if I wanted to go all the way. A little was all I needed.

I heard running feet in the corridor, and Lachie's voice shrieking, "Mum!"

She lunged as my eyes flicked toward the sound, sure she'd caught me off guard. Instead my claws burst from my fingertips, as long as swords but stronger than any steel. I'd slashed her throat before she'd even realised what was happening.

Behind me Ben gave a strangled cry as blood sprayed from her throat. As I retracted my claws the door burst open behind me. She fell against me, then the knife slipped from her hand and she collapsed at my feet.

A woman screamed, and I turned to find two horrified nurses staring at me, with Lachie desperately trying to see around them.

"You killed her! You killed Amy."

"Keep him out! Don't let him see." I sank to my knees on the bloody floor, only now beginning to shake. What the hell was *that*? Like a faint yellow mist rising from the body? "She attacked us. Out of nowhere. She was trying to kill Ben!"

The first nurse hesitated, her face a mask of shock. "Amy would never … Why would she …" She swallowed hard, glancing between me and the body on the floor, and pulled herself together with an effort. "Are you hurt?" Then, to the other nurse: "Where the hell is security?"

She knelt beside me and tried to urge me to my feet. I must have looked a sight, spattered in blood, hair across my face like a madwoman. Ben said something to the other woman, who nodded and drew Lachie gently away.

The door snicked shut behind them. No sign now of the yellow mist. Had I imagined it? Everything had happened so fast. I gave the nurse a brief, mainly true version of events.

She kept shaking her head, her eyes drawn over and over again to the body of her co-worker on the floor, as if she couldn't make sense of my story. I was having trouble myself. If she wasn't a shifter, how was she connected to the shifter world? It wasn't as if shifters had human moles planted all through the community, just in case they needed to assassinate someone. Not even a dragon like Elizabeth had that kind of reach.

Could it be a goblin seeming? One of Elizabeth's people— or even Alicia's—wearing a borrowed face to get close to us? In which case things were going to get mighty interesting when the spell wore off and the dead body suddenly looked like someone else. But it was the best explanation I could come up with.

I finished by saying I'd accidentally cut the woman's throat as we struggled over the knife. The nurse didn't even bother to take the would-be killer's pulse. It was painfully obvious she no longer had one.

"The police will be here soon. It will be all right," the nurse kept saying, though the expression on her face said different. Clearly she was having trouble imagining how anything could be all right in a world where such strange and random slayings could occur. She wrapped me in a blanket, as if she expected me to go into shock. The poor woman looked as though she needed it more than I did.

I tried my best to act shocked, but now the danger was past I felt nothing but the deepest satisfaction. That woman had threatened my mate, and if I could kill her again I would.

Perhaps that was the most shocking thing of all.

CHAPTER TWO

We spent two more hours at the hospital, answering the questions of every uniform that went past, watching the parade of police and hospital staff coming and going. Photographers and forensics, and whole hordes of other people whose jobs I couldn't even guess at, made their way into the room, then reappeared, checking me out as they went past as if they couldn't quite believe what I'd done. The nurses gave me a wide berth, though eventually one came with a wheelchair and took Ben off to be examined, ignoring his protests that he was fine.

A uniformed officer showed me to a tiny room that boasted a ripped-up couch and a microwave that had seen better days, then lurked uncomfortably outside the door. I'd cleaned the blood off my face and hands, though my clothes were a mess, and I sat, still wrapped in my blanket, with Lachie on my lap. His head drooped onto my shoulder—by now it was close to nine o'clock at night, and high time he was in bed.

The cop at the door stood up straighter as someone appeared: a small hard woman in plain clothes. She waved him away with a flick of the hand that spoke of authority and entered the room. A large man followed her.

"Good evening. I'm Detective Hartley and this is Detective Franks. I'm sorry for the delay; we got here as fast as we could. We'd like you to come with us to the station."

I eyed her suspiciously. She wore no jewellery apart from a wedding ring, but her dark trouser suit looked expensive. That, combined with her confident air, gave the impression she was higher up the food chain than the people I'd already spoken to. "Why? Are you arresting me?"

"No. We just want to do an interview while the details are still fresh in your mind."

"Can't it wait until tomorrow?"

Her polite expression didn't change, but a sharpness entered her voice. "A woman has died here, Ms O'Connor. I think that warrants a little inconvenience."

I nodded and went to find Ben, Lachie slumped against my shoulder like a drugged monkey, arms and legs dangling. He was really too big to carry around like a toddler, but I didn't care. I couldn't get enough of him, the weight and shape and feel of him in my arms, half-afraid he might disappear from my life again if I let him go.

The lights were still on in the corridors, but most of the rooms were in darkness. Blue-grey vinyl floors stretched ahead of us, empty now that visiting hours were over. I followed the sound of voices to the nurses' station and found Ben in a small waiting area next to it, his face grey with fatigue in the stark light. He still wore his pyjamas.

"Get dressed," I said. "The police need to speak to me at the station. We're leaving."

Both the nurses behind the desk looked up at that.

"You can't do that!" said one.

"He still needs to be here," said the other. "We're just waiting on another bed."

I glared at them. "What he *needs* is to be somewhere where people aren't trying to kill him. And no offence, ladies, but your hospital isn't doing such a great job on that front."

"I'll have to call the registrar on duty," said the first one.

"Call anyone you like. But as soon as he's got a pair of pants on, we're out of here."

"And shoes," Lachie mumbled sleepily into my shoulder. "He might hurt his feet."

Ben hauled himself out of the chair. "I'm good to go. Got nothing but pyjamas here anyway."

"Mr Stevens, please wait for the registrar. I'm sure he'll advise against this."

"Sorry." He didn't sound it.

The officious one stood and came around the desk. "You'll have to sign a form saying you're discharging yourself against doctor's orders."

"If you've got one right there, he'll sign anything you like," I said. "Otherwise, we're leaving."

"But—"

I turned my will on her, reaching into her mind and taking control. I might have sworn off enthralment, but I had nothing against a temporary compulsion. She stood frozen like a deer in the headlights, helpless in my gaze.

"We. Are. Leaving."

And we did.

***

"Are you okay?" Ben asked, breaking the long silence in the car. Oncoming headlights flashed across his face like strobe lights in the darkness.

"Fine. You?"

"You killed that woman."

Oh. I changed lanes and wondered how to answer that.

A week ago I would have had a hard time killing a person, even in self-defence. If I'd had to, I'd have been a blubbering mess afterwards. Ben probably thought I was heading for a mental breakdown, alarmed by my cool.

In fact, deep down—or maybe not so deep—a new resolve had hardened. Leandra wouldn't have thought twice about destroying a threat, and now neither did I. That didn't mean I didn't regret the necessity. But I wouldn't be falling apart any time I had to eliminate some low-life who threatened me or the people I cared about. Shifters saw such things differently to regular humans.

"She was trying to kill you. And me. I didn't have much choice."

"If you'd held her off till the nurses came—"

"What? She might have knifed one of them? Or Lachie? Would that have been better?"

"We might have been able to question her."

Detective Hartley would have liked that. Hell, I would have liked that. Bad enough to have people lining up to kill you. It was even worse when you didn't know who was at the head of the queue.

"I doubt she would have told us anything."

"But at least we wouldn't have been driving to the police station now, would we? Are they going to charge you?"

"I don't think so. It's pretty obvious it was self defence." At least, that's how it should look to someone who didn't know about shifters. "Detective Hartley said they just wanted to do a formal interview. She seems like the type that wants everything done by the book."

He made a noncommittal noise and stared out the window. Detective Hartley had told me to meet her at Chatswood police station, which wasn't far away. We were soon cruising down Archer Street looking for a parking spot.

The police station loomed on the corner of Archer Street and Albert Avenue, a big glass and concrete box that spilled golden light onto the dark street. I felt a shiver of apprehension as we entered. The Leandra side of me sneered at my nerves. What did a dragon have to fear from human law enforcement?

"Pretend you're my nephew," I whispered to Lachie as Detective Hartley came to greet us. No point taking chances. Accidental deaths were hard enough to explain without adding miraculous resurrections as well.

"Mr Stevens! I didn't expect to see you here. I thought you weren't well enough to leave hospital yet." Her glance travelled across his bandaged arm in its sling before coming to rest on his face.

He shrugged. "Hospital didn't seem so appealing any more."

"Well, since you're here, we can take your statement too." She led us from the reception area to the interview rooms. "If you could go with Detective Franks, Mr Stevens, you can talk to him while I ask Ms O'Connor some questions."

Ben followed Detective Franks, and Detective Hartley smiled at Lachie.

"What about you, young man? Would you like to wait with Constable Eaton here while I talk to your mum?"

"She's my auntie, actually."

A young woman in uniform offered Lachie a friendly smile. "Would you like a jelly bean?"

That sealed the deal. Lachie went off with her without a backward glance, while I followed Detective Hartley into the small interview room.

We faced each other at the table and she pressed the button to start the recording. After she'd recited the standard warnings and asked a few preliminary questions she got stuck straight into it. "How well did you know Amy Johnson?"

"Not well at all. I'd seen her a couple of times before, when I was visiting Ben."

"And how did you get on with her?"

"Fine. To be honest, I didn't pay her that much attention."

"So you never argued with her? There was no friction between you?"

"No, nothing like that. I don't think I ever said more than hello."

The guy who'd taken my initial statement at the hospital had asked this too. Was all this checking and double-checking standard procedure, or had Detective Hartley decided something seemed screwy?

"Please tell me again what happened."

"I came back into the room—"

"Where had you been?"

She interrupted a lot more than the first guy. No detail too big or too small. Maybe that was how you got to be lead detective on a case.

"I was going home, but when I got to the car park I couldn't find my keys. We were coming back to check if I'd dropped them in Ben's room." They had been under the bed, against the wall. One of the police officers at the hospital had retrieved them for me.

"And where was Ms Johnson when you came in?"

"Standing right next to the bed, holding a pillow over Ben's face."

"What did you do then?"

"I told my nephew to run to the nurses' station, and then I tried to stop her."

"Did you shut the door?"

"What?"

"Did you pause to shut the door before you tried to stop Ms Johnson suffocating Mr Stevens?" She pulled out a notebook and flipped through until she found the page she wanted. Must have belonged to the officer who'd questioned me at the scene. "The two nurses who came to your aid said the door was shut when they arrived."

She looked up, an expression of polite interest on her face. I paused. No telling what was going on behind that attentive mask, but I had a feeling she didn't miss much.

"I … guess I must have, then. I was probably trying to stop Lachie from seeing what was happening. He's only ten, you know." I didn't actually remember shutting the door, but it was a smart move if you knew you were probably going to use unusual methods of winning a fight. Unless, of course, some detail-obsessed detective decided to take it as an admission of premeditated murder or something.

She regarded me steadily. "Most people would have stood there and screamed for security. You're remarkably cool under pressure, Ms O'Connor."

It sounded more like an accusation than a compliment. I'd have to try harder to be unremarkable.

"There wasn't time to wait for help. I had to do something."

"And you're positive Mr Stevens didn't know Ms Johnson either before he was admitted to hospital?"

That was about the fifth time someone had asked me that. Some of my irritation crept into my voice. "Asking me again won't change my answer, you know."

Detective Hartley smiled, a professional expression that didn't reach her eyes. "You'd be surprised how often things come back to people afterwards, once they've gotten over the shock. It doesn't hurt to jog their memory."

I had a feeling Detective Hartley was never surprised by the things people suddenly "remembered". Perhaps I was too calm for someone who'd supposedly just killed an attacker with their own knife. Or maybe it was the not-screaming thing. Note to self: scream blue murder next time you get attacked in public. It makes the cops happier.

"Why do you think Ms Johnson attacked Mr Stevens?"

I sagged against the hard plastic chair. That was a damn good question. If only I knew the answer. "I have no idea."

"According to her co-workers, Ms Johnson was a dedicated nurse, and not the violent type. They'd never even heard her raise her voice to anyone." Detective Hartley glanced down and read from another page of the notebook. "Divorced, two grown children, never been in trouble with the law. We checked: one speeding ticket seven years ago. Went to church every Sunday." The sudden snap of the notebook closing made me jump. "Why does a person like that take it into their head to kill someone they hardly know? It doesn't make sense."

"Plenty of bad people go to church every Sunday. She had that knife. That seems like she must have been planning something."

"True." She eyed me as if she'd like to ask about my own church-going habits. "But if she planned to smother him, why did she need the knife?"

Well, damn. Should have kept my mouth shut instead of sending her chasing after more riddles. I didn't need someone like her poking around at the moment. I had enough to deal with.

"Does Mr Stevens have any enemies? Can you think of any reason why someone would want him dead?"

Half a dozen off the top of my head, but none she needed to know about. Hell, I'd been so sure Elizabeth would leave him alone. Could it have been Alicia, trying to get to me through him? A supporter of Valeria's looking for revenge? Or, God forbid, even Jason?

I'd described everything twice already, but Detective Hartley walked me through the rest of the scene again, lingering over every detail, before finally agreeing I could leave. Ben and Lachie were waiting outside the interview room. I half expected her to tell me not to leave town, the way they did on TV, but all she said was that she'd be in touch.

"Here's my card," she said. *Detective Senior Constable Ellen Hartley, Chatswood Criminal Investigation.* "Call me if you think of anything else."

"Sure." Not a chance, lady.

CHAPTER THREE

The drive home was quiet. Home. Wherever that was these days. Leandra owned two Sydney properties, one a townhouse in The Rocks, the other a much larger place out the back of Arcadia, an hour's drive from the city. Both were way more luxurious than the rundown suburban house Lachie and I had called home. Both held troubling memories from Leandra's point of view. The country place had been the site of Jason's first assassination attempt. The townhouse was where she died, after he got it right the second time.

And of course where she tricked her way into my body, leaving her own to die. So not exactly bursting with happy memories from my point of view either.

Nevertheless, we were staying in the Sydney townhouse, partly for its closeness to Royal North Shore Hospital, and partly because it suited Garth's paranoia—it was small enough to defend with the handful of security we had. If he'd had his way we would have gone completely to ground, somewhere anonymous with no association with either Leandra or Kate, but I'd had enough of hiding in cheap motels. To win the proving I had to re-establish my dominance fast, and hiding wouldn't do that. With the great game at a shell-shocked standstill for now, it seemed a good time to regroup. Let Alicia waste time licking her wounds. I would be forging ahead, growing stronger every day.

Unless … I stopped at a set of lights on the Pacific Highway and frowned at the lone car heading across the intersection. Unless this *was* Alicia, back in the game already?

Normally I wouldn't even consider it. When Valeria had taken trueshape and come arrowing out of the heart of the bushfire like an angel of fiery death, where had Alicia been? Struggling hand-to-hand against Valeria's forces with the rest of us, choking on smoke and blistered by a hundred flying sparks? Or even up in the roiling sky, taking on Valeria dragon to dragon?

Not bloody likely. She'd been hiding in her special fireproof bunker, waiting, as usual, for someone else to do the dirty work until she could emerge, make-up unsmudged. It was hard to believe she'd hatched from the same clutch as the rest of us. Her whole strategy so far had consisted of "hide and hope the others kill each other off".

But now she had Luce on her side. My hands clenched the wheel till my knuckles whitened. Luce was *my* security chief, but now she was bound to Alicia by an arcane ritual, forced to aid her instead of me. Just thinking about it made me want to hurt someone. Preferably Alicia.

Luce wasn't the type to cross her fingers and hide. She was a wyvern with all the natural wiles of her kind, plus a go get 'em attitude that made her as unstoppable as a force of nature.

Luce would be prodding Alicia into action, making her own luck as usual.

"People say I'm lucky," she'd told me once, not long after we started working together. "But I've noticed the harder I work, the luckier I get."

So I could totally see Luce dragging Alicia out of her comfort zone and making her actually do something for a change. The tricky part was seeing why Luce would think attacking Ben would be the best move for my sister.

I glanced across at Ben. He had his eyes shut, head tipped back against the passenger seat, but he wasn't asleep—unlike Lachie, whose heavy breathing from the back seat was the only sound in the car. Obviously I'd be distraught if I lost him, but from a practical point of view targeting him didn't make a lot of sense. She'd be better off taking out Garth, if she could. In her absence he was my right-hand man. Ben had connections to the heralds that might prove useful, but he was hardly a key player.

Much as I hated to admit it, it was more likely that Ben's past as a herald was coming back to bite us in the arse. Or, more specifically, his sudden exit from the ranks of the heralds. We'd always known there could be a price to pay for that change in allegiance, and it looked like the bill was coming due. Elizabeth must have decided to make an example of him.

She had a history of doing that—like the time she called me and my remaining sisters into her study in the aftermath of the disastrous Presentation Ball. I hadn't fully realised until that moment what a cold-blooded killer she was.

***

We stood in front of Elizabeth's massive mahogany desk like naughty children called before the headmistress. It was impossible to think of her as our mother. Dragons didn't do motherhood, not in the way that humans and other shifters understood it.

Her cold blue gaze travelled across each of us in turn. By coincidence, or perhaps unconsciously, we'd lined up in order, oldest to youngest. Valeria stood with her arms folded across her blood-spattered chest, chin lifted in challenge. That pale blue satin would never be the same again. Most people would trash it, but it wouldn't surprise me if she kept it as a souvenir of her first kill. Because, despite her denials, I was one hundred per cent certain she was responsible for the bomb blast.

Next to her stood Alicia, her stark black-and-white ball gown still pristine. She'd been way across the other side of the room when the bomb went off. Ingrid, closest to me in age, was next in line and similarly unruffled. Now that Monique was dead, she was the only brunette among us. I looked a wreck compared to her, with a scrape across my cheek and raw patches on my hands and elbows where I'd been thrown to the stone flagging of the terrace. My chiffon skirts were sadly torn but I'd had a lucky escape, thanks to Luce's quick reactions.

Monique, who should have been standing on my other side, hadn't been so lucky. It was her blood that stained Valeria's dress and coated the broken walls and floor of the throne room. Plus a few other people's outfits, which were going to need epic dry-cleaning. There wasn't much else left of our youngest sister, and Elizabeth was seriously unamused.

Oh, not because Monique was dead. We were expected to kill each other off. Last woman standing got to inherit our dearest mother's throne. She just didn't appreciate the battle beginning in her own throne room, with such destructive results. Not to mention the possible risk to her precious person.

An ornate grandfather clock in the corner ticked solemnly as Elizabeth let the silence lengthen, each swing of its massive pendulum reproaching us for disturbing the peace of the queen's domain. I stared down at the carpet beneath our feet, following the intricate swirls and flowers of its design, and tried not to draw our mother's attention. She disliked me enough already.

"The Presentation Ball is intended to introduce the candidates to the domain," she said at last, her voice as icy as her gaze. "It is not meant to host the outbreak of hostilities. Such breaches of etiquette are not to be tolerated."

Trust Elizabeth to label the murder of one of her own daughters as a "breach of etiquette".

"It could have been anyone." Valeria's blue eyes, so like our mother's, were wide with a very unconvincing innocence. "Why assume it was one of us?"

Elizabeth shot her a scathing glance. "I believe the expression in these cases is *cui bono?*"

Who benefits, indeed. It had to be one of us.

"Perhaps an enterprising shifter, trying to win favour ..." Valeria persisted.

"Oh, give it a rest." Alicia rolled her eyes. "We all know it was you. Who else has a griffin on staff?" She turned to Elizabeth. "Are you going to let her get away with this?"

"If you mean, am I going to fight your battles for you, Alicia, then no." Elizabeth didn't seem to care much for any of us apart from Valeria, but I swear her lip curled as her gaze rested on Alicia. "But when I find out who was responsible they will be punished."

Right. I had no doubt Elizabeth was pissed, but pigs would fly before she punished Valeria for anything. Valeria was the golden girl, firstborn and favoured to win the proving.

The door opened, admitting Gideon Thorne and two men in dark suits, part of Elizabeth's security team. Thralls, by the look of them. Their gaze went straight to Elizabeth when they entered, and never wavered from her face as they waited, hands clasped loosely in front of them.

Thorne's aura shone a brilliant red, though not as bright as the queen's. Apart from the thralls, everyone in the room was outlined in dragon red. We were probably the six most powerful dragons in the domain, though the light of half of us would flicker and die soon enough. Thorne would most likely outlive us all. He'd been around for centuries and had the knack of ingratiating himself with the right people. Nasty little bootlicker.

He perched on the corner of Elizabeth's desk, the only one permitted to sit in her presence, and indicated the thralls.

"These are the ones."

"You were responsible for security tonight?" she said to them.

"Yes, ma'am."

"Did you search each guest as instructed?"

"Yes, ma'am."

"And yet someone managed to smuggle a bomb into my throne room."

There didn't seem to be an answer to that, so they said nothing, though I noticed one of them swallowed convulsively. Even thralls, near-zombies though they were, responded to imminent danger.

"It's very disappointing," she said in a conversational tone, then waved her hand at Thorne.

He nodded, and before anyone could react, sabre-like claws burst from his fingertips, and he slashed the throats of both thralls in one smooth swipe. They were dead before they hit the floor.

Alicia leapt back to avoid getting blood on her dress. Even Valeria looked shaken by the casual violence. Thorne's claws disappeared as fast as they'd come, and he pulled a snowy white handkerchief from his pocket and wiped his hands, all without moving from the spot.

"Let's have no more disappointments," said Elizabeth. "My home is off limits for your duelling in future. Understood?"

What else could we say?

"Yes, ma'am," we chorused.

CHAPTER FOUR

We drove across the Harbour Bridge, its great steel girders criss-crossing above our heads, their huge size making the cars below look like tiny coloured toys. Five nights ago Valeria had been perched up there like some nightmare bird, even her great size diminished by the mighty bridge. I'd swooped across this deck, though there'd been no headlights lighting it up then, no traffic at all, the bridge closed for the big New Year's Eve fireworks display. I'd flown all around it, ducking and weaving as I tried to stay ahead of Valeria's slashing claws.

It was hard to believe now. Everything looked so normal. The only reminder of that night was the missing dove. The fireworks had ended, as they did every year, with a waterfall of fireworks fountaining from the deck of the bridge into the harbour and the lighting of a symbol that was meant to hang from the top of the arch for the whole month of January. This year it had been a dove, symbol of peace.

Unfortunately two warring dragons had knocked it askew, and the damaged symbol had been removed the next day. Just as well I wasn't superstitious. That was one bad omen.

I took the turn-off for The Rocks and threaded my way through narrow streets, quiet now, past the clock tower, up through the Argyle Cut and home. The houses here had been built before Henry Ford ever dreamed of the automobile, so there were no driveways or garages attached to the narrow homes. Street parking was always hard to find, but I didn't bother looking. I might be keen to reassert my strength, but I wasn't stupid. Walking the streets of The Rocks late at night with a small child and an injured man for company was asking for trouble I didn't need.

I double-parked outside the house. Garth must have been watching for me; he came bounding down the front steps before I even had the door open, Steve on his heels. They were both big hulking guys, and with the light behind them they looked like a badass Tweedledum and Tweedledee. Up close, though, no one would mistake them for twins. Garth, with his buzz-cut greying hair and care-worn face, was probably twice Steve's age, but the differences in temperament were even greater. The big werewolf scowled at me as he scooped Lachie out of the back seat, whereas a welcoming grin split Steve's dark face as he slipped behind the wheel. But they were both good at their jobs: the car disappeared and we were safe inside in a matter of seconds.

"You're late," Garth growled as I followed him upstairs to settle Lachie into bed.

"What are you, my mother?"

He didn't even blink. "If I was I'd bloody ground you for coming home at this hour. Where the hell have you been?"

"You knew where I was! At the hospital."

"You left for the hospital at five. For a short visit, you said."

In Lachie's room I pulled down the sheet and he laid Lachie on the bed. The poor kid didn't even stir. Though Garth continued to glare at me he took off Lachie's shoes and socks with gentle hands.

I felt a little guilty. A new emotion for the part of me that remembered being Leandra. Tomorrow I'd have to send one of the guys out to buy me a new mobile phone. I'd lost mine in all the excitement last week and hadn't had a chance yet to replace it.

"Something came up."

Something in my tone alerted him. He stiffened, then almost dragged me into the hall, his nostrils flaring.

"Whose blood is that? Are you hurt?"

Normally he would have noticed it the minute I came in. Werewolf noses were very sensitive. Too busy telling me off to listen to his senses.

"Not mine, and no." I laid a calming hand on his arm. "Chill, Garth. It's okay. Come downstairs and I'll tell you all about it."

The front door opened as we reached the bottom of the stairs, and Steve came back in. We joined Ben in the lounge room, where he'd subsided into an armchair. The room was small by Leandra's standards—she'd always preferred the country property—but in the old part of The Rocks nothing was newer than a hundred years old, and all the buildings were crammed in, rubbing shoulders with their neighbours. Nobody had big lounge rooms around here. She'd done it up nicely, though, with plenty of antique furniture and expensive-looking paintings on the walls. No one who saw the room would be surprised to discover her favourite colour was red—the chairs were covered in red velvet, and their wooden arms were stained a deep rose that matched the dominant colour in the rug that covered the floor.

"And what's the one-armed wonder doing here? Thought he had a few more days in hospital?"

"Hospital got a bit too lively," Ben said without opening his eyes. "Hello, Garth. Nice to see you too."

Steve and I sat down side by side on a velvet-covered lounge, which creaked as it took Steve's muscled weight. He was half-Maori and built like a tank. Garth prowled back and forth across the Persian rug, unsettled, while I gave them a brief rundown of the events at the hospital and our visit to the police station. His aura flared with bright orange streaks, and his normally grey eyes were ringed with yellow, sure signs of the inner wolf's distress.

"I knew I shouldn't have let you go without me," he said.

"You can't tag along everywhere I go. We were fine."

"We need more men," Steve said, in his deep, slow voice. "We can barely protect you here, much less when you go out."

I huffed out a frustrated breath. He was right, of course. The problem was how to find them.

"Oh, for God's sake sit down, Garth. You're going to wear a hole in the carpet."

The werewolf sank into a chair with bad grace. Its delicate lines had been built for smaller people, and he looked enormous in it. Enormous and grumpy. "Anyone we recruit now is suspect. Alicia or Elizabeth could plant someone on us."

But if we couldn't find allies they'd have little trouble finishing us off. Catch-22.

"Unless we take people we already know," Steve said. "What about the rest of the old team?"

Only six of Leandra's eleven thralls had signed on again. Two Garth hadn't been able to locate and the other three obviously didn't like my chances, as they'd refused to have anything to do with me. I'd offered bucket loads of cash, but money could only buy so much. Since I'd refused to enthral them, I couldn't force them to change their minds. They were lucky they'd only been enthralled by Leandra for a few months, or they would have been left comatose when she died.

Apart from them, the old team had consisted of Jason, now playing for the other team, and Luce, ditto. Oh, and the werewolf pack whose alpha had already refused to help me last week.

Garth shook his head. "No go."

Steve hesitated. "Maybe … some more thralls?"

"Seriously?" He knew how I felt about thralls. The world looked very different when you'd been on the other end of a dragon's mental powers, and I was a changed woman. No more thralls for this dragon. "You've been a thrall. You think that's any way to live? Unable to do anything except follow orders? Barely able to think for yourself?"

He shifted in his seat, clearly uncomfortable, like a puppy that knew it had done something wrong and was waiting to be kicked. He'd been pretty happy to hear I'd had no intention of enthralling *him* again. "I'm not saying it's the best answer.

Maybe just for a little while. They wouldn't know any different—and we need the manpower."

"No. Not an option."

I missed Luce. She'd made a great head of security. As Leandra I'd hardly had to think of such things before, she made everything run so smoothly. And now she was trapped in Alicia's camp, bound by magic to my worst enemy. Or maybe my second-worst enemy. I had a few to choose from.

Not only did I miss her advice and her strong, capable presence, she was now actively working against me. In fact I was more afraid of Luce than of Alicia. Luce would be hatching some diabolical plot while we flailed around here.

"Goblin magic," said Garth. "If we bought a seeming, we could get close enough to Alicia to get rid of her, and then Luce would be free. Problem solved."

Well, it was a nice idea, if not quite as simple as he made out. Goblin magic was complex stuff, and there weren't too many mages around with the necessary skills. It couldn't be any old seeming. Valeria's pet griffin Nada had used a seeming to sneak into the Presentation Ball and bomb Monique into tiny little pieces, but that had been a big, busy occasion, and the seeming had only been a general one, designed to disguise her real features, but not make her look like anyone else in particular.

To get close to Alicia we'd need a particular seeming, and for that we'd need hair or fingernails of an actual person in Alicia's camp. With that, an experienced mage could make a disguise that looked exactly like the targeted person—except for their aura. The spell couldn't disguise auras, which made it a lot less useful, since Alicia would immediately see a problem if, say, one of her leshies suddenly turned up with the orange aura of a werewolf.

"The problem is finding a clan willing to deal with us," said Ben. "Most of them don't have a powerful enough mage, and the ones that do are sitting out the proving."

"I know a guy," Garth said.

"Right. You know a guy." Ben looked supremely unconvinced. "A goblin mage."

"Yes. Blue Munroe."

"I thought he was dead?" said Steve.

"Nobody's seen him in months," said Ben. "Not even the heralds know where he is."

"I do. Or at least, I did." Garth shrugged. "I reckon I could find him again."

Last time I'd had dealings with Blue he'd still been living with his clan. He'd done the security work on this house and the Arcadia property for Leandra, nearly a year ago. After what happened to Monique at the Presentation Ball, Luce had insisted on a security upgrade. She hadn't been too impressed with him, though, and had given him the third degree.

"So the security system is only triggered when a hostile crosses the property boundary?" she'd asked once he'd finished his explanation of the magical defences he'd put in place. For an exorbitant price, I might add. Not that he'd see much of the money: the clan chieftain who'd negotiated the fee would probably keep most of it.

"That's right." He was a skinny guy with big round glasses and a floppy orange fringe that made him look a little like a red-haired young John Lennon, and nothing at all like someone capable of working complicated magic.

"So what if someone fires from an adjoining building?"

"Well … nothing, I guess."

"Or if they land on the roof? Does the protection extend above the ground?"

"Ah … Not as such." He pushed his glasses back up to the bridge of his nose, looking as though he'd rather be anywhere else.

She folded her arms and gave him her trademark glare, eyes narrowed. Luce was built like a delicate Chinese doll, so tiny that she had to look up at him to do it. "So basically this spell of yours is pretty limited."

"Well, yes—no!" He jiggled from foot to foot, wilting under her gaze. She might only be small, but no one did intimidation like Luce. "It's my best spell. Not many mages can manage a spell of this intricacy, you know."

I took pity on him and sent him away soon after. Months later I'd heard he left his clan.

"Didn't he skip out on a wedding or something?"

Garth nodded. "He was supposed to marry the clan chief's daughter. He wasn't too keen on the idea, so he went into hiding."

"I remember that!" Steve grinned, teeth very white against his dark skin. "Blue the Reluctant Bridegroom, they called him. Apparently the bride had a face like the back of a bus."

"I think the problem was more that he didn't want to be under the thumb of the chieftain's family," Ben said. "Any more than he already was, that is."

Some clans treated their mages like princes. Others acted as if they were no more than performing monkeys, a resource to be used up by the clan rather than a person. From memory Blue's clan had been one of the latter.

"So how did you find him?" I asked Garth.

He shrugged and looked down at his feet. "Got lucky. I knew him from before."

The way he said "before", I knew he meant before he became a wolf. Interesting. Garth hated talking about his past.

"You think you could find him again?"

Another shrug.

"How much use is he going to be, even if you do find him?" Ben asked. He ran a hand through his already tousled curls. "Getting something he could use in a seeming would be almost impossible. And if we can get that close to Alicia in the first place, why do we need the seeming?"

"You got any better ideas?" Garth growled.

"What about Trevor and the pack? They worked with Leandra before."

Right. Being in hospital, he hadn't caught up on all our adventures. Garth and I exchanged a look. "We tried to get him on-side last week. No deal."

"Although that was before he knew about Leandra," Garth pointed out, forgetting to glare at Ben as the thought struck him. Poor Garth probably missed Luce even more than I did. He made a great second, but he didn't like being in command.

Well, we were all in unfamiliar territory here.

"True." Blue seemed a dodgy option at best: *if* we could find him, *if* he could work any useful magic for us. "Set up a meeting," I told Steve. No point antagonising the pack leader by having Garth do it. Even if he hadn't been exiled from the pack, he would never win any awards for diplomacy. "Tell him Leandra's back and wants to see him."

Ben shifted uneasily in his chair. "But she's not ... You're not—"

I sighed. How many times were we going to have this discussion? "Yes, I am." The fact he didn't like it didn't make it any less true. I hadn't exactly asked to be in this situation myself, but there was no point pretending I was the same person I'd always been. Hell, I doubted I even qualified as human now. "I'm not the same old Kate O'Connor any more. There's no going back."

CHAPTER FIVE

Nevertheless, there were times I felt a lot more Kate than Leandra. Leandra would have run screaming from the scene at the breakfast table next morning. Dragons just didn't do family. Case in point: my lying scum of an ex-husband. However lousy he'd been as a husband and father—and trust me, he defined a new low in lousy—he'd probably done the best he could given the staggering self-centredness of most dragons.

Lachie was shovelling Coco Pops like there was no tomorrow when I entered the kitchen. A chocolate-brown milk moustache was smeared across his upper lip, and the guilty look on his face said he knew full well he should have been eating something healthier. Judging by the speed at which he was chomping through the bowl, he'd probably figured on destroying the evidence before I came downstairs. Or maybe he thought that if Garth could get away with eating sugar-coated crap for breakfast, he should be able to as well. The big werewolf sat beside him, a chocolate-smeared bowl the only sign of his crimes against breakfast.

I smiled at Lachie and decided to overlook the sugar explosion in his bowl. Parental discipline had kind of gone out the window lately. It was so good to have him back I was turning into one of those pushover mothers who let their child do anything they wanted. Soon I'd have to bring us both back to reality—but not yet.

Ben sat on his other side, reading the newspaper. This back part of the house was a modern extension, open-plan and full of light. It looked out on the Japanese-inspired garden where Leandra and I had had our fateful meeting. It was only a small garden, though big by the standards of The Rocks. From here I could see the spreading jacaranda tree where she'd waited for me, and the patch of grass where she'd died. I shuddered and turned my attention to pleasanter things.

Sunlight streamed in the big windows behind Ben and Lachie and gleamed in the reflections on the polished table. It lit their curly heads, one big, one small. They could have been father and son having breakfast together. There was a superficial resemblance—they were both tall and lean with curly hair, though Ben's was black where Lachie's was a mid-brown. I paused in the doorway, my heart caught for a moment by might-have-beens. What would our lives have been like if I'd married Ben instead of Jason?

But then Lachie wouldn't have been Lachie, and I couldn't regret the choices that had brought him into my world. As for Ben ... we were together now. Better to look to the future than dwell on the past. Assuming we survived long enough to have a future, of course.

He looked better this morning. He'd shaved, and in clothes instead of pyjamas he no longer looked like he might collapse any minute. The arm in its sling and a little bruising on the right side of his face were the only signs left of his injuries.

Ben smiled at me, but Lachie's expression was troubled. He hunched over his bowl as if he carried the cares of the world on his slight shoulders.

"Did you sleep well?" I dropped a kiss on his hair as I headed for the coffee machine.

"All right." He slurped up the last of the chocolate-coloured milk in his bowl and pushed it away. "How long are we going to stay here?"

Uh-oh. I'd been expecting a conversation like this. "In this house, you mean?"

He nodded. "I want to go home."

"Don't you like it here?"

"It's okay. But it's not home. I miss my Lego, and my old room."

His eyes flicked to the side, to Garth, and Dave, who was unstacking the big dishwasher. *And there are all these strangers living with us.* The poor kid had been living in a boarding school for the last seven months, for God's sake. He'd probably had it with sharing his living space with crowds of people.

I met Ben's eyes over Lachie's head, and saw sympathy there. Just the three of us—a little family together—sounded pretty good to me too. But we both knew there was no going back to that little green house in the suburbs, at least not any time soon, and maybe never. I took my time making the coffee, then sat down opposite at the long wooden table. Its gleaming surface was the colour of honey, warm and golden. The matching chairs were a touch too modern for comfort, and I shifted on the hard surface, trying to get comfortable.

"We could get you new Lego, you know. All the Lego you wanted."

His frown deepened. God, he looked like his father when he did that. "It wouldn't be the same. They don't sell some of the old stuff any more. All my old Ninjago, and the Star Wars sets. Why can't we just go home?"

His voice wobbled a little on the last word. An overwhelming desire to punch Jason right in his smug face seized me. If he hadn't started this with his scheming, Lachie and I could still be living our quiet little lives, untouched by all this shifter madness.

I took a deep breath. "Honey, what did Dad tell you about why you had to go to boarding school all of a sudden?"

He sniffed. "I told you, he said you'd died."

"I know, but why couldn't you stay with him? Most people don't move into boarding school when their mums die. Did he say?"

His bottom lip started to tremble. He looked down at his bowl, unwilling to meet my eyes, and played with a drop of milk on the table, smooshing it around with the tip of his finger. "He said he was too busy working to look after me, and that Uncle Ben was going to keep an eye on me. He said I should tell everyone my name was Lachie Stevens, so no one would say Uncle Ben wasn't allowed to visit."

A single tear rolled down the soft curve of his cheek. Poor little guy. My heart broke all over again. He must have felt so abandoned, when his own father didn't have time for him, and even his identity was stripped away. But Jason couldn't have left his surname unchanged for fear other dragons would find him.

I reached across the table and took his clenched fist in my hands, cradling it between them, smoothing his small fingers straight. Dave clattered around, putting away cups and plates and cooking implements with enough noise to give us at least the illusion of privacy, carefully not looking our way. Nice guy, Dave. Cooked like a pro, too.

"And now you know that was a lie. I wasn't dead—but I thought *you* were. Dad used magic to stage an accident and convince everyone that you were dead. Me, Gran, Auntie Simone, your teachers, all your friends at school—we all believed it. And Dad changed your name and hid you away so no one would know it was a trick."

Except Ben, of course. I didn't look at him, not wanting to see the guilt on his face. He'd been coerced into being part of Jason's scheme with typical dragon ruthlessness. No need to burden Lachie with the details. Let him harbour whatever illusions about his father he still could.

"Why did he do that?" His brown eyes swam with unshed tears.

"He was trying to look after you. He'd done some bad things, to some powerful people, and he was afraid they might pay him back by hurting you."

In an interesting twist of fate, one of them was me. Me, Leandra, that is. In fact it was more of a pre-emptive strike on Jason's part. He'd been planning to change sides, so arranged Lachie's "death" before he betrayed her.

It seemed likely he was more worried about Valeria, though. If all had gone to plan, Leandra would have been dead as soon as he left her, so who was he hiding Lachie from? Ever-pragmatic, he'd decided Valeria had the best chance of winning the proving, so he'd switched sides—but he didn't trust her, and wanted to make sure she couldn't use Lachie as a hold over him if it didn't work out.

Maybe one day I'd ask him, if he ever showed his face again. Right before I killed him for all the pain he'd caused us. For months of loss and grieving. For Lachie's lonely nights in his boarding school bed.

For making me have this conversation with our son.

"Some of those people are still mad at Dad. And now they're mad at me too, for killing Valeria. We need to keep you safe. That's why Garth and Steve and Dave and all these other guys are living with us now. We wouldn't all fit in our little house in Rembrandt Street, would we?"

Garth snorted, and got up to take his bowl to the sink. He'd seen how small that house was.

"Couldn't they be like guards, and go sleep somewhere else?"

"No, honey."

"Well, what about when the bad guys stop being mad? Can we go home then?"

He turned pleading brown eyes up to me and I sighed. It nearly killed me to dash his hopes. "You know, everything's a bit messed up now. I'm a dragon and you're a ghost. What do you think people will do if we go back and tell them you're not dead after all?"

He sniffed and scrubbed one hand across his eyes. "They'll say, 'hey Lachie, we're glad you're not really dead'."

Ben laughed. I smiled too, some of the tension leaking out of me. "Well, sure, but after that? They're going to want to know why Dad tricked them—and then they'll start asking *how* he tricked them—and then all sorts of things are going to come out that we'd rather they didn't know."

He was a perceptive kid. "About dragons and stuff, you mean?"

"Yeah. About dragons, and who killed Valeria, and why. I might have to go to jail if the police find out it was me. There'd be people following us around with cameras all the time like they do with movie stars, and scientists asking questions and wanting to do tests on us."

And probably an assortment of religious nutjobs trying to save us or kill us, depending on their particular brand of nutjobbery. It would be a nightmare. It didn't take much imagination to see why Elizabeth wanted to keep the shifter world under wraps.

If I won the proving, the whole headache would land in my lap. And I had to succeed: the only options were win or die. Running a shifter kingdom sure wouldn't be any easier with every man and his dog on my back about Lachie's miraculous return from the dead.

"So we can't *ever* go home?" The tremble was back in his bottom lip. "But my Lego …"

He burst into tears. I leapt up, scraping my chair across the tiles, and rounded the table, feeling like the world's worst mother. You were supposed to protect your kid from the kind of trauma that he'd been through. The poor little guy had been so brave, but there were limits to even the bravest ten-year-old's endurance. It wasn't fair, and I could never make it up to him, but I'd walk across broken glass just to try. I swept him into a hug, feeling his bony little arms clutch me tightly, his thin frame heaving with sobs.

"I'll get your Lego, okay? Don't cry, Monster. It'll be all right."

Garth's ears pricked up. "Not a great plan, going back there."

I glared at him as Lachie sobbed harder. He stood on the other side of the long island bench that separated the kitchen from the eating area, leaning forward in unconscious menace. Well, probably unconscious. I wouldn't put it past him to try to strong-arm me into doing what he thought best. "Too bad."

"There could be—" He glanced at Lachie and changed whatever he'd been about to say. "Other people might have been there."

Well, clearly other people had been there. My next-door neighbour, Tanya, for one, and the police who responded to her panicked call the night Garth attacked me in my own kitchen. It took a minute to realise what he meant.

Someone could have set a trap for me in the hope I'd return.

I sighed. Would life always be this screwed up? "It's not very likely, Garth."

Neither Elizabeth nor Alicia would waste a moment shaking the dust of a place like our old home off their feet, if they even deigned to set foot in it at all. It would never occur to them that I might want to go back there.

"Still possible, though."

God, he was nearly as stubborn as Ben. If only Luce were here I'd have the trifecta. Why did I seem to be surrounded lately by people who insisted on arguing with me?

"Then you can come with me and frighten people off with that scowl."

He shook his head. "You need someone like Blue to check it out. Disarm anything magical."

"We've already established that Blue is missing in action, and I doubt there's another goblin mage this side of Brisbane."

"I can find him," he insisted.

"Fine." I was sick of arguing already and it was only breakfast time. "Go find him. You've got twenty-four hours. If you're not back by then, I'm going without you."

CHAPTER SIX

Finding a single goblin in all of Sydney was never going to be an easy job, however good Garth's werewolf nose or however many dodgy connections he could tap for information. When he wasn't back by dinner time I rang him, to check he hadn't been attacked by any murderous nurses.

"Still looking," he said, and hung up. Our Garth was a man of few words.

When there was no sign of him at breakfast the next morning I felt a stirring of unease, but I refused to ring him again. Maybe next time I wouldn't challenge a pig-headed guy like Garth to accomplish the near-impossible in a mere twenty-four hours. He'd use up every last second of it, determined not to fail. And he'd be even more cheerful than usual after a night with no sleep.

I was still sitting at the breakfast table in a patch of morning sunlight, nursing a cup of coffee, when Lachie wandered in, his eyes bright with hope.

"Is Garth back yet?"

"You two must be related," Ben muttered, grinning at me.

"Yes, but he's only asking because he wants his Lego back."

The kid practically quivered with excitement at the prospect. "I could go with you if Garth doesn't come back in time."

"I don't actually have to go the very second the twenty-four hours is up," I pointed out.

He turned a shocked look on me. "But you promised."

Oh, Lord. Those big brown eyes. I glanced at Ben.

He shrugged. "You might as well. I doubt anyone will have targeted the house. And Garth's not going to turn up any faster if you sit here worrying about him."

True. I could take Steve as back-up. In fact, it might even be better that way. Get it done before my paranoid werewolf got back and started demanding more time to hunt down a goblin mage who didn't want to be found.

But when Steve and I opened the front door on our way out, guess who was coming up the steps?

"Found him." Garth flashed me a triumphant grin.

"So I see." His big hand was clamped firmly around the bicep of a tall scrawny guy with a shock of bright orange hair. He'd lost so much weight since I'd last seen him that I wouldn't have recognised him except for the hair and the John Lennon-style glasses. He stank of eau de Jack Daniels, and he swayed a little as he blinked at me through the round lenses.

"Who are you? Where's Leandra?"

I sighed. "Let's talk about it on the way."

Garth marched him toward the car. It was hard to say whether the hand on his arm was holding him up or stopping him from running away. A little of both, perhaps. He tripped over nothing—his own feet, maybe?—and nearly rearranged his face against the side of the big four-wheel drive.

"On the way where? Where are you taking me?"

Before we attracted too much attention from passers-by Steve whisked the back door open and Garth shoved him in, then climbed in beside him. Steve and I got in the front and Steve pulled out from the kerb smoothly.

"Garth?" Blue's voice sounded whiny, like a tired child. "Where are we going? You said you were taking me to Leandra."

"I explained this already." Garth's brows drew together in a scowl that suggested he'd been through it more than once. "Leandra changed bodies. Now she's part of Kate. This is Kate."

He sounded like he was reciting from a book for beginning readers. *This is Leandra. This is Kate. See Leandra in Kate!*

Blue stared at me from under his floppy orange fringe, his face screwed up in confusion. He must be completely smashed. With all the windows closed the car reeked of alcohol. I could see the wheels turning as his brain struggled to catch up with what his ears had just heard. When the confusion soured into a sullen expression I knew he'd caught on.

"So you're one of *them*?"

"One of who?"

"A dragon."

Garth gave him a flat stare. "You got a problem with dragons now?"

"The whole world's got a problem with dragons. Nasty beasts." Spit flew from his mouth and landed on Garth's arm.

He wiped it off. "Remember your manners."

"Why? This one's different, is she? Doesn't go around using people and taking what she wants?" He laughed, showing yellowed teeth. "Yeah, right."

I almost stopped the car and kicked him out. What use was a drunken, hostile goblin? I couldn't compel him; he was a mage. He'd have to be a lot drunker than he was to forget his magical defences against manipulation.

But Garth had gone to a lot of trouble to find him, so I gritted my teeth.

"I have a simple job for you, and I'm prepared to pay well."

He laughed again, a bitter sound. "Yeah, that's what the last dragon said too. *All you gotta do is make a changeling, Blue, and the money's yours. Easy as falling off a log.* Then as soon as the job was done he tried to kill me."

I stiffened. There couldn't be that many dragons requesting changelings. Had Blue helped Jason set up Lachie's fake death?

I turned back to face front before I could say anything I might regret. If Garth wanted the guy's help so much, he'd have to persuade him on his own. I could hardly stand to look at him.

I stared out the window and tried to ignore the angry conversation going on in the back seat. We were heading across the Bridge, the blue water below showing white tips. Another glorious summer's day in Sydney. Already the sun shone white-hot, promising a scorching afternoon. I wore shorts and a sleeveless top. The car was air-conditioned but my house wasn't, and it had been shut up for a while. With a bit of luck Tanya would have cleaned out the fridge for me. If not there could be some nasty surprises in there.

She was a great neighbour. She'd been keeping an eye on the place for the last week, while I was supposedly in Brisbane visiting my sick mother in hospital. As far as I knew Mum was in her usual good health—that had been a spur-of-the-moment lie to cover up the world-shattering truth.

The reason I'd had to leave home in such a rush sat in the back seat, arguing with the goblin. Blue was complaining about being "used" again. His nasal whine grated on my nerves. It was a relief when Garth snarled at him and he finally shut up.

I sat back, happy to let the journey pass in silence. Steve drove with his usual competence, but left me to my thoughts. He wasn't much for chitchat, usually, more interested in computers than people.

A cowardly part of me hoped Tanya wouldn't be home, but really it would be better to get it over with than leave her hanging. Tanya was a force of nature, a powerful personality. Who knew what she'd do if she decided there was something fishy about my continued absence? She might ring the police. Or worse—my mother. And that conversation would go downhill very fast. It would be news to Mum that she'd had a heart attack.

We pulled into the driveway at last. The place looked smaller than I remembered, though not quite so unkempt as usual. Tanya must have sent Roy over to mow the lawn. The blinds were down and the house lay still, dreaming in the morning sun. A feeling of unreality crept over me—as if the familiar house with its green paint and its sagging gutters shouldn't be here any more. It belonged to a different time, to a person who no longer existed.

"So, what now?" I asked as the four of us got out of the car.

Blue eyed the house with suspicion. "I'm not doing this for you, I'm doing it for him." He looked at Garth. "And then we're even, right? One job, and then you leave me alone."

"One job," Garth agreed, though he didn't look too happy with the deal. He'd probably been hoping to win the proving with the aid of his pet goblin mage. I reckoned we were probably better off without the scrawny goblin. He was even less impressive than when Luce and I had met him last year. At least then he'd been sober.

"Wait here," he said.

He approached the front steps, though he didn't set foot on them, and sniffed the air. God knows how he could smell anything over his own stink, but he stood there a long time. Then he set off around the side of the house and disappeared from view.

"What's he doing?" The sun beat down on our heads, and I could feel its bite on my bare shoulders. A lizard crept out onto one of the rocks that bordered the overgrown garden. I felt like an idiot standing on the driveway doing nothing.

Garth shrugged. "Don't know. Goblin stuff."

I rolled my eyes. Goblin stuff. Let's hope Tanya wasn't home. If she saw us loitering in the front yard, I doubt "goblin stuff" would satisfy her curiosity.

Imagine if I'd brought Lachie. Tanya would have had a heart attack—and five minutes later every person she'd ever met in her life would have heard about Lachie's miraculous return from the dead. Plus she'd hound me in order to get every last detail out of me—and I'd probably cave, too. Tanya was relentless.

But we were saved from Tanya's curiosity when Blue reappeared and beckoned us over to the steps.

"You got the key?"

I offered him the front door key. "Did you find anything? Is it safe?"

"Perfectly safe," he said. "But there's a tell-me on the lock here."

"What's that?"

"A trigger spell. As soon as someone goes inside, it alerts whoever set the spell."

"Cheaper than surveillance," said Steve. He had an approving gleam in his eye. Probably already trying to figure out how to write a computer program that would do the same thing.

"So we go in the back door," said Garth.

Blue gave him a pitying look. "It doesn't work like that. It's only anchored to the lock. It covers the whole house."

"I wonder who set it?" Steve stared at the door as if he might see the spell if he looked hard enough.

I sighed. Yes, that was the big question. We didn't know who would come running if we triggered their magical alarm.

"Can you get rid of it without setting it off?" I asked.

Blue sniffed and turned away as if offended. "I *am* a mage."

He spoiled the effect by catching his foot on the first step, which nearly sent him sprawling across the veranda. Garth made as if to catch him but Blue waved him off. He climbed the steps with the exaggerated care of the truly drunk, then crouched by the front door.

He laid the key on the doormat and pulled a tiny knife from his pocket.

Steve's eyebrows shot up and he looked at Garth in surprise. "Didn't you check him for weapons?"

"It's just ceremonial," Garth muttered, but he looked surprised too. The goblin must have managed to hide it from him.

Blue used the tip of the knife to pierce his finger. He squeezed a drop of blood out and let it drip onto the key, droning something dirge-like in the goblin tongue. I looked uneasily over my shoulder, hoping no one could see this peculiar performance. The dirge seemed to go on forever, until abruptly he stopped and inserted the bloody key in the lock.

He unlocked the door and pushed it open. "All done."

"That's it?" said Garth. "The tell-me's gone?"

Blue clumped back down the stairs and stopped in front of him. "Just said so, didn't I?" He held out the bloodstained key, but when Garth would have taken it he didn't let go, sticking his long nose right up into the werewolf's face instead. "So we're even now. No more night-time visits?"

"Fine. Whatever."

"Good." He released the key and headed down the driveway. "And don't tell my family you saw me."

"What about the money?" I asked. Was he just going to leave?

"Keep your blood money," he snapped over his shoulder. "And leave me out of your dragon squabbles."

He staggered down the street like a scarecrow that had escaped its field.

"Strange guy," said Steve. "Friend of yours?"

"Kind of." Garth watched him go with a troubled frown.

I was glad to see the back of him. Quite apart from a strong desire to beat the living crap out of him for his part in convincing me my son was dead, something about him set my teeth on edge.

"Let's go."

I bounded up the steps, eager to be done with the house and its bittersweet memories so I could get back to my miraculously alive child. Lego in hand, of course. I entered the dim hallway; all the blinds were drawn to keep out the heat. The sharp eucalyptus smell of disinfectant lingered in the air, probably from when I'd thrown up the channel stone on this very spot last week. Garth was right behind me. "Can you believe it's only a week since we met?"

That had been my first inkling of how my life was about to change—coming home and being attacked by an intruder in my kitchen. An intruder who had turned into a wolf and tried to tear my heart out. Happy times.

"Should have killed you then and saved myself a lot of trouble." He prowled around the tiny house, checking every room, assuring himself it was safe. If he'd been in wolf form his hackles probably would have been standing up. Not a happy camper, our Garth.

"I love you too."

His mouth quirked in spite of himself. "Don't make promises you can't keep."

I stared at his muscled back as he disappeared into the kitchen. Hadn't been expecting *that* answer. Smart arse. At least he hadn't completely lost his sense of humour. He hadn't quoted *Star Wars* in days, which was a bad sign. Something was definitely eating at him.

I'd hoped reuniting him with some of Leandra's team would help him, but he still seemed to be struggling. Wolves were pack animals. They liked togetherness, but they *loved* order. A pack was a hierarchy where every member knew their place, and how they related to every other member. Simple. Clear and certain.

First he'd lost his mistress, and the thralls had scattered. Then he'd lost Luce, the person he relied on to tell him what to do. Now life was full of new faces and uncertainties, and a lot of responsibility for making sure those uncertainties didn't prove fatal had fallen on his broad shoulders.

I knew how he felt. All our lives had been turned upside down in the last week, but Garth's way of coping seemed to be digging his heels in and trying to control every last little detail, like his insistence on finding the goblin. Although, as it turned out, that hadn't been such a bad idea. Whoever the tell-me had summoned would have been bad news.

I stopped in the doorway of Lachie's room. Funny how, even knowing he was still alive, the weight of all that remembered sorrow pressed down on me, gathered in this room. I hadn't moved a thing; it was still exactly as it had been the day our lives unravelled, his school bag dropped on the floor by his chair, books spilling out onto the carpet next to pieces of Lego and a lone sock. The other one had probably been kicked under the bed, but I'd never looked. The room was like a shrine to my lost son, both a solace and an unbearable reminder of the bright little spark of life I'd thought forever extinguished.

I drew in a shuddering breath. Garth's keen eyes missed nothing. He laid a big hand on my bare shoulder, but all he said was: "Guess the kid really likes Lego."

"Yep."

Apart from the pieces in various stages of construction all over the carpet, there were models on his bedhead, on top of his chest of drawers, and lined up along the shelves of a bookcase that had room for only a handful of books crammed into one corner. Still more lurked unseen behind the doors of his wardrobe.

"I'll bring in the boxes then."

CHAPTER SEVEN

The doorbell rang while we worked and Garth leapt up as though stung. He and Steve exchanged a look, and Steve's hand slipped under the jacket he wore despite the heat.

"Oh, come on, guys. It's probably just Tanya."

"Stay there," said Steve. "I'll check."

I followed him down the hall, ignoring his warning glare. Steve's muscled bulk was intimidating, but I'd been glared at by experts. And I wasn't having Tanya dropping dead of a heart attack because a giant with a gun opened the door to her. "No assassin is going to ring the door bell."

Sure enough, my neighbour stood on the door step, looking like she'd come from the gym, her breasts jammed into a skimpy Lycra top and her dark hair tied back in a jaunty ponytail. Her suspicious frown at being greeted by a hulking stranger cleared when I pushed past him, and she grabbed me with a cry of delight.

"You're back! How are you, hon? How's your mum?"

She caught me in a crushing bear hug, despite her tiny size, and enveloped me in a cloud of her signature perfume, sweet and floral.

"I'm good—Mum's good—we're all good," I laughed. "Tanya! I can't breathe!"

"Sorry!" She eased off the pressure a bit. "It's so good to see you."

When she finally let go I smelled like the Estée Lauder counter at David Jones and I had a crick in my neck.

"It's good to see you too. Thanks for looking after the place for me."

"No problem, honey. Any time." Steve had faded back into the bedroom, but Garth lurked in the background, and she looked him up and down in blatant assessment, a predatory gleam in her eye. It was her dearest wish to see me hook up with someone—anyone, she didn't care—and she'd taken my prolonged singleness as a personal challenge. "Who's your friend?"

I hurried to make introductions. Garth nodded hello then disappeared to join Steve, leaving us to chat. We went into the kitchen, where I discovered she had, in fact, cleaned out my fridge, and emptied the rubbish bin too—on top of cleaning up the shattered mess Garth and I had left after our fight.

"He seems nice." Never one to waste an opportunity, she moved straight to digging-for-goss mode. "Nice" wouldn't have been my choice of adjective, though if muscled-up guys were your thing, he was certainly easy on the eye. "Surly" probably came closer, but Tanya was an incurable glass-half-full kind of person. "Where did you meet him?"

I smothered a laugh. She'd never believe me if I told her the truth.

Or maybe she would. After New Year's Eve, a lot of people were finding it easier to believe in things they never had before.

Our meeting in this very room had left more than a few gaps in the china collection displayed in the old-fashioned dresser. I moved in for a closer look. As I'd feared, Grandma's willow-pattern plate hadn't survived the experience. I ran my hand lightly over the pepper grinder, back on its familiar shelf, a smile tugging at the corners of my mouth. Never underestimate a pepper grinder in a fight.

"Garth? Feels like I've known him for ages."

I picked up a mug that sported a big new chip, rubbing my thumb over the rough spot.

"Now you're back you can check if anything's been taken," Tanya said. "The police will want to know."

"Sure." I turned the mug over in my hands, wondering which was the lesser of the two evils: ignore the police and risk them chasing me up over the supposed burglary, or file a report and draw Detective Hartley's attention to a burglary complete with random blood stains connected to my already-sullied name.

"I had to come in when I saw a strange car in the driveway," Tanya said. "I wasn't sure it was you. Why didn't you tell me you were coming back? I could have picked you up at the airport."

"No, no, it was fine. I had Garth."

"Have you?"

"What?"

"Had Garth."

I choked. I hoped he hadn't heard that. Werewolf ears were pretty sharp. "God, Tanya, don't you ever stop? He's just a friend." *And thanks very much for putting* that *idea in my head.* As if my dragon libido needed any encouragement to start thinking inappropriate thoughts about my employees.

She pouted. "You always say that. What about that gorgeous hunk of man flesh you work with? What's he going to think when he sees you running around with this Garth guy?"

"Actually—" I could feel my cheeks warming as the image of a naked Garth persisted. "Actually, Ben and I are, um … together now."

"Really?" She clapped her hands and jumped up and down on the spot like a little girl. An oversexed little girl. "Ooh, that's fabulous. About time!"

"Yeah." I grinned. It *was* pretty fabulous, despite everything. And what I felt for Ben went much deeper than any random dragon attraction to a well-built werewolf. "You won't be seeing much of me any more. I'm moving in with him."

"Wow! That was quick."

"Well, we've been friends for such a long time—we know each other pretty well already. Now that we've realised how we truly feel about each other, there doesn't seem much point waiting around."

"True. Didn't I tell you you'd be perfect for each other? You should have listened to Mama Tanya ages ago."

"Yeah, yeah, you were right." I rolled my eyes. "So how've you been? How are the girls?"

"They're good. I can't wait for school to go back, though. They're always fighting!"

I nodded in sympathy, though I knew she didn't mean it. She adored those kids. She liked nothing better than having them home where she could stuff them with some good Italian home cooking.

"We'll miss you. What are you going to do with this place? Rent it out?"

"I haven't had much chance to think about it yet."

"Well, don't make a decision too fast. Just in case, you know? And keep your bank accounts separate! A girl can't be too careful these days."

"Yes, Mum."

"I'm serious!"

"I know, I know. Don't worry."

"Can't help it, hon. I'm a mum. That's what we do. And I wouldn't want to see you get hurt again."

Her usually mobile face held a rare serious expression, and I felt an unexpected wave of emotion, glad that somebody cared. But relationship problems were the last thing on my mind at the moment. Well, maybe not the last thing—but they were pretty far down the list. First I had to keep Ben alive to have a relationship *with*—and then I had my own issues to deal with. The proving didn't end till either Alicia or I was dead. Like Highlander: there could be only one.

Garth popped his head into the kitchen. "Do you want the rest of the stuff, or just the Lego?"

"Ah …" There wasn't much beside Lego. A couple of boxes worth of books, maybe, some board games. Would last summer's clothes still fit Lachie? Boys grew so fast at this age.

"What are you doing?" Tanya asked.

"Packing up Lachie's stuff. I decided you were right, it's silly to keep hanging on to everything." God, I felt so bad. If only I could tell her the truth—but it was too dangerous. "I'm going to donate it all to charity."

I guess that answered Garth's question.

"So pack it all up?"

"Yeah, thanks."

Tanya put her hand on my arm as he left the room. "Good for you, hon. I know it must be hard, but I think it's the right thing to do."

I gave her hand a quick squeeze. "Thanks. Well, I guess I'd better get back to it. Give Garth a hand."

"Sure. I won't hold you up. You're probably in a hurry to get back to that gorgeous feller of yours. I know I would be!" She grinned suggestively, then her face fell. "Can't believe you're moving out, though. We'll miss you."

She pulled me into another fierce hug. Certainly no one could ever accuse Tanya of hiding her feelings.

"I'll miss you too."

She swiped at her eyes. "Oh, look at me, my mascara's probably all over my face. I can't believe how quickly things can change."

"I know." God, did I know. This time last week I'd been a grieving mother, living a lonely, broken life, with Tanya and Ben my only friends. This time last week I'd been human.

Now I had my beautiful boy back—an amazing, life-altering plus in the great scales of the universe. On the downside, I was no longer fully human, but some strange dragon-human hybrid, with my life at stake in a deadly game to see who would inherit the throne from my mother the dragon queen. Or maybe that was a plus too? It was hard to tell. I found the whole people-trying-to-kill-me thing far too distracting.

And of course there was Ben: the change in our relationship was *definitely* a plus.

"The world's a funny old place sometimes, isn't it? I mean, look at that business with the dragons on New Year's Eve. What do you reckon? Think there really are supernatural creatures hidden among us?"

"Don't know. It seems a little hard to believe, right?" My eyes flicked to the damaged cupboard door, still hanging by one hinge. The door that I'd slammed into the snarling werewolf's face. "Like, if it *is* true, how come we've never had any hints till now?"

That's probably what I'd be thinking if I was still plain Kate. And Lord knows, if anyone should have suspected, I should have. For crying out loud, I'd been married to a dragon for five years—how could I have missed it completely? I mean, sure, it's not the first explanation that springs to mind if your husband starts acting a little strange, but not even a hint? In five years?

No one would think it possible. No one who wasn't in the know, that is. To other shifters it seemed entirely reasonable. Dragons had powers of persuasion bordering on total mind control. In the right circumstances they could convince a human black was white. Leandra had managed to entrance me into cutting her open, extracting the channel stone that controlled her magic and swallowing it—all while she was dying of poisoning. And I hadn't been able to remember doing any of it afterwards. Covering up any little indiscretions or diverting suspicion in a wife would have been child's play for Jason in comparison.

"I know, right? That's what I think too, though Roy's a believer. I always said he read too many of those stupid fantasy novels. Have you seen that new video?"

"What new video?"

"It came out this morning. YouTube crashed, they had so many hits. It shows you how they did it. Just search dragons and CGI."

"CGI?" Even though it was in my own interest to act convinced, I couldn't help sounding incredulous. Who the hell would believe that? "That was done with *computers*? Says who?"

"Oh, they're not saying it was *done* with computers. They had remote-controlled models. They used CGI on the video to make them look bigger and hide the engines."

I opened my mouth to argue. Surely anyone who'd been there wouldn't buy that story. Those dragons were huge—way too big to be remote-controlled craft. And the way we'd moved, so organic, so clearly not robotic.

Still, even though it was New Year's Eve and thousands of people *had* seen it in person, there were still millions who hadn't, who might possibly be persuaded by this new "truth".

"There's more than one video on the Internet, though. Are they all supposedly doctored like this?"

Tanya shrugged. "Most of them are a bit blurry, you know, or taken from too far away. It makes it look more convincing if there's more than one, from different users. But there's only that one that the news programs have been replaying where you can actually see much. Someone spent a lot of effort planning this."

Someone certainly had spent a lot of effort—but on this new cover-up, not on the original "stunt". It had to be either the government or Elizabeth, and my money was on Elizabeth.

"Makes you wonder why they bothered, doesn't it?"

"Probably some massive publicity stunt. Bet you someone comes forward in a few days and it'll turn out to be part of an advertising campaign for a new beer or something."

"Probably." I moved toward the door. She'd talk all day if I let her.

Thankfully she got the hint. "Well, I'd better leave you to it. Call me, okay? Let me know how you go."

I promised I would and she finally left, though not before waving goodbye to both Garth and Steve. I went back into Lachie's room and found the guys had stripped it nearly bare, so I grabbed a suitcase out of the hall cupboard and packed a few of my own things too. Leandra had the best of everything, and her clothes fit me pretty well, but we'd been two different people. Her taste in music, for instance, sucked. And she didn't appear to own a single pair of running shoes. Too busy prancing around in designer outfits.

Lucky we'd brought the big car. Even with the back row of seats laid flat we barely managed to squeeze everything in. Poor Steve had boxes piled up all around him. I felt a wrench as we pulled away from the kerb, and had to resist an urge to wave goodbye to the old house. Who knew when I'd see it again? But Garth already thought I was mad enough.

He kept glancing in the rear vision mirror as he drove, a preoccupied look on his face.

"What's wrong?"

"We've got someone on our tail. No, don't turn round!"

I froze guiltily, then tried to pretend I hadn't had any such intention. Not that I would have been able to see past the piles of boxes.

"Who is it?"

"Don't know. I don't recognise the car. They're sitting two cars back."

"Are you sure they're really following us?"

I don't know why I should feel so surprised. People had followed me all the time when I'd worked as a herald delivering messages for shifters, though at the time I'd had no idea of the real nature of my job. I thought there were just a lot of secretive people in the world who were prepared to pay well for keeping their messages private—and a whole bunch of other people busy trying to find out where those messages were going. Delivering the messages undetected had been like a kind of game.

When I thought about it now it didn't make that much sense, but at the time I'd been in a very different headspace. With Lachie dead I didn't give a crap about anything else, and

I moved through the world in a kind of fog of despair, detached and completely lacking in curiosity. In fact I'd liked the thrill of adrenalin being followed always brought. It was the only time during those dark months that I'd ever felt alive.

"Of course I'm sure." Garth changed lanes and took a random left turn. In the rear-view mirror on the passenger side I caught a glimpse of a white sedan making the same turn. The driver had dark hair, but I couldn't make out anything else in the tiny reflection.

"Is that them? In the white car?"

"Yep." Garth checked his mirror again as we drove through a roundabout. "It's a woman. Seems to be alone. She's hanging back now—she's let that guy in."

A car entered the roundabout from the right and slotted in behind us. The woman in the white car now sat two cars behind again.

"What do you want to do?" I asked.

He gave me a toothy grin. The big werewolf seemed to enjoy the adrenalin rush as much as I used to.

"What would Luke do?"

In the back seat Steve groaned. I shook my head. Garth and his damn Star Wars obsession. "Probably blow them up. Sadly for you, this is a Mazda, not an X-wing."

"Faith you must have," he croaked in his best Yoda voice. "Show you I will."

I groaned too, but in truth I wanted to grin back. Garth so rarely showed a playful side. Always worrying. Always scowling. He looked about ten years younger when he smiled.

Maybe he wasn't as old as I'd thought. I was glad he wasn't freaking out.

For a time nothing happened. We continued along Epping Road. The sun shone and a catchy tune played on the radio. Around us the traffic flowed normally. The woman in the white car never got closer than two cars behind.

We'd stopped for three red lights before we found ourselves the first car in line at the next one. We were in the middle lane. Garth stopped the car. The cars on either side pulled up too.

Then he floored it, charging through the intersection as the cross-traffic started to move. Horns blared, but no one hit us. We were through and the intersection behind us filled with cars from the cross street. The woman in the white car couldn't follow, trapped behind stationary cars.

Garth roared down Epping Road, doing at least fifty over the speed limit. Two intersections later he picked his gap and ran the red arrow, turning off into a residential area. I clutched at my seat as we skidded through the turn. Then he ducked and weaved through side streets, still heading in the general direction of the city, as Lego rattled and slid around in the back. I held on tight and hoped there were no police around.

Finally he slowed to a more sedate pace, a smug look on his face.

"We won't be seeing her again."

"I may not be seeing my stomach again any time soon either. Where'd you learn to drive like that? A dodgem car ride?"

He grinned. "You talk too much. I definitely should have killed you."

I grinned back. "You and whose army, Skywalker?"

77

CHAPTER EIGHT

Lachie was overjoyed to be reunited with his beloved Lego. Even Garth had to smile at the squeals of delight as each new set was carried in from the car. I left them to it and went to Google "Sydney dragons CGI".

I found Tanya's video straight away. Was this supposed to be the same CGI program used by the big special effects studios? But those big movie effects took months. How could people believe this had been done in a matter of days?

"Come look at this," I called to Ben once I'd watched it through. He came into the study and stood behind me, massaging my neck with his good hand, as I hit replay.

The world watched in shock and amazement as two dragons fought over Sydney Harbour in the early hours of New Year's Day, the voiceover began. The familiar footage rolled and Valeria stooped upon me once again. I shifted uncomfortably in my seat at the memory. That had been too close.

Dragons exist! The supernatural live among us. Or do they?
On screen I fled under the Bridge, Valeria in hot pursuit.

How could anyone doubt the evidence of their own eyes? Here they are, captured on film for all the world to see.

I backwinged and landed briefly on the bridge before taking off again. I'd been dropping Lachie to safety, to free myself up to fight Valeria, but the view was too distant to see the small figure stumbling from my cradling claws.

But how closely is the world looking?

The camera zoomed in, as it always did at this point in the footage, and the picture shook, presumably because the cameraman's hands were shaking too. None of the videos I'd seen were perfectly polished. Despite the presence of a gazillion TV cameras around the harbour earlier in the night, this had taken place at least two hours after the fireworks had finished, and the camera crews had all gone home. Only amateurs, mostly with iPhones, remained to capture the action.

But this time, as we took to the skies again, the familiar footage shook even more than usual. A dark, boxy mass could be seen under the bellies of the two dragons. Both dragons moved far less naturally.

Close enough to notice the engines that powered these two "dragons"? Notice how slowly they're moving now? What if we speed this footage up again and add a little CGI magic?

As if at the touch of a magic eraser, the engines gradually disappeared and the jerky movements became graceful, showing realistic muscles flexing beneath golden skin.

Let's see that again.

The screen split in two, and the same piece of footage played on both sides. But one side had the "before" image, with engines showing and jerky robotic dragons. The robotic dragons appeared smaller against the backdrop of the Harbour Bridge. The "after" side showed large, lifelike dragons waging acrobatic war.

Are you still amazed that dragons exist? Or are you just amazed at what computers can do these days?

I spun in my chair to face Ben. "What do you think?"

"Pretty impressive. Plays well to the sceptics. Elizabeth, I suppose?"

"Probably. Either her or the government, but she seems the most likely candidate. I can't imagine the government getting its act together this fast, for a start. And they haven't got her money to throw at something like that. It must have cost a bomb."

"And she has more to gain from sowing doubt."

I grinned, swinging in the chair. "Oh, I don't know. I heard yesterday some African country was considering declaring war on Australia. That might have stirred them up in Canberra."

"Really? Why?"

"Something about wiping out all the black magicians we're supposedly harbouring."

He snorted. "You can't believe everything you read on the Internet."

"Apparently not. Do you think many people will believe this? What about all the people who saw it in real life?"

He leaned against the desk, looking thoughtful. "Most people won't take much persuading. They don't want to believe it, so they'll grasp at any plausible explanation. And if the media run with it … Things don't have to be true to be believed. Ask any politician. As long as you shout it long enough and loud enough you wear people down."

"True. If it muddies the waters enough we'll only have a few crackpots convinced we're real by the time it all dies down."

"Let's hope so. The last thing we need at the moment is more publicity."

A proving was hard enough to keep secret at the best of times, with people turning up dead all over the place. Having the eyes of the world on us made it that much more difficult. And I already had the police interested in me. I couldn't afford to feature in any more of their reports.

I turned back to the computer and checked my Twitter feed. Predictably, it was running mad with speculation. I watched tweets fly past at a furious rate. The world was still enthralled by the dragon spectacle.

I suppose that was to be expected. It was a huge story, at a very quiet time of year, and everyone had an opinion. At least it was keeping Elizabeth too busy with damage control to take any action against me for causing the whole mess.

Ben leaned over my shoulder. "What's this *not the Middle Ages* hashtag?"

I ran a quick search, and my heart sank as I scanned the resulting column. The tweets flashed past almost too fast to read, and it wasn't hard to see why. Talk about a hot topic. Seemed like half the world wanted to get out the pitchforks, and the other half was trying to persuade them that this was "*not the Middle Ages*".

We're all Australians. This is #nottheMiddleAges

Civilisation has moved past the age of witch hunts. #nottheMiddleAges

You can't accuse someone of being a werewolf just because you don't like them. #nottheMiddleAges

I winced a little at that last one. It would be happening soon, if it wasn't already. True or not, people would be accused. Neighbours would insist they had a right to know; they had children to protect, and before you knew it someone's house would be firebombed. Maybe someone would take pot shots at the old lady who lived in the creepy old house, or kill a little boy's dog because they thought it was a werewolf. Someone else would be driven out of town. Someone would lose their job, or their girlfriend—or their life.

Humans were so goddamned tribal. If you weren't Us, you were Other, and Other was to be feared. And where Fear walked, its big brother Hate followed in the shadows, growing stronger and more powerful.

I blew out a heavy sigh. Not that people would always be wrong to fear. God knows there were plenty of shifters only too ready to do them harm. I just felt sorry for the innocent ones caught up in the mess, and the humans who'd never heard of shifters who would now be victimised just because.

A tweet caught my eye and I frowned. *Dead woman a dragon?* I clicked the link and arrived at a feature article in the *Sydney Morning Herald.*

"Damn. Look at this."

Ben read aloud, his breath stirring my hair. "*Sources close to the coroner have suggested there could be a link between the mystery woman pulled from the harbour in the early hours of New*

Year's Day and the dragon battle that took place on and around the Harbour Bridge that morning. Sources close to the coroner? What does that mean?"

"Don't know." My thoughts flashed to Detective Hartley. The death of the "mystery woman" would be treated as a murder investigation. Would that one cross her desk too? But nothing tied Valeria's naked body to me. I was jumping at shadows. "I guess cause of death is pretty obvious. She'd have a giant hole through her chest. But I don't see how the coroner can link that to the dragons, even if he can prove that she died at roughly the same time as the dragon hit the water."

"He'd have to officially recognise the supernatural first," Ben said. "And that's not going to happen, especially with Elizabeth doing her damnedest to convince people it's all a giant con trick."

If only everyone *would* be convinced. The spectre of the Middle Ages loomed over me. If people died, it would be my fault, but what choice had I had? Once Valeria had turned dragon there'd been no other way out.

In other news, the Prime Minister announces the formation of a special taskforce to investigate allegations of supernatural activities in Australia. Taskforce Jaeger will begin its investigations with a review of evidence and eyewitness accounts of the alleged dragon sightings over Sydney Harbour in the early hours of January 1st.

I sighed and rubbed at my face. Alleged dragon sightings. Right. Not even one o'clock in the afternoon, and I was already exhausted.

Ben dropped a kiss on my hair. "Don't sweat it. They've got nothing. Let's focus on more important things."

There sure were a lot of those. We had to find more men, and I desperately needed allies in the shifter community. I had to keep Detective Hartley at bay, keep my nose clean and keep Ben alive. I had to find out who'd tried to kill him and where Jason had got to.

"Which ones?" I asked, feeling the weight of all those enormous and often-incompatible responsibilities.

He turned the chair around and drew me gently to my feet. For once we were alone, which was pretty unusual these days, though my enhanced hearing picked up other voices elsewhere in the house. A bright square of sunlight lay on the carpet, and dust motes danced through it, swirling with the movement of our bodies. He stood a head taller than me, though I wasn't a short woman, and I lifted my face to his.

"Lachie will be busy for hours with his Lego. I thought we might have a little nap. Afterwards, of course."

"Afterwards?" He stood very close. I gulped in a deep breath, full of his fresh woodsy aftershave and a warm Ben-smell. My pulse sped up. "But your arm ..."

"I have an injured arm. I'm not *dead*."

"True." I pressed against him and felt his body respond. "In fact, you seem ... rather lively."

Amusement glittered in his eyes. His good hand slid down my back, producing little shivers of delight, and cupped one cheek firmly. "Come upstairs and I'll show you just how lively."

I wound my arms round his neck and pulled him down for a kiss. The world would just have to burn without me for a while. "Thought you'd never ask."

CHAPTER NINE

Sex is a wonderful stress release. Dr Ben was prepared to prescribe a great deal of it, but even his enthusiastic assistance couldn't produce more than a temporary relief. I had an appointment with Trevor, the leader of the Sydney werewolf pack, the next morning, and my nerves grew as the time ticked away till the meeting.

Garth and I waited in the study. Leandra had preferred to call it her office, but come on—who was she kidding? Sure, she had the big antique desk, the plush carpet and visitors' chairs so padded you could lose yourself in them. She had state-of-the-art computer equipment and a bank of filing cabinets that looked the part, but she barely worked. Those cabinets were so empty you could have hidden a body in them. She lived off the interest from a bucket load of investments, but the most she ever did in this room was sign a few papers. She had an accountant and a financial planner who handled everything for her.

She hadn't even earned the money in the first place—it was the "seed capital" a dragon queen provided to each of her queen daughters when they left her protection to face the rigours of the proving. It wasn't much of a risk for the queen—only the winner got to keep it. The losers' assets came back to their mother, and if they'd managed the money well, often with a substantial profit. Leandra—or her financial advisors, at least—had turned a small fortune into a significantly larger one.

I was now the beneficiary, and determined Elizabeth wouldn't see a penny of her money back.

Garth sighed and checked his watch for at least the third time since sitting down across the desk from me. The chair next to him awaited his brother, the pack leader. It amused me to receive Trevor from the position of power behind a desk, as he'd done to me only last week. I wanted him in no doubt as to who was in charge.

"Do you want me to call you when he gets here?" I asked, as Garth shifted restlessly. Not for the first time that morning, I rearranged the pens on the red leather that was set into the desk top. His nerves were catching. "You could go make Steve's happy life miserable instead of waiting around."

I'd considered not having him present at all. Though they were brothers, Garth was an exile. Some pack leaders might take offence at his inclusion in the interview. But I had Trevor pegged as a fairly level-headed guy, and last week he'd seemed to reject Garth more because of pressure from the rest of the pack than from any personal inclination.

Besides, Garth might be able to push his brother to join us in ways I couldn't. I had to take every advantage I could find.

"I'll wait," Garth growled.

Yesterday's playfulness had disappeared. Grumpy Garth was back.

"When's full moon?" I asked.

The scowl deepened. Asking a werewolf when full moon was due was like accusing a woman of having PMS. But it was a valid question. The proximity of full moon did affect werewolves' moods, no two ways about it. And if Trevor was feeling its pull he'd be more prickly and unreasonable than normal.

"Not for eight nights."

That was common too. Ask a schoolteacher how long it is till the holidays, and they'll answer you to the hour. Werewolves were the same. They knew exactly when to expect the moon. It was never "about a week" or "in a fortnight". Eight nights. Eight nights exactly until they were forced to change, whether they wanted to or not, and either run wild or lock themselves safely away. Any other night they could take wolf form or not as they wished. But on full moon they couldn't resist the pull of their darker nature.

Full moon night was a bad night to meet a werewolf.

Not that there was ever a great night to meet a werewolf. I'd had personal experience in how terrifying such an encounter could be.

"How long have you been a werewolf?" I asked on impulse.

Also not a polite question in shifter society, and for a moment I thought he wouldn't reply. Leandra had taken him on as a favour to Trevor after the pack leader had been forced to exile him from the pack. She'd found him a useful addition to her team, but she hadn't been interested in his personal history. Whereas I felt very close to him, despite only meeting him a week ago, in less-than-ideal circumstances. Funny how bonding it can be to dig up a grave together. They should include it in team-building management courses. But I still knew very little about him. He'd mentioned last week that he'd been turned, but hadn't gone into detail.

"Sixteen years," he said eventually. "Coming up seventeen in June."

Leandra had assumed he'd been born shifter, as most wolves were. Turned werewolves were rare, which was just as well, or the secret existence of werewolves wouldn't have stayed secret very long. Only a person who was bitten on the night of full moon would become a werewolf—and didn't I wish I'd known *that* the night Garth attacked me and I was panicking about transforming. Unfortunately for the victim, wolves were so crazed by the influence of the moon that night that the attacks were usually too frenzied to leave survivors.

"And Trevor? Was he turned at the same time?"

"No. He's a born."

I blinked. "But you're brothers. How does that work?"

"He's younger than me. Mum was turned after she had me."

"What about your father? Was he turned too?"

"He died." He crossed his arms and stared down at the carpet, as if he'd found something fascinating in its design. "She met Trevor's dad after she joined the pack."

I stared at the top of his bowed head. His defensive posture made it clear he didn't like discussing this. I supposed I could drag it out of him if I had the patience for playing twenty questions, but really, it wasn't any of my business. I was only trying to distract myself from my own nerves. I shifted the pens again instead.

It made sense, though. Ever since I'd discovered Garth wasn't born a werewolf I'd been wondering how on earth his brother had managed to work his way up to pack leader starting as a rank outsider. Though packs weren't strictly dynastic, it was more common than not for the offspring of a pack leader to become leader in turn, and absolutely unheard of for a newcomer to the shifter world to make it that far. Trevor was an unlikely enough candidate as it was, given his relatively small physical size and his rather bookish air.

Not that I had any illusions about his mild-mannered exterior. I knew he could be a ruthless bastard when the situation called for it.

Before I could change my mind and subject Garth to a thorough grilling on his personal history, Steve knocked on the door. The ruthless bastard himself followed Steve into the room, looking surprisingly small next to the big half-Maori. Garth and I both stood.

I offered my hand, and Trevor shook it. His grip was firm but not crushing. He was shorter than his brother, only a little taller than me, and looked to be in his early thirties, though his hair had already started to recede.

"Please, have a seat. Can I offer you something to drink?"

Trevor sat—though not till after Garth did. Wolf dominance games were as natural as breathing to them. He declined a drink, so Steve left, closing the door with a definite click, cutting off the noises of the house.

In the silence Trevor cocked his head to one side, an expression of polite puzzlement on his face.

"Not that I'm not happy to see you survived the … drama … since we met, but I understood this meeting was to be with Leandra."

"It is." I leaned back in my chair, projecting a relaxed assurance I didn't feel. "You're speaking to her."

He frowned and looked around as if expecting Leandra to jump from behind the filing cabinet. "I don't understand."

"At our last meeting you said you couldn't take sides with me against Valeria. You said if only Leandra herself were standing in front of you asking, your answer might have been different."

"I remember what I said. And my answer hasn't changed. If Leandra wants something from me she can ask me herself."

I put my hands flat on the desk, the leather inset giving slightly beneath my fingers, and leaned toward him. "She is. I am. I *am* Leandra."

He rose from the chair, his expression chilly. "Don't waste my time. I know what Leandra looks like. And I've seen her on the news, like every other man and his dog, killing Valeria, so I know she's still alive. Is she injured? Is that why she's hiding?"

I didn't move. Inside I reached for the rest of my essence. Only a little. It got easier every time. Claws as long as sword blades sprang from my fingertips with a tiny snick, and Trevor flinched.

"Let me put it another way. Leandra and I have merged into one personality." I lifted one hand from the desk, not in a menacing way, but so he could clearly see the curve of dragon claws, harder than steel. "You won't be seeing her old body again, but rest assured, she's here. Please sit down."

He subsided into the chair, eyes fixed on the wicked length of my claws. I willed them away and folded my hands on the desk top.

He glanced at his brother. "Is this true?"

Garth nodded. "Every word."

"Bloody hell." He looked back at me. "You'll have to tell me the story."

"Some other time, perhaps. Today I'd like to discuss a mutually beneficial arrangement such as we used to have."

Good Lord, I even sounded like Leandra. Well, at least that might convince him I was telling the truth.

"Ah." He drummed the fingers of his right hand lightly on the arm of his chair. His fingernails were short and very clean. Anyone further from the popular image of a werewolf would be hard to find. There was nothing wild or unkempt about him. Even the faint shadow of stubble on his cheeks looked more city chic than weekend hangover. Werewolves always had a problem with fast hair regrowth. He wore a tie and a long-sleeved blue business shirt, as if he'd just stepped out of the office.

Quite possibly he had. He had a thriving accountancy practice. I could see that logical mind stepping through the options as he sat there, fingers moving in a quiet rhythm.

"I assume you've heard about the bounty?"

"What bounty?" Garth growled, instantly alert.

I tensed too, though I tried to hide the fact. "Bounty" was not a good word.

"I see you haven't. Elizabeth has set one on the heads of two former heralds: Ben Stevens and Kate O'Connor."

"How much?" Garth asked.

"Half a million for Ben—"

"Half a *million*? Shit. We'll have all the world and his brother taking pot shots at us."

Elizabeth must be majorly pissed. Half a million was a fortune, and guaranteed every second shifter would be gunning for Ben. We were lucky we'd only had to fight off one attacker so far. I'd never heard of such a big bounty. Usually they were more like fifty grand, and only the regular bounty-hunting crowd took much notice.

"—and one million for you."

I stared, too shocked to hide my reaction. So much for letting the proving take its course. The bitch was determined to see me fail.

"She calls you the abomination," he added helpfully. "I didn't know what she meant before, but I guess I see it now."

"What's that supposed to mean?" Ever quick to take offence, Garth leapt to his feet.

I waved him back to his seat. "Chill, Garth."

"That came out badly," Trevor said, inclining his head in a gesture of apology. "I meant that I can see why she thinks you're a threat. When I thought you were just a herald I couldn't imagine what you'd done to get so far into her bad books."

I nodded in agreement. "Valeria was her favourite daughter." If I'd ever doubted that before, here was the proof. Elizabeth hadn't lifted a manicured finger to help her two heralds when they were kidnapped by Valeria's forces, even though violence against heralds was meant to be answered with swift punishment. Yet now that we'd taken sides with Leandra, however unintentionally, she'd gone all fire-and-brimstone on us. Was it possible Valeria had actually cleared the whole kidnapping-of-heralds thing with her first? Surely not. That stunt had been all Nada's idea, part of her long vendetta against Jason. More likely Elizabeth had let it slide, thinking Valeria was about to win and the point would be moot. Only now she wasn't happy with how things had turned out. "I'm sure she thought Valeria's victory was a done deal."

"Then you went and destroyed the favourite in front of the whole world."

Yeah. That obviously hadn't gone down too well. "She may even be as upset about the publicity as the actual killing. She's always been so paranoid about the shifter world being exposed."

Trevor sat back and rested one ankle on the other knee. His socks had blue TARDISes on them. "And now here we are, with our arses hanging out in public."

"Exactly." I regarded him thoughtfully. Though he looked relaxed and confident, he still hadn't actually said he would support me. "Though some of us have our arses hanging out further than others. Which is why I wanted to talk to you."

Though he didn't move, he no longer looked so relaxed. "I'm not sure there's much to talk about. My situation hasn't changed since last time we had this conversation."

"But mine has. I'm a full dragon now, and I've just destroyed my greatest enemy."

"And earned yourself a million others. How long do you think you'll last with a million-dollar price tag on your head?"

"As long as it's long enough to destroy Alicia, it doesn't matter. If I win the proving Elizabeth can't touch me." I leaned forward, wishing I could compel him. But once the effect wore off we'd be back to square one. Part of me wanted to try anyway. This man had been Leandra's to command. The part of me that used to be her raged at having to beg. "But to do that I need your help."

"And I wish I could give it." He rose and walked to the window. Werewolves had a terrible tendency to pace when they were unsettled. Sunlight caught the golden stubble on his face, making him look like he'd been attacked by a kid with a glitter bomb.

Obedience bought with threats could always be re-bought by someone wielding bigger threats. I had to have his willing co-operation. I forced myself to sit still and master my temper.

Garth had no such constraints. He swivelled round in his chair, his expression black. "Do you *want* Alicia to win?"

"For what it's worth, no, I don't." He threw a frustrated look his brother's way. "But what does it matter to a werewolf which dragon arse sits on the throne? They're all the same."

"Kate's not."

"It doesn't matter anyway. Elizabeth is still queen, and if you think I'm going to stand against her you must be moon-touched." He turned back to me. "I'm sorry, I really am, but I can't help you. Officially my hands are tied."

Well, there was an opening if ever I heard one. I gritted my teeth. I couldn't afford to be proud. I'd take any help I could get. "But unofficially?"

He spread his arms in a *who knows* gesture. Combined with his own soft orange aura, the sunlight streaming in the window outlined him in a glowing light. He looked like a Renaissance saint bestowing benediction. "Unofficially a couple of my people might be looking for a change of pace. Pack life doesn't suit everyone."

Garth was all ears. "Who?"

"Jerry and Mac. I think they'd be willing to join your team."

"Will they fight? We're not a halfway house for werewolves wanting to escape the pack, you know."

I snorted. It had worked out all right for him. "We can always use a good man."

Trevor laughed, though I didn't see the joke. "They're very good. And I think they'll jump at the chance. I'll let you know."

"As long as they understand the danger." I needed genuine commitment, not the dead weight of unwilling conscripts. If they thought the pack was bad, wait till they tried being hunted by half of supernatural Sydney.

Trevor sobered. "There are all different kinds of danger."

CHAPTER TEN

I understood the joke the next day, when two young werewolves turned up and introduced themselves as Jerry and McKenna. Two female werewolves.

Jerry fit the werewolf stereotype beautifully. Her short pink hair stood up in gelled spikes and she'd clearly only stopped adding piercings to her ears because she ran out of flesh. She wore a cropped black top, which displayed the full sleeve tattoo on her right arm. Crucifixes and roses featured prominently in the design, along with a surprising number of butterflies.

McKenna looked barely old enough to vote, and had the biggest blue eyes I'd ever seen outside of an anime character. Her light brown hair had natural-looking blond streaks. A couple of strands had escaped her ponytail and curled softly round her face. Anything less like a werewolf would be hard to imagine.

"You could have told me they were girls," I said to Garth after they'd gone upstairs to settle in.

He dropped into the chair across from me and put his feet up on the desk. "Why? Does it matter?"

"No … Guess not." Wolves were wolves. They all fought like trapped animals, and were damn near unstoppable. I glared meaningfully at his giant clodhoppers till he took them off my desk. "I was just surprised. Jerry and Mac? Not your average girls' names."

He grinned, unrepentant. "There's nothing average about those two."

"They look so young." Sometimes Leandra's pragmatism won out, but other times Kate's motherly instincts were aroused. Mac, in particular, made me uneasy. She could have been playing with Lego herself only a few years ago.

"Leandra wouldn't have cared."

I couldn't read his expression. Was that a criticism or not? Did he think Leandra had changed for the worse?

I guess the real question was whether or not she could still win. All our lives depended on it. There was no backing out once a proving got started: you either won or you were worm food. No middle ground.

The doorbell rang and I pushed it out of my mind. No point worrying. It was beyond my control now. We'd both changed, and the new me that had been formed would have to deal with whatever crap the shifter world found to throw at her.

And there sure seemed to be a lot of it.

Steve filled the doorway with his bulk. I was on the computer again, hunting for any mentions of "Taskforce Jaeger", but the only official word was the original bland announcement. Other than that it was all speculation. "There's a herald at the door."

I rolled my chair away from the desk and stretched, easing the kinks in my neck. "Did you check his Hermes charm?"

"Of course." He looked offended at the question. "He's legit. But I've got three of the guys watching him."

"I'll get Ben," Garth said, as untrusting as I was. Is it still paranoia if everyone really *is* trying to kill you?

"Tell him to be careful."

It could be a genuine message—or it could be an assassination attempt. I waited, nerves jangling, till Ben came in.

Relief rushed over me. "All clear?"

"Yep. I knew the guy. He's the real deal, and the package checks out."

Ben knew all the heralds working in Sydney. There wasn't any kind of guild or association; they were more like contractors to the queen, but there weren't that many of them. For most the business had been in the family for generations. He perched on the corner of the desk next to me and handed over an envelope, in the familiar buff colour. I'd delivered a few of these myself.

I turned it over. The insignia stamped into the red wax that sealed it was an unfamiliar design. Not from Elizabeth or Alicia, then. I broke the seal and slid out the dragon scale inside.

Bigger than my hand, it had a soft metallic sheen like pewter. At first it showed me only my own hazy reflection, then, as it warmed in my hand, words started to appear, dancing across the surface in lines of fire. As soon as I put it down they'd disappear again. Only my touch could bring them to life. Such was the paranoia of dragons. It was why they didn't deal in emails or phone calls. When they had something they wanted kept secret, nothing beat a method of communication that would only be visible to the intended recipient.

I scanned the message.

"It's from Carl Davison."

Garth's eyes widened. He crowded in next to Ben, craning his neck to try to read the message. "The software guy? He's a dragon?"

Ben frowned. "I thought he was one of Elizabeth's cronies. What does he want?"

"He wants to meet with me." I checked my watch. "In less than an hour. He says I need to know what my sisters are doing."

Ben was right. Carl was pretty high up in Elizabeth's court. How could I trust him? But if he had information for me, could I afford to ignore that?

"What does he mean, sisters?" Ben looked as puzzled as I felt.

I leaned back and stared at the ceiling, thinking hard. My turn to put my feet on the desk.

"Maybe it's a typo," said Garth.

I snorted. Dragons didn't make typos, not on scales. There was no writing or typing involved, just pure will. If he said sisters, he meant it.

But what *did* he mean? I'd had four originally: Valeria, Ingrid, Monique and Alicia. Alicia was the only one still alive. Valeria and Ingrid I'd killed myself. Monique had been blown into itty bitty dragon pieces by a bomb of Valeria's that had almost wiped me out too. There hadn't been a body left to see, but I'd been sure she was dead.

Could I be wrong? Could she somehow have escaped the blast?

If she had, she'd been lying so low for the last year that there hadn't been so much as a whisper of her existence. I found that very hard to believe. Not a single sighting? Not even a hint, in a whole year, of something odd going on behind the scenes?

In a relatively small shifter community like Sydney, where everyone watched everyone else, and the proving was like some giant free show where the non-combatants sat back with their popcorn to enjoy the spectacle, it seemed hugely unlikely. What did she gain by basically putting her entire existence on hold like that?

But what was the alternative?

I sat up, slamming my feet to the floor, and gazed at Ben in horror. "There must be another sister."

There had been six eggs in that clutch. The sixth egg had supposedly never hatched. It happened sometimes, and I'd never given it any thought until now.

I tossed Carl's scale on the desk, its message fading as it left my hand. It lay like a pool of quicksilver, glinting against the blood red of the leather desk top. My mind raced. "Elizabeth only declared the five of us, but she must have kept one back."

But why? Dragon queens were notoriously unsentimental about their offspring. Her current attitude to me was pretty clear proof of that. She'd have to be very sure that this hypothetical sixth daughter far exceeded her sisters' abilities, or risk putting a weakling on the throne. But if she was as good as all that, why not let her join the proving and destroy the rest of us in the usual way?

I slammed my hand on the desk top. "God *damn* it. And all this time I thought Valeria was the favourite."

"That doesn't make any sense," said Ben. "How could she know which daughter was strongest if they didn't all compete?"

Garth looked from one to the other of us in confusion. "What the hell are you talking about? I have enough trouble keeping up with pack politics, much less this dragon shit."

"Well, this dragon shit just got a lot stinkier." I rubbed my forehead, feeling a headache threatening. Stress could kill you—as long as the bounty hunters, your mother, your sisters and half the people you knew didn't get there first.

"Elizabeth laid a queen clutch, twenty-six years ago. You know queens do that, right, when they're nearing the end of their lives?"

"Yeah, and when the daughters grow up they fight and the winner becomes the next queen."

"Right." As if I was likely to forget *that* part. "But the eggs don't all hatch at the same time. There can be as much as five years between the first hatching and the last. In our case it was only about eighteen months." Or so I'd always been told. "Valeria was first, and Monique was last."

"How is that fair? The older ones are bigger and stronger."

"True. Which is why the hatchlings are reared separately, and the proving doesn't start till the queen judges they're all ready."

"But why does she care? If the queen's about to die, what difference does it make to her who takes over?"

"Dragons are very territorial. If they don't make sure they have the strongest possible successor, they risk having a queen from another domain move in and take over. No queen can stand the thought of her bloodline being wiped out and one of her rivals stealing her throne. Anyway, when she thinks they're ready, you get the Presentation Ball, where the candidates are officially introduced and the proving is announced."

"Though some don't wait for that," Ben pointed out. "If you can believe the legends, Elizabeth finished off her sisters before the last one was even out of nappies."

"Maybe that's why she was so careful with us. The first time I met my sisters was at the Presentation Ball—though I tried once before that."

CHAPTER ELEVEN

I was twelve years old and convinced I already knew everything. I'd devoured every book in the farm's small library, and could rattle off the powers and weaknesses of every type of shifter like a regular little encyclopaedia. I knew the colours of their auras and their special abilities plus the personal histories of every shifter in my mother's court. On top of that I knew all the turning points in my mother's long rule, and was pretty well acquainted with the courts and histories of the other queens too.

And then Mr Saunders arrived to teach me economics and human history.

Well, economics I could at least see the use for. After all, when I was queen I'd have a huge business empire to oversee. Though my servants would do the actual work, I would need to understand what was going on. But human history?

I sat at my desk in the library. I'd been having lessons here since before I could read, and the wooden surface of the desk showed my evolving handwriting skills, with various sets of my initials, snatches of poetry and the occasional swear word carved into it. From here I could look out over the paddocks of the farm and see cows and horses grazing, and maybe the odd hawk circling far overhead. Some days whole afternoons slipped by in a kind of dreaming haze, but today I lounged back in my seat and glared at Mr Saunders.

"Why should a dragon bother learning human history? What do I care what the monkeys have been up to?"

Mr Saunders was an old man, the first old person I'd ever known. The permanent staff at the farm were all my mother's thralls, mostly young, fit men apart from the middle-aged couple who posed as my parents. Supposedly I was too sickly to attend school or get out much, and they were homeschooling me. The only other people I saw were my mother—very occasionally—and slightly more frequently, her right-hand man, Gideon Thorne. And since they were both dragons, they looked even younger than my middle-aged guardians, their bright red auras blazing with good health.

Mr Saunders' wisps of white hair and thick-lensed glasses fascinated me almost as much as they grossed me out. Thank God I would never look like that, with half my face sagging down my neck and my shoulders rounded with age. If he'd had an aura it would have been flickering and dull, but he was human, so no aura cradled him in its soft glow.

Still, he could sit up straight when he wanted to, and he did so now, giving me a disapproving look from under his thick white eyebrows. Those eyebrows were a shocker too, with random hairs curling off in all directions. Someone needed to do him a favour and introduce him to a pair of scissors.

"You have to live in the human world," he pointed out. "You need to understand it. And you have a lot of work to do if you are to catch up with your older sisters."

I was always being reminded that my whole life was a competition with the sisters I'd never met, but the way he spoke sounded more specific, as if he actually knew these elusive girls.

"Have you met them? My sisters?"

I sat up straighter too, hands flat on the pitted surface of the desk, eager for the answer. I'd seen photos of them, but that wasn't the same as meeting them in real life. All my life I'd had information about these girls shoved down my throat, but personal anecdotes would be so much better than dry facts.

"Some."

He heaved his creaky old body out of the armchair across from my desk and turned to study the view through the French doors. Outside chickens strutted across the lawn under flapping sheets on the line. The library where I had my lessons was at the back of the old farmhouse. Beyond the clothesline and the low hedge that marked the boundary of the mown lawn, the fields stretched off into the distance until the rough paddocks met the foothills. It was a pretty scene, but too familiar. I watched the hawk wheel off into the blue in envy. I wanted new sights in my life. New people. People my own age. The only teenagers I saw were the ones in the sitcoms I loved to watch whenever my guardians decided I'd done enough study for the day.

"Which ones? What are they like?"

"Like you." He stood with his gnarled old hands clasped behind his back as he gazed out at the fields, framed on both sides by tall bookcases stuffed with books. "They ask too many questions instead of doing their work."

I glared at his back, hot resentment coursing through me. How would he like to be cooped up here with only thralls for company? I was a future queen, but he turned his back on me as if I was no more than a thrall myself.

And he wasn't even a shifter. Just another stupid monkey.

Though, for some reason, not an enslaved monkey. I'd probed his mind the first time he came, expecting to find the usual enthralled fog, but his thoughts were clear. Now, as I stared at his back, a bold new idea came to me.

Before I could think better of it, I sneaked into his mind again. I was getting better at it. He didn't move or give any sign that he'd noticed my presence. I'd tried practising on the thralls, but entering their minds was like trying to wade through molasses, with nothing inside to catch hold of anyway. This was the first unguarded mind I'd had the chance to play with.

I pushed as gently as I could. I didn't want to scare him away, or have him telling tales to my mother or Gideon Thorne. Outside a cow stared my way, huge brown eyes vacant as her jaw moved in rhythmic circles.

"But my questions are important." I added as much mental persuasion to my words as I dared. I didn't want him to end up as mindless as that cow. "How can I win the proving if I don't understand the other candidates? As my teacher, isn't it your duty to teach me about my sisters? They're more important to me than stupid human history."

He turned to consider me. Oops. Maybe that had been a bit heavy-handed.

But then he nodded.

"Perhaps you're right. Well, then." He settled himself in the armchair again and smiled. "If you finish your work quickly, we'll have time for some questions at the end of the session."

I guess that would do for a start. Feeling rather pleased with myself, I picked up my pen and got stuck into it.

Every day Mr Saunders answered more of my questions. I learned that Valeria had a quick mind but only used it if the lesson interested her. Mr Saunders didn't approve. He also thought she wore too much eye make-up for a girl who was barely fourteen. Alicia was very pretty, liked reading and had a terrible fear of spiders. Ingrid ate too much and sometimes wasn't very nice to her servants. That didn't seem so bad. Maybe Mr Saunders had been on the receiving end of some of her insults. Monique was younger than me and still seemed rather babyish in her ways. She had a pet cat called Mouse.

"Where do they live?" I asked, putting some mental pressure behind the question.

"You know I can't tell you that," he said reprovingly. "You are kept separate for a reason."

"I wish *I* had a cat."

"You have dogs here, don't you?" He seemed surprised. "And horses? Why do you need a cat?"

I shrugged. The dogs were working dogs, and I was rarely allowed to ride the horses. The thralls were probably afraid I'd ride off into the sunset and never come back. If I had a cat it could be a pet of my very own, something to cuddle up with in the long slow afternoons.

But more than a cat—more than anything—I longed to meet my sisters. Sometimes I daydreamed that we all lived together like the Brady Bunch, with a mother and a father. We would fight over little things like borrowing each other's clothes, but underneath the bickering we'd be best friends.

Mr Saunders' stories had brought my sisters alive in my imagination. If we could only talk together face to face, maybe we could find a way out of the proving. Maybe we could really be sisters, instead of rivals. The more I thought about it, the more logical it seemed. Who wanted to kill all her closest living relatives? I certainly didn't. It seemed to me that the monkeys, inferior though they were in almost every way, actually had the edge on dragons when it came to families. All the people in those TV families seemed happier for having their family around them, and they all stuck together when times were tough.

An idea began to take shape as 1 pushed Mr Saunders harder, thirsting for every last drop of information he could give me. He knew where my sisters lived. He had a car. All I needed was his devoted co-operation.

All I needed was a thrall of my own.

It was surprisingly easy. I'd never enthralled anyone before, but I'd imagined the subject would resist, that there might be some difficulty. But I surged into his mind, unstoppable as the tide. One minute he was drilling me on the causes of World War I, the next he was blinking at me, his mouth forming a little surprised "O".

"Mistress," he breathed, and I smiled at the look of devotion on his face.

After that everything fell into place. My new thrall brought me something to slip into the drinks of the thralls who had night shift. All I had to do then was wait until the rest of the household was asleep and sneak out.

The old clock in the hall was about to strike midnight when I slipped out, avoiding the floorboards on the wide veranda that always creaked, and hurried down the steps. The big sky above glittered with stars but they cast little light.

I wasn't afraid. Country nights are always dark. There were no streetlights on our dirt road, but I made my way to it easily enough. The working dogs, chained up for the night, barked as I passed, but no one paid any attention. All our defences aimed to stop people coming onto the property. Nothing stopped me from leaving.

My feet found the dark road, and I strode along it with a bounce in my step. I should have tried this before. Freedom felt good. Frogs croaked in the ditch beside the road, and something rustled in the field as I passed: a fox, perhaps, or a cow shifting in her sleep. I'd told Mr Saunders to wait where our road joined the main one into town, a couple of kilometres from the farmhouse. Sound travelled at night, and I didn't want the noise of his engine to wake anyone.

I half-expected to hear a car start up behind me, and one of Elizabeth's thralls to come chasing after me, but the only sound was the crunch of my sneakers on the dirt road. As I walked I wondered how my sisters would react. Would they be pleased to see me? I had gifts for all of them in my backpack: a favourite book for Valeria, my old teddy for Monique. Valeria looked the most like me: we both had long blond hair and were tall for our age. Maybe we'd have a special bond, though she was the oldest and I was fourth in line. Did she think the way I did about the proving? What a stupid, wasteful system it was. Surely if we put our heads together we could come up with something better, and then we wouldn't have to be kept apart any more. We could all grow up together, just like a real family.

When I reached the meeting place there was no Mr Saunders to greet me, no car idling by the side of the road. Was I late? I squinted at my watch but it was too dark to read the numbers. I thought I'd left plenty of time, but I'd never actually walked that far from home before. Maybe I'd gotten it wrong.

I shifted anxiously from foot to foot. Was that a car in the distance? Maybe he was the one running late. Stupid thrall. Now I'd stopped walking I could feel the bite of the cold night air through my thin jacket.

The noise of the car's engine got closer, and soon I could see the headlights approaching. I waited a little back from the road, half-hidden by the overhanging branches of a tree, in case it wasn't Mr Saunders.

But I recognised the bulk of his big Ford when he pulled up, so I opened the passenger door with relief and climbed in. The interior light didn't come on when the door opened.

"You're late," I said as the car pulled out onto the road again.

"Sorry to keep you waiting."

My heart leapt into my throat. That wasn't Mr Saunders' voice; it was—

"Thorne! What—where's Mr Saunders? What have you done with him?"

"I've done nothing with him. I daresay he's asleep in his bed, considering how late it is."

"But ..."

My heart still stuttered from the shock of finding Gideon Thorne behind the wheel. How was this possible? I'd enthralled Mr Saunders! He couldn't have betrayed me. So how did Thorne get here?

"You didn't really think we'd let an untethered human anywhere near you, did you?" It was dark in the car but I didn't need light to hear the sneer in his voice. "Saunders is my thrall. It's possible to disguise the signs if you know what you're doing."

Which clearly you don't, that tone implied.

My pride in having enthralled my first servant deflated like a punctured balloon. "So I didn't really enthral him?"

"Of course not." His voice snapped with impatience. "You can't enthral someone who's already in thrall to another dragon."

"Then why did he let me think I had?"

The car turned in at the gates of my very own farmhouse. It had taken less than two minutes to drive the distance that had taken me twenty minutes to walk in the dark. The lights at the front of the house were on, and I slumped in the seat, feeling dispirited. Looked like the other thralls had only been pretending to be asleep, too. What was the point? All that effort, and here I was, right back where I started.

"To see what you would do." He switched off the engine and sighed. "Sadly, you have proven to be a great disappointment. I was thrilled when Saunders said you were pumping him for information on your rivals, but this—this is appalling." He indicated my backpack with revulsion. "What kind of dragon takes *presents* for her enemies?"

I shrank away from the fury and disgust on his face, lit by the floodlights from the veranda. I struggled to understand.

"They're my sisters. What should I have taken?"

"A gun? A knife? Poison, perhaps." The front door of the farmhouse opened, and two thralls stepped out onto the veranda and stood with folded arms. Clearly they were just waiting for me to come slinking home, tail between my legs.

"What difference does it make if you were going to stop me anyway?"

"But I wouldn't have."

I stared at him. He made an impatient gesture. "Oh, go inside. I can hardly stand to look at you."

I fumbled for the door handle, stung by the look on his face and the weight of his words. He wouldn't have stopped me if I'd intended to kill my sisters?

I slammed the door and marched past the waiting thralls, head held high though my legs were trembling. Safe in my own room again, I locked the door and threw myself on the bed.

The episode hadn't been a complete waste of time. I learned two valuable things that night. The first was that I wasn't safe in my own home. If one of my sisters decided to try to kill me, Thorne would let them make the attempt, would even applaud it.

The second thing was that I hated Thorne. I vowed to dedicate myself to preparing for the proving. I'd show him—and my mother—that I could be the strongest, most ruthless fighter ever. I would be queen, whatever it took.

And then Thorne would pay.

CHAPTER TWELVE

Ben, of course, wanted to come. Being unable even to cut up his own food hadn't done anything to affect his protective instincts, which were as strong as ever.

"I can still fire a gun one-handed," he said.

"Let's hope it doesn't come to that." I leaned in and rested my face against his for a moment. The bright light from the window showed the unhealthy yellowish tinge to his tanned skin. Dark shadows lurked under his eyes. He was still a long way from his usual strength. "Stay here and look after Lachie for me instead."

Lachie was lying on his tummy in front of the TV, chin propped in one hand. Totally absorbed in some superhero cartoon. His new theory was that all the superhero stories were real, and that they were actually all shifters. I'd asked him how many shifters he knew who wore their undies on the outside and were allergic to kryptonite, but he'd waved away my objections.

"Details, Mum."

"Dave and Thommo are here," said Ben. "Rob too. The house is full of people. He doesn't need me."

"They're not family," I said.

"And I am?"

"You know you are. Family isn't about blood."

"Oh? What is it about then?"

"Love."

His breath caught as he gazed down at me. Somehow this conversation had gotten very serious.

And then he laughed. "Damn you, woman, how can I argue when you say things like that?" He swept me into a fierce one-armed hug. "You know I can't refuse you anything. Fine. I'll stay home and be good, even though the little turkey won't notice if the house explodes as long as the TV's on."

I kissed him, glad to see him smile. "You need the rest anyway. I worry about you."

He snorted. "Well, that only seems fair. I worry about you too."

In the end I left Steve behind as well. The away team consisted of Garth, two of the ex-thralls, and the two werewolf girls. It was kind of cosy, even in the big car, with six of us.

Eric and Alex, the two ex-thralls, were armed to the teeth. Their jackets concealed a number of suspicious bulges. Leandra was a lot more comfortable with firearms than I was, but even I had to admit they were a necessary evil in the current situation. The three werewolves probably all had knives hidden away somewhere. A knife was a daytime wolf's best friend. At four o'clock in the afternoon they wouldn't be able to change if we ran into trouble. Not that traumatising a bunch of office workers with rampaging werewolves in a busy place like North Sydney would ever be a preferred option anyway. Shifters had had quite enough publicity already.

We crossed the Bridge, joining the stream of traffic leaving the city. Peak hour was already underway, though being school holidays it was nowhere near as bad as usual. With a bit of luck we might even be able to find a parking spot when we got there.

The address Carl had given me turned out to be a low-rise office block on the outskirts of North Sydney. The ground floor housed a dentist and an empty rug shop with *Closing Soon! Hurry, last days!* still plastered across the front window. The parking gods smiled on us; there was an empty spot a few doors down, which was even more of a miracle considering a busy building site was right next door. A multi-storey office tower was going up, its concrete and steel reaching for the sky behind the white hoardings that blocked it off from the street, and the thunderous rat-a-tat of jackhammers filled the air.

Eric got out and fed the meter, looking like any businessman on his lunch break in jacket and tie, his short beard neatly groomed, while Garth and Alex moved warily down the street. Garth wore his usual T-shirt and dark jeans; he said he only dressed up for weddings and funerals. Today the T-shirt featured the Death Star and the words "Home Sweet Home". Alex trailed in his wake, looking uncomfortably warm in his jacket. Summer in Sydney was no place for a jacket; his face glistened with sweat, bright red. He looked like a retired boxer, or maybe a footballer. He'd probably been quite handsome before someone had spread his nose half over his face.

Plenty of cars passed, and there were several people on the street; I could see Garth's tension in the way his head moved from side to side, trying to see everything at once. The noise from the building site would be adding to his stress, assaulting his sensitive hearing and making it impossible to hear the approach of enemies. And if there was one thing werewolves hated, it was being sneaked up on. They disappeared into the foyer while the other two wolves and I waited in the car.

"Do you think it's a trap?" Jerry asked.

I swivelled in my seat to look at her. Chewing gum, she looked the picture of casual who-gives-a-toss with her tatts and her flaming pink hair. She was dressed all in black, with black combat boots that laced halfway up her shins. One arm lay casually along the back of the seat, but beneath the surface I sensed an undercurrent of nerves, which wasn't a bad thing. Nothing wrong with nerves if they kept you alive. Some shifters figured they were bulletproof, and found out the hard way they weren't.

"It's always a possibility." I shrugged. "But Davison's not stupid. Elizabeth won't last forever. It makes sense to hitch his wagon to someone else's star."

"Wish it was dark," Mac muttered. She shifted restlessly on the seat next to Jerry. I had trouble picturing Mac as a ravening beast, despite her clothing matching Jerry's tough look. If she made as cute a wolf as she did a girl, she'd have preschoolers lining up to pat her and kiss her fluffy nose.

"He probably picked the time so you guys couldn't change," I said. Any dragon who followed the proving would know by now of the werewolves in my camp. Jerry cast me an anxious look. "But that doesn't prove he's planning a double-cross, just that he's taking precautions. You know how paranoid dragons are."

She nodded, and we got out of the car at Eric's signal. The thunder from the building site pounded my sensitive dragon hearing, and I saw Jerry flinch as the wall of sound hit her. The three of them watched the street, while I ignored the noise and the butterflies fluttering in my stomach as best I could and tried to recall everything I knew about Carl Davison.

He was young for a dragon; only about a hundred years old. It was a measure of his ambition that he'd risen so high in Elizabeth's court in that relatively short amount of time, shouldering aside older dragons. According to some sources, he was a regular visitor in her bed, but that was hardly surprising. The combination of long life and healthy sexual appetites meant that, for the older dragons like Elizabeth, there would hardly be a male dragon left she hadn't slept with. And probably quite a few of the females too.

The human persona he'd adopted was that of a businessman who'd taken the stock market by storm with a start-up software company a few years back. It had been so successful it now had the big market players looking nervous, and Carl's fortune was made.

In fact, he'd most likely already amassed a fortune in a previous "life". One of the drawbacks of living for centuries without ageing was that you had to arrange regular "deaths" and reinvent yourself in a new place. That had been easier before photography became widespread, but the real problems had only started with the rise of the Internet. With facial recognition software and global connectivity it was much harder to start over if your face was already well known.

Still, no one had been caught out yet, and people like Carl continued to build their fortunes and enjoy the high life. He was a regular in the society pages, a real hit with the ladies with his dark good looks and goatee that proclaimed him not just some boring businessman, but an artistic soul. An artistic soul with money. He had B-graders lining up to hang off his arm.

His other big claim to fame from a shifter point of view was the number of wyverns he had on staff—three that I knew of. Wyverns generally preferred to keep to themselves. He must have a lot to offer if he could coax three of them into joining him.

Garth waved us in, and it was a relief to put a closed door between us and the thunder of the jackhammers next door. I glanced around as we entered the foyer, a narrow space between the dentist and the empty shopfront. A faint smell of urine lingered, as if no one came here but homeless people and drunks. The space opened up further in, to a lift lobby with three lifts and a door to the stairwell. A board on the wall listed the building's tenants. Level two, where we were meeting Carl, housed a firm of solicitors.

If Carl owned the building I bet it wasn't one of his more profitable investments. The décor of the foyer was dated, and it looked as though the cleaner worked with one eye shut. Only two of the lifts showed lights on their display; the third one appeared to be out of order. More likely, the place had nothing to do with him, and that was why he'd chosen it as a rendezvous point.

"Stay here," Garth said to Alex. "Make sure no one sneaks up on us."

Alex nodded, his sweating face serious, and took up position where he could see the lifts and the two doors. Eric called the lift and the rest of us stepped in. It smelled a little musty, and the worn carpet was badly stained, as if they'd had a water leak that no one had bothered to fix. I certainly wouldn't feel too confident of my lawyers' skills if they worked in a place like this.

Confidence was in pretty short supply at the moment. All of us were on edge. Garth looked positively grim. Werewolves didn't like enclosed spaces, and he burst out of the lift the minute the doors opened like the cork from a bottle of champagne. If anyone had been waiting for the lift he would have scared three years' growth out of them.

But no one was there, and it wasn't hard to see why. The double doors opposite the lift were locked. The lawyers' company name was still written on the glass, but the rooms beyond held nothing but carpet, showing darker patches where furniture had once stood.

Garth turned a full circle in the foyer area in front of the doors. "So where is he?"

Eric tried the doors again, but they were definitely locked.

"Maybe he's late," I said, trying not to feel insulted. Wolves weren't the only ones who played dominance games. Usually the person who arrived last had the most power.

Jerry pulled something from her back pocket that looked like a Swiss army knife, but turned out to be a set of lock-picking tools. In a moment she had the doors open. Luce would have been proud.

"May as well have a look," she said. Without waiting for orders she strode inside. Mac and Eric hurried after her, and after a minute, so did Garth and I.

It didn't take long to confirm our initial impression: the place had been abandoned, probably some time ago. The air smelled musty and stale. The only sign of life was the odd cockroach, skittering for cover as we disturbed it.

Garth checked his watch as we filed back out to the lifts, clearly uneasy. "Where the hell is he? If he's not here in two minutes, we're leaving."

I caught his eye, knowing what he was thinking. If it was a set-up, we'd taken the bait. Enemies could be closing in right now to spring the trap. I had my mouth open to tell him to call Alex when the lift pinged. I turned toward the sound with relief. Davison was here.

It took me a second to react when the doors opened. Yes, Davison was here. A body lay on the floor of the lift, its head kicked into the corner like a discarded soccer ball. Underneath all the blood the head sported a natty little goatee and a look of surprise.

Frozen with horror, I was still staring when the door to the stairs flew open and bodies started pouring through.

Garth snarled and hurled himself on the first man through the door. The guy's gun went flying as he hit the floor, and he scrabbled at Garth's big hands as they closed around his throat.

The next two managed to get shots off before Eric took them both out with a neat bullet to the head, his feet planted wide and his arm unwavering, a look of calm concentration on his bearded face. At least the racket from the building site next door should hide the noise of gunshots from the outside world. And that was the last coherent thought I had for the next few minutes.

In front of me Jerry collapsed with a howl like a wounded animal.

There were too many bodies for the small space. My claws snapped out between one breath and the next as I leapt for one of the attackers. His gun roared and I felt a stinging pain in my shoulder.

I stumbled as I landed, but my claws still caught him, half severing his head. His blood sprayed me as he went down, and another took his place. My ears rang from the gunfire and the terrible unearthly screeching noise Jerry still made. What was wrong with her? I couldn't spare a second even to look.

I could hear Garth shouting. From the corner of my eye I saw dainty little Mac tackle a guy twice her size. I turned to help her, but I wasn't needed. The man was dead before he even hit the ground, blood fountaining from his slashed throat. Mac stood over the body, teeth bared, dripping knife in hand. I caught her eye and she gave me a feral grin.

No more gunfire. I looked around, bemused, as the last attacker bolted for the safety of the stairwell. With a roar Garth lunged after him.

"Garth, wait!" I yelled. "Jerry's hurt."

He turned back, frustration plain on his face, but he let the door slam shut. Jerry's shrieks were like nothing that ever came from a human throat before, high and agonised. She writhed on the dirty carpet like a trapped animal. I sank down next to her.

"What's wrong? Where are you hurt?"

She couldn't answer. I don't think she even knew I was there. Her T-shirt was covered in blood, and I ripped it open, searching for the bullet wound.

Behind me Mac gasped.

Garth knelt next to me, his face grim. "Silver bullet."

A small, neat hole in the top of her breast peeked over the unexpected red lace of her bra like some baleful third nipple. Monstrous black lines radiated out from it as her veins swelled in reaction to the poisonous metal. I gripped one of her hands, though I doubt she felt the pressure. She burned to the touch. Before our eyes the black lines twisted across her skin, mapping the poison's spread.

All shifters were susceptible to silver poisoning, but werewolves reacted particularly badly. It would take a hundred such bullets to kill a dragon. One would only make us sick. But one was more than enough to bring agonising death to a wolf.

Mac sank to the floor on Jerry's other side, leaning over her doomed friend with a look of such anguish on her face I had to look away.

"Can't you help her?" she begged. "You have to help her!"

I felt sick. Removing the bullet would make no difference now. Nothing could stop those evil black lines from spreading, carrying death through her veins.

Tears streamed down Mac's pretty face.

"Eric could …" I gestured at the gun, hating to say it out loud. "It might be kinder."

Jerry still cried out, but her screams had faded to whimpers. Her once-spiky hair lay flat and sweat-soaked against her scalp. She struggled now to breathe.

Mac shook her head once, emphatically, and leaned down to bring her face close to Jerry's ear. I didn't hear what she whispered. Jerry probably didn't either.

"Where the hell was Alex?" Garth growled. He crouched next to me, his face as black as thunder.

I met his bleak gaze. Was Alex dead? We both knew the lack of warning from him was a bad sign.

Jerry struggled for breath, each more laboured than the last. Her face had quickly become so discoloured and swollen she was unrecognisable. Greenish foam burst from her lips. Then her eyes rolled back in her head and she went still.

I got to my feet, feeling shaken. Jerry looked as though she'd been attacked by a psychotic tattooist. Her skin was covered in crazed black lines, her face and neck swollen and shiny with sweat. No one spoke.

Then Garth looked at me and he surged to his feet, face drained of colour. "You're bleeding!"

I'd forgotten that stinging pain in my shoulder. Hastily I ripped my shirt open to inspect the wound.

"It's okay." Surprisingly enough, it was true. "It actually doesn't hurt that much."

"Let me see." Garth pushed my hands aside with urgent fingers. "Are you sure? Wouldn't they have all the guns loaded with silver?"

"It would take more than a silver bullet to kill me."

"Yeah, but you don't want to be out of action with silver fever for a week, either, do you?" He laid an anxious hand on my forehead, checking for any sign of fever. Touching Jerry had felt like laying my hand on an oven door.

Dragons were notoriously hard to kill. It took something like bane leaf poison, which had killed Leandra, or a catastrophic severing of the brain/body connection. Like Carl Davison's grisly end. My eyes strayed toward the lift, but the doors had shut again, hiding the body within. Our bodies healed with supernatural speed, even from injuries that would kill a human or lesser shifter. Already the pain in my shoulder had dimmed, and I felt a weird movement inside, as if something were burrowing its way out.

That would be the bullet, being forced out by my healing body.

"Relax, Garth." I put a hand to my shoulder. It really was the most peculiar sensation. I gritted my teeth, feeling as if some parasite were chewing its way through my flesh. Best not to think about it.

In a moment I could feel the lump, a pea-sized mass rising toward the surface. Then, with a little welling of blood, it broke the skin and I caught it between thumb and forefinger and yanked it out with relief.

"See? Nothing to worry about."

I held the bloody little lump of metal out to Garth, who took it.

Then he yelped and dropped it back into my palm.

"Damn it!" He sucked his fingers.

"What's wrong?"

He showed them to me. The burn marks were already blistering. "That's definitely silver."

I turned the bullet over, perplexed. Though the effect wouldn't be nearly as obvious on me as it was on Garth, there should be *something*. Some reaction, some sign. But my shoulder barely ached, and I felt none of the dizzy sickness I should be experiencing from silver fever. As if it were no more than an ordinary bullet.

Still, now wasn't a good time to stand around pondering the mysteries of the universe. Garth seemed to realise it at the same instant I did.

"We need to leave," he growled.

I nodded and shoved the bullet into my pocket. At a word from Garth, Eric bent and picked up the small form of the dead werewolf, while Garth helped Mac to her feet. Then he checked the other bodies for ID, but predictably they carried none.

I sighed. Did it even matter who they were, or who'd sent them? I had so many enemies. I could take my pick. I had to do something about thinning their numbers before someone managed to thin me right out of existence. Although I would like to know whose door to lay Jerry's death at. Someone would wish they'd never dreamed up that little double-cross.

At least I could rule out Carl Davison as a suspect. The lift doors had closed, but when I pressed the call button they slid open again, revealing their gruesome cargo. I stepped inside, trying to avoid the pool of blood soaking into the carpet, and squinted at the gory head in the corner. Yep. Definitely Carl Davison. The stock market would have a meltdown when word got out.

We took the stairs to the ground floor, not trusting the lifts any more. Didn't want any more nasty surprises. Alex lay against the wall, out of sight from the street, as if someone had dragged him there. My heart sank.

Garth tried to see in three different directions at once as he crossed the empty foyer to Alex's side, jumpy as only a werewolf under threat can be. He knelt and laid his fingers to the pulse point in Alex's neck, then looked up in relief.

"He's alive."

As I joined him Alex groaned, and in a few moments Garth had him sitting up, groggy but functional.

"What happened?"

Alex felt gingerly at a lump on the back of his blond head. "Not sure. Two guys came out of the lift, and I was watching them when someone hit me from behind. I don't know where they came from—I didn't hear a thing. Too much bloody noise from next door."

"You good to go?" asked Garth.

"Sure. Just give me a minute." He got to his feet and laid one hand on the wall, swaying a little. For the first time he noticed Jerry in Eric's arms, her pink head lolling against his shoulder.

His eyes widened. "What happened?"

"Tell you later. Let's get out of here." I could see our car from here. It wasn't far. If we made sure no one got close enough for a good look at Jerry, people would probably assume she'd collapsed. It would still draw attention, but that couldn't be helped. No one was running and shouting, or pointing at our building in alarm, so the noise from the building site must have covered our brief gun battle. "Garth, check the street." I caught at his muscled arm. "And be careful."

He nodded and stepped outside without hesitation, though he must have felt like a sitting duck. There were two guys smoking on the opposite pavement outside the door of another office block. Legitimate smoke break or enemies watching for us?

They paid him no attention, apparently absorbed in their conversation. He ducked back inside.

"There's a group of women coming this way. When they're past we're good to go."

Eric faded into the background with his burden, while the rest of us stood watching the street. Soon enough, five women dressed in neat office attire strode past, the sound of their conversation drowned out by a chorus of jackhammers and nail guns. Once they'd passed Garth stepped out again, then motioned the rest of us to follow.

As he reached the car a figure rose from its crouch between our car and the next, gun levelled at Garth's chest. He had no time to react. A shot rang out …

And the unknown gunman crumpled to the ground. The women scattered, screaming, while the two smokers stood rooted to the spot. Across the street a small dark-haired woman lowered her gun and slipped into an alley between two buildings.

"Run!" Alex shoved me hard in the direction of the car.

We ran.

With great presence of mind, considering he'd just escaped death by a fraction of a second and the keen marksmanship of a complete stranger, Garth stepped over the body, jumped in and started the car. We all piled in, Mac diving over the middle seat into the back, Eric and I manhandling Jerry's body in with us.

In a second we were roaring down the street. The smokers had found their wits and hurried inside. Hopefully no one had held it together well enough to note the licence plate of our car.

I glanced down the alley as we passed, but there was no sign of our mysterious benefactor. She was a damn good shot, whoever she was.

CHAPTER THIRTEEN

"Who the *hell* was that?" Garth eyed me in the rear-vision mirror.

"I wish I knew. I can number my supporters on two hands—hell, most of them are in this car—and I have no idea why anyone else would be running around taking out my enemies."

"It looked like Luce." Eric's voice held a cautious hope. He cradled Jerry against his shoulder, heedless of the blood smeared across his jacket and the white shirt beneath. He didn't look so debonair any more.

It *had* looked like Luce in the brief glimpse I'd caught—small, dark-haired, Asian appearance. But she'd had a Japanese look to her, and Luce was Chinese. Besides which …

"We're lucky it wasn't. Luce would have been taking shots at *us*, not our enemies. She's Alicia's now, body and soul."

And therefore bound to do whatever she could to further Alicia's cause. Defending my people didn't come under that heading at all.

Eric shrugged. "I was just hoping she'd found some way around the binding."

"There is no way." Though if anyone could find it, it would be Luce. The word "determined" could have been invented for her. "Luce won't be free till Alicia dies."

"Let's hurry up and kill the bitch, then," said Garth, ever the pragmatist.

Amen to that, brother. It would certainly help to have Luce back in our camp. Alicia's death couldn't come soon enough for me. The problem would be staying alive long enough to bring it about, with the bounty hunters out in full force.

"Who were those guys?" Eric asked. "And who killed Davison?"

I looked down at Jerry's still face. At least they'd paid for her death, but who'd sent them? It could have been any one of dozens of players. Not Carl Davison, apparently. Was he just collateral damage, or was there more to it?

I sighed. "They could have been bounty hunters. Or maybe someone got wind that Carl was talking to me and decided to shut him up."

Eric raised one eyebrow. The effect was quite saturnine, with his dark hair and beard. "Makes you wonder what he was going to tell you."

"Sure does. And why they didn't want me to know."

I guess it was even possible that Davison's death and the attack on us were unrelated. It would be a huge coincidence, but stranger things had happened. Hell, stranger things seemed to be happening to me on a daily bloody basis. The fact was, I had too damn many enemies. No matter how fast I ran, one of these days someone would catch me. Somehow I had to take control. Act instead of react.

"We've got to do something," I said. "We can't go on like this."

Everyone fell silent. The mood in the car was dark. How could it not be, with Jerry's body cooling on our laps? I hadn't even gotten to know her, and now she was dead, just for trying to help me. I couldn't bear to look at her swollen, distorted features; I stared out the window instead. City streets slid by, a whole world of people living normal lives, going to work, coming home. Lucky bastards.

The sooner the bloodbath of the proving was decided, the sooner life could go back to normal for all of us.

"Anyone know where Jerry's family lives?" I asked. "Mac?"

Her poor parents would be devastated. No one knew better than me what losing a child felt like.

Mac sniffed. When she spoke her voice was still choked with tears. "I don't think she has any. She came up from Melbourne last year. I never heard her talk about anyone back home."

"We'd better take her to Trevor, then. He'll know."

"After we get you home," Garth said. "Every minute you spend outside you're a target."

Besides, Garth wouldn't be welcome at Trevor's house. In the end we agreed that Garth, Alex and I would return to The Rocks, then Eric and Mac would continue on to Trevor's with Jerry's body.

"Mac, you don't have to come back with Eric. I'd understand if you wanted to go back to the pack after what's happened."

"There's nothing for me there," she said. "I'll stay with you."

Trevor had said there were different kinds of danger when we first discussed Mac and Jerry joining me. What was so bad at the pack house that she preferred risking her life with me?

Garth double-parked outside the house; as usual, the street was parked out. The three of us slid out and Eric quickly took the driver's seat and pulled away. Garth took me by the arm and hustled me toward the house, as if I were an old lady needing his help to stand up. Damn werewolves got so protective sometimes, they were worse than wyverns.

A car door slammed down the street, and a woman I recognised got out. Damn. How did Detective Hartley get a parking spot practically on my doorstep? And what the hell was she doing here, obviously waiting for me to arrive?

"Garth." I nodded toward the oncoming policewoman.

"Inside," he said to Alex. "Get those guns out of sight. Warn Ben."

Then he moved to shield me from the street with his body while Alex disappeared into the house, his long legs taking the steps two at a time.

"Hello, Detective." I offered the policewoman a polite smile as she joined us. "What can I do for you?"

"I have a few more questions for you," she began, then her eyes took in my torn shirt with its suspicious rust-coloured stain. Her tone sharpened. "Is that blood?"

"Tomato sauce," I said, keeping that bland smile plastered on my face. "I'm a very messy eater sometimes."

"Really." I could tell she didn't believe me. Her keen eyes lingered on the hole in the middle of the stain, where the bullet had entered. I still had the damn thing in my back pocket. Lucky she couldn't see that. "Do you mind if I come inside?"

"Not at all. Please—" I gestured for her to precede us up the stairs, where Garth leaned past her and opened the door.

As we came into the hall Ben appeared from the lounge room, a worried look on his face. Alex had disappeared.

"Hi, honey!" My face was starting to ache from my forced smile. "Would you mind entertaining Detective Hartley for a moment while I duck upstairs and change my shirt? Won't be long!"

I could see he was busting to give me the third degree, and would much rather have followed me up the stairs than deal with a suspicious policewoman, but he smiled and invited her into the lounge. As I took the stairs two at a time I heard him offering her coffee or tea.

Something stronger would have suited me. In the safety of my own room I sank down on the bed. Now the crisis was over my hands started to tremble, and I dragged in deep breaths as if I'd just run a marathon. Jerry was dead. So were Carl Davison and half a dozen others. Two of them I'd killed myself.

I stared at my shaking hands. Long, elegant fingers, smooth palms. Fingernails kept short and practical. No sign now of those deadly claws. It seemed impossible that these hands had just killed two people.

Even harder to believe that I felt no regret. More than anything else, that told me how much I'd changed from the old Kate. She could never have killed anyone.

Of course, she would be dead by now if Leandra hadn't taken over. So would Lachie. I ripped off my stained shirt and threw it into the corner. I had no time for regret. Regret got people killed. Staying alive, keeping Lachie and Ben and everyone I cared about alive, was a task that required total focus. Regret was a luxury for people whose every waking moment wasn't taken up with the struggle for survival.

Quickly I dragged on a clean shirt. A shower would have been nice, but Detective Hartley was waiting. I ran a damp flannel over my arms and hands instead to remove any traces of blood. Best not to upset the nice detective.

Garth waited outside my bedroom, lounging against the wall with his muscled arms folded. He straightened when I appeared.

"Let me look at that bullet wound."

"It's fine." I pulled the neck of my shirt down to show the shiny new pink skin on my shoulder. "Stop fretting."

"I'm not fretting. It was bloody silver." He held me still while he inspected the newly formed scar. His big hands were warm and surprisingly gentle on my skin.

"Truly, Garth, I'm fine."

He shook his head. "I don't understand."

"Me either. Guess I'm full of surprises these days."

"I hate surprises."

"Where's Lachie?" I had a detective to see to.

"Don't know. Do you want me to find him?"

"Just make sure he stays out of sight while Detective Hartley's here."

The last thing I needed was trying to explain away my supposedly dead son to the police. If the cloud of suspicion hanging over my head got any bigger there'd be one hell of a storm breaking soon.

Ben and Detective Hartley both looked up as I entered the lounge, Ben with relief, she with that sharp look I was coming to dread, the one that took in everything and noted it down to be used against me later. Her eyes ran over the clean shirt, my messy hair, my hands, before coming to rest again on my face. I had to fight the urge to check myself again for blood stains. She, of course, was perfectly groomed, with a crease ironed into her trousers so sharp you could have cut yourself on it, and her hair pulled back in a neat ponytail.

"Sorry to keep you waiting." I sat next to Ben on the lounge and laid a reassuring hand on his knee. *See? I'm fine.* His hand covered mine briefly and gave it a squeeze. *Thank God.* "Now, how can I help you? You said you had some more questions?"

"Yes."

She considered me for a long moment, head tipped to one side like a bird of prey. She perched right on the edge of her seat, as if holding herself in readiness to leap up and arrest someone. The light from the window behind her cast her face into shadow. I wouldn't be surprised if she'd positioned herself that way on purpose, the better to observe us while obscuring her own features.

"Have you found out why that nurse attacked Ben?"

"Actually, my questions relate to a different woman."

"Oh?" I offered her a look of polite confusion while my mind spun. What now? Surely not …

"Do you know a woman named Valeria Grey?"

Oh shit. Now the dragons were coming home to roost. "No. Should I?"

"She is—or rather, was—a wealthy property developer. Lived in a mansion in Mosman. Also owned a penthouse apartment at the Toaster and several other luxury properties. You sure you don't know her?"

"Positive. Why?"

"I'm sure you've heard of the body that was pulled out of the Harbour on New Year's Eve, not long after the supposed dragon battle?" She put a definite emphasis on *supposed*. Detective Hartley was obviously not a believer. I nodded. "That was her."

"That's unfortunate. But what does it have to do with me?"

"Crime Stoppers has had a lot of calls about it. Your name was mentioned. More than once. So I'd like to ask you a few questions."

Great. Probably half the shifter community of Sydney had been wearing out their redial buttons, trying to curry favour with Elizabeth by dropping me in the shit.

"I'm a suspect? You think *I* killed her?" I injected as much disbelief as possible into my voice.

"Not at all. But there could be a connection with Nurse Johnson's motive for attacking you and Mr Stevens. We have to explore every possible angle." She was nowhere near as good a liar as I was. "These questions are just routine. We have to tick all the boxes."

Ben shifted uneasily. He could probably tell she was lying too. "Maybe we should have a lawyer present."

I shot him a warning look. "Don't be silly. If Detective Hartley says it's routine I'm happy to help."

"Thank you. You don't have to say anything unless you wish to, but anything you do say may be used in evidence." She pulled out a notebook and pen. Then she passed me a photo. "Do you recognise this woman?"

Valeria, with her golden hair piled up in that braided coronet style that had always annoyed me, as if she were claiming the crown before she'd earned it. Subtlety was never her strong point. Looking at her smug face again made me want to punch something.

I handed the photo back. "Never seen her before. That's her? The woman from the harbour?"

"Yes. Could you tell me what you were doing on New Year's Eve, Ms O'Connor?"

What I was doing on New Year's Eve—that was a tale and a half. The telling of it would blow a rational policewoman's mind. Dragons and leshies and gory slaughter, oh my. From her previous tone she seemed to fall firmly in the *it's all a hoax* camp. I had no desire to change her opinion.

"I was home, watching the fireworks. We have a pretty good view of the harbour from the upstairs rooms."

"You didn't leave home at all?"

"Not until after midnight."

"Did you go to Ms Grey's house at Mosman?"

"No."

"Where did you go?"

"We decided to go for a walk and enjoy the party atmosphere down at the Quay."

"You and Mr Stevens?"

"And Garth, our friend."

I wished I could say I'd been home all night, but it would be easy enough for her to discover, if she didn't already know, that Ben had been admitted to hospital in the early hours of New Year's Day, so there was no point pretending we'd gone to bed like an old married couple and slept the sleep of the just.

"I see. And what time was that?"

"I'm not sure." I looked at Ben and he shrugged. "Maybe around one o'clock?"

"And is that when you were hurt, Mr Stevens?" Her pen skated across the notebook's page, taking everything down.

"I don't know what time it was," Ben said. "The details are a bit hazy."

"Do you remember how you were injured?"

"Some drunk attacked me with a broken bottle."

That was the story we'd given at the hospital. It seemed plausible, considering the amount of alcohol consumed that night and the number of drunks still staggering around the streets till sunrise.

"And did you go with him to the hospital, Ms O'Connor?"

"No."

"Why not?"

"We'd split up. I was watching a street performer and the guys went to find a drink. The first I knew of the attack was when Garth found me and told me Ben had been rushed to hospital."

"So what did you do then?"

"We followed him to the hospital, but it took a long time with all the traffic and the road closures. Really, Detective, I can't see how any of this is relevant to the murder of some poor woman in Mosman. You did say she'd been killed in Mosman, right?"

"We're still waiting on the coroner's report as to that." She wasn't giving anything away. "Thank you, you've been most helpful."

She rose, and we stood up too. "Well, you know where to find us if you need us."

As soon as the front door closed behind her Ben whirled and grabbed me. "My God, what happened? Jerry's *dead*? Are you hurt? What the hell was all that blood on your shirt?"

Garth and Steve appeared, as if magically summoned by the sound of the front door closing, wearing identical worried frowns.

"Yes, Jerry's dead. Silver poisoning. We were ambushed."

"So it was a set-up? Davison wasn't there?"

"Oh, he was there all right." Quickly I ran through the details. Steve nodded along to the tale; Garth must have filled him in while we talked with the detective.

When I told him how I'd been hit Ben insisted on seeing where the bullet had entered. He was as bad as Garth. No more now than a small, slightly puckered circle of shiny pink skin on my shoulder, in a couple of days it would look like an old scar, faded to white. My shoulder ached, but as if I'd been punched, not shot.

His fingers brushed my skin, tracing the small round mark. When I caught his gaze his eyes were troubled.

"I'll never get used to this."

"This what?" Being shot at? Being a constant target? I'd be happy not to get used to that myself.

"You." He gestured impatiently at my shoulder. "Your new … powers, or whatever you want to call them."

I clenched my teeth on a hasty retort. That look in his eyes hurt. I wasn't some kind of monster.

"That's just me. Some things have changed, sure"—*ooh, understatement of the year, Kate*—"but I'm still me."

"Are you? You seem pretty calm for someone who just killed two people."

"Would you rather I'd let them kill me?"

"No, of course not! I'm just saying …"

"Saying what?" *Please don't look at me like that. We can make this work.*

He turned away, his face bleak. "That's a dragon attitude. That nobody else's life matters. I just thought you'd be more shaken up about it."

"I didn't choose this!" I grabbed his chin and forced him to look at me. "Of course I'd prefer to be human, but I didn't get a choice." Just think, I could still be happily oblivious of the shifter world and all its dangers. We could be a regular little suburban family, just the three of us, and our biggest worry would be how to make the monthly mortgage repayments. But I couldn't change what had happened. And I'd kill anyone who threatened me and mine without shedding a tear. If that made me inhuman, then so be it.

"I'm sorry." He moved closer, and dropped an apologetic kiss on my hair. "I'm just afraid of losing you. The real you."

"Don't be. I'm right here."

He needed time, that was all.

I turned to Garth. "Is Eric back yet?"

He shook his head. I guess we hadn't been with Detective Hartley that long. But I wouldn't be happy until he made it back safely—and Mac too, if she came. She'd said she would, but the fellowship of the pack might be tempting now she'd lost her friend. I'd seen a new side of her in the fighting, but choosing a group of strangers and certain danger over the security of the pack was a lot to ask of a young woman on her own. Today had made it clearer than ever how at risk we were outside these walls.

And even inside. My enemies were doing their damnedest to bring me down without even setting foot out the door. Dobbing me in to the police for Valeria's death—more than one call to Crime Stoppers, she'd said. They were probably all doing it—Jason, Elizabeth, Alicia, and anyone else Leandra had pissed off over the years. A whole spiteful army of informers busting a gut to be the first one to hang me out to dry. What next? DNA samples to prove I was related to Valeria?

At least that wouldn't work now I'd switched bodies.

"Oh, shit."

"What?" The three men were instantly alert.

They didn't need DNA. Something far less high-tech could trip me up any day. It all depended on how good Detective Hartley was at her job.

And I had a feeling she was very good.

"I've just thought of something. I told Detective Hartley you were injured in The Rocks. But the ambulance records will show they picked you up in Mosman."

"Told you we should have got a lawyer." For once Ben took no pleasure in being right.

That would teach me to stop trying to talk my way out of situations. Now I'd dug a deeper hole.

I sat down and let my head fall back against the back of the lounge. What an awful day.

"And you know what else? If they find out Valeria was at the Toaster on New Year's Eve, and they think to check the concierge's visitors' log …"

Garth groaned. "Your name will be on it."

CHAPTER FOURTEEN

Mac did return, but she spent the evening in her room, and I didn't see her again until lunch the next day.

It was a subdued group around the kitchen table, just me, Garth, Ben and Lachie. We ate in shifts. Alex and Steve had already eaten, and were out doing a regular sweep of the street, checking for anything that looked suspicious, anyone who seemed too interested in the house. Being in the heart of the tourist district of Sydney gave them some advantages, since they could blend into the ever-changing crowds. Unfortunately some of the locals were starting to catch on to the same faces doing regular patrols. The guy who owned the café across the street was convinced some major actress lived here, and didn't mind sharing his views with half his customers.

Eric and Rob would be in shortly. They'd been watching the back lane all morning and making sure the boundaries of the property were secure. Then it would be the turn of Dave and Thommo to take the outside shift.

And apart from Mac, that was the sum total of my group.

"Mum?" Lachie watched me with a thoughtful expression, his salad abandoned on his plate.

"Mmm?"

"Who killed Jerry?"

"I wish I knew, honey." I had no answers myself.

"Why are people attacking us?"

I blew out a frustrated breath. "A couple of reasons, but the main one's that my mother's not very happy with me killing Valeria."

His eyes widened. "*Grandma's* attacking us?"

"No!" Good God, no. The thought of my respectable suburban mother being tied up in this was enough to lighten my dark mood. I still hadn't told her about Lachie's miraculous resurrection. God, I was a bad daughter. She *would* kill me when she found out I'd kept that news from her. "No, I meant my dragon mother, Elizabeth."

"How come you have a dragon mother now?"

"It's a long story, but you've seen me turn into a dragon. That happened when a dragon called Leandra started sharing my body."

"Is she still in there? Can I talk to her?"

"It doesn't work like that. We're kind of one person now. But anyway, it's her mother, the queen, who's unhappy with me. In fact, her whole family was unhappy with me." Fortunately most of them were now dead. "They're not very nice people."

"Can't Dad help us? You said he was a dragon too."

I sighed. How do you tell your child his Dad's not a very nice person either? In fact, that double-cross of Carl Davison seemed just Jason's style. It wouldn't surprise me at all if he'd been involved.

"Dad's not really on our side. But no one knows where he is anyway." And that was about the best spin I could put on it. I indicated his plate. "Are you trying to distract me from the fact that you haven't touched your salad? Because it's not working."

"I've eaten heaps!" His little face twisted into an outraged expression. He shoved another forkful into his mouth and chewed ostentatiously. "See?"

"That's great work. Keep it up."

Ben's plate also sported a suspicious amount of salad, though, like Lachie's, it bore no trace of the spaghetti bolognaise that had come with it. I gave him a meaningful look.

He rolled his eyes, but started crunching dutifully on lettuce leaves. What did men have against vegetables?

Lachie pushed cucumber around his plate, trying to hide it under a lettuce leaf, but his mind obviously still dwelt on our conversation.

"I wish we could find Dad. I bet he'd help us if I asked him."

I paused, my fork halfway to my mouth. "I wish we could find him too, Monster."

Just not for the same reasons.

When Mac walked in I did a double take. She'd hacked her hair off short in a kind of demented pixie cut, messy and uneven. She looked like she'd been attacked by a blind man wielding a pair of garden shears. A bare patch at one temple suggested she'd started shaving and then thought better of it. A shocked silence fell over the room.

"What happened to your hair?" Lachie asked. When even the attention of a ten-year-old boy is caught by a haircut, it's got to be pretty drastic.

"Felt like a change," she said, lifting her chin.

She was a wreck. Her eyes were puffy from crying, and huge dark circles underneath them showed how little she'd slept. With her hair so short she could have passed for fifteen. A lost and broken fifteen. My heart went out to her.

Dave paused in loading the dishwasher, taking in her woebegone appearance. He was a short, stocky man, about Garth's age, with an open, friendly face. Already he treated Lachie like a favoured nephew, and I could see an urge to take Mac under his wing too in the softening of his expression. "There's spag bol here."

Dave was a firm believer in the power of a full stomach to improve any situation. Must be his Italian heritage. Though he was as handy with a gun as any of the other guys and had a mean right hook, he did most of the cooking. The only thing he liked better than cooking was opera, and he could often be heard singing at the stove.

No one was singing today, of course.

"As long as you've got a strong stomach," Garth said, scraping up the last bits of sauce with a hunk of bread.

"Didn't stop you coming back for seconds," said Dave. "Don't listen to him. Italian mothers have begged me with tears in their eyes for this recipe. But did I give it to them? No way. Best spag bol you'll ever have, trust me."

He plonked a huge serving on a plate and handed it to her. She sat next to Garth and got stuck into it. Grief obviously didn't affect her appetite. That was werewolves for you—walking stomachs.

They could have been father and daughter sitting there together. I had no idea how old Garth was. Somewhere in his early forties, maybe. Though his body was fit and strong his short military-style hair was greying at the temples, and lines of experience cut deep grooves into his face. He looked like a guy who worked out a lot, with muscles on his muscles and the thickest neck I'd ever seen. Went with his stubborn thick head.

Shame he was probably too old for her. Apart from the stubbornness thing, and of course the frequent bouts of grumpiness, he was a great guy. I wouldn't exactly say his bark was worse than his bite—he was a dangerous man—but he certainly improved as you got to know him. He should be making some lucky werewolf lady happy by now.

He looked up from his now gleaming empty plate, as if sensing my gaze on him. Wolves hate to be stared at. It's a dominance thing. His eyes were a clear grey-blue in the light from the window, and probably his best feature. For all that I snarked about his monobrow he wasn't a bad-looking guy.

Guiltily I shifted my gaze. Now was not the time to be thinking how hot my employees were. Actually, there was never a good time for that. Ben was my partner, and he was enough for me. Damn Leandra and her oversexed dragon urges.

I focused on Mac's sad face instead.

"I'm glad you came back," I said, "but are you sure you want to stay? Maybe you should take some time to think it over."

She laid her fork down. "Why do you keep asking? You think because I'm young I can't hack it? You saw what I did yesterday."

She cast a sidelong glance at Lachie, and I was glad she didn't go into detail in front of him. The image of her feral grin as she stood over the body of the man she'd just killed, knife dripping, was still crystal clear in my mind.

"I'm not questioning your ability."

"What, then? Is it because I'm gay?"

I blinked. Didn't see that one coming. Lachie's ears pricked up. Garth stared down at his empty plate as if it were the most interesting thing he'd ever seen. You could have heard a pin drop.

"Oh. You didn't know? I thought Trevor told you."

"No, he didn't." And neither had Garth. I cast him a reproachful look.

Suddenly it all made sense. Big macho werewolves were notoriously homophobic. If she and Jerry were more than friends, some of the guys in the pack would have made their lives hell. However strong a leader Trevor was—and he ran a very tight pack—he couldn't be everywhere at once, and a certain amount of bullying was a natural result of the hierarchical structure of pack dynamics anyway.

No wonder they wanted out.

"So what's the problem? It's not as if you can afford to turn anyone away. You need all the help you can get."

"That's true. Forget I asked." Sometimes I still thought too much like the old Kate, worrying about people's feelings. That kind of thinking would get us all killed. "I'm glad to have you."

She nodded and went back to shovelling spaghetti. Already her plate was nearly empty. The clink of her fork against the plate filled the silence.

Lachie watched her, speculation in his eyes. "Do you like Lego?"

Silly me. Here I'd been, imagining he was pondering her sexual orientation, when he'd already dismissed that and moved on to something *really* important.

"Let Mac finish her lunch in peace."

"No, it's all right." The poor girl was probably glad of the diversion. "I don't mind. What sort of Lego?"

His face brightened. Ben rolled his eyes, well aware of the dangers of encouraging Lachie to talk about Lego, and we shared a grin. She could be there for hours.

"Star Wars is the best …"

"Hear, hear," said Garth, our resident Star Wars freak. Today was actually the first time in three days he wasn't wearing a Star Wars T-shirt.

"… but I like all sorts. Ninjago, Lego City, Power Miners …"

He reeled off a whole list while she finished her food. A wave of love surged through me. His little face was so animated, and his skinny arms described big enthusiastic patterns in the air as he talked. I could still hardly believe he was here, alive and whole. I wanted to touch him constantly, as if to reassure myself that it wasn't a dream. He was the sun my world revolved around.

As soon as Mac laid down her fork he leaned forward confidentially.

"I have this app on my iPod. It's awesome! I can make Lego stop-motion animations with it. If you like, you can help me make one."

Okay, so maybe he was a tad obsessed, but the kid had a heart of gold. I'd told him we all had to be extra nice to Mac because she was so sad about her friend. In his mind, he was offering her a huge treat.

"That'd be cool," she said.

Though her smile didn't light her sad blue eyes, he didn't notice. She got up and allowed him to tug her from the room with his usual impatience to get started on the latest creative masterpiece. Every member of the team would be expected to admire it the minute it was finished.

"That's the last we'll see of Mac for a while," said Garth, a satisfied look on his face. I could tell he was worried about her too.

"Why didn't you tell me she was gay?" I asked.

He shrugged. Sometimes he could be so infuriating. "Don't care who she sleeps with."

"Well, neither do I, but I feel like an idiot for not realising Jerry was her partner." And I'd even been imagining her matched up with Garth. I wasn't usually so unobservant— there were just too many demands on my attention lately.

"Poor girl," said Ben.

"What's with the haircut?" Dave asked as he cleared away the last plates.

My turn to shrug. "Maybe it's a kind of tribute to Jerry? Keep her memory alive kind of thing?"

Garth raised a sceptical eyebrow.

"Well, I don't know. I'm no psychiatrist. Grief can make you do crazy things." That much I did know. Plenty of experience there.

Eric and Rob came in, bringing the scent of outdoors and rain-washed air with them. I glanced out the window and saw that the day had turned grey.

"Something smells good," Eric said. "What's for lunch?"

"Dave's special spaghetti bolognaise," said Ben. "Apparently it makes Italian mamas weep."

"Hey! That's not what I said," Dave protested, but he was already on his way out the door to find Thommo. No one ever slacked off on their shifts under Garth's watchful eye.

The two men were soon tucking in with enthusiasm. I lingered over my coffee and watched them. Rob was the baby of our team. His face still bore traces of acne, and he tended to communicate in grunts. The only time you heard his voice much was when he and Eric talked guns, which was a favourite topic for both of them.

"Saw Mac going off with Lachie," Eric said, pushing away his empty plate. He ate with the same efficiency he did everything, in small economical movements. He wiped his mouth with a napkin, then folded it neatly and centred it on the plate. "She all right?"

"Probably not," I said. "But she's putting a good front on it. Nice shooting yesterday, by the way."

"Thanks." He shrugged off the compliment as if it meant little, but above his neat beard his cheeks coloured slightly. Not many people could shoot as well as he did at the best of times, much less under fire themselves. If he hadn't taken out two of our opponents so quickly Jerry might not have been the only person we were mourning today.

It was a good team I had here, despite its small size. But it wouldn't be enough on its own.

"We need to stop chasing our tails, guys. Every man and his dog is out to get us. Even the police are joining in the fun. We have to stop reacting to things and take the initiative."

"What do you want to do?" asked Ben.

"We should move." Garth jumped in before I could answer. "We're too exposed here. This place is barely defensible. The street is on our doorstep, the lines of sight are bad, there's buildings overlooking us. It's a nightmare. And if that idiot in the café keeps mouthing off we'll have paparazzi thrown into the mix as well."

He had a point. We'd stayed here initially because it was handy to Royal North Shore, and more secure than a hotel, but it wasn't ideal. Unfortunately, neither was our other main option.

"Arcadia's a much bigger boundary to defend."

The house at Arcadia was set on fifty hectares in a secluded valley, with its own guesthouse and stables. It had a state-of-the-art security system and walls high enough to keep out any but the most determined human intruder. There were a few surprises for any uninvited shifter guests too, courtesy of some very expensive goblin magic.

It was also the house where Jason had nearly killed Leandra with a bomb disguised in a clock. Nowhere was a hundred per cent safe.

"Yeah, but it's set up properly, and maybe I could talk Blue into joining us out there."

"What use is a drunk goblin mage?"

"We could sober him up."

"Garth, I know you think goblin magic is the answer, but frankly Blue doesn't impress me. He wasn't exactly keen to help us out the other day, was he? He couldn't wait to see the back of us."

"He's good at what he does."

"Maybe, but I can't enthral him, so I can't force him to co-operate. And the last thing we need is a mage who's not loyal." Just thinking about the damage a deliberately botched spell could cause made me shudder. No, I definitely didn't need help like that.

Garth sighed and switched to a different tack. "Even without Blue, Arcadia's our best option. It's more secure than this place, and the neighbours are a long way away."

And wolves loved space. Although, come to think of it, being away from the city would be an advantage come full moon, and that was what? A week away now? Arcadia held some bad memories for me, though.

"I don't know that open space is such a great idea," said Ben. "Look what happened to Alicia."

The three of us had been there when Valeria took trueshape and blasted Alicia's bush property into charred ruins. The searing heat of the flames, the choking smoke, the stench of burned human flesh—I shook my head, trying to shake the horrible memories away. And while her people had screamed and died, Alicia had hidden in her fireproof bunker, leaving them to fend for themselves against a dragon.

"That's not going to happen again." Alicia was nothing like Valeria. Witness the cowering in the bunker. There was no way she'd pull the same stunt.

"Let me send a couple of the guys out to open up the house and do a security sweep," Garth said.

"It doesn't have any better magical security than we do here." But even as I spoke I recalled Luce quizzing Blue about sniper fire and how he'd squirmed when she'd pointed out that anyone could land on the roof here without triggering the defences.

Garth got that familiar mulish look on his face. I could tell he was gritting his teeth. "You said yourself we had to take the initiative. Being based here isn't helping, so let's shake things up."

I nodded reluctantly, aware that there was no compelling reason to stay now Ben was out of hospital, and my resistance to the idea came from Leandra's dislike. Although the damage had been repaired, she hadn't been back to Arcadia since Jason's "birthday surprise" had blown half the back of the house off. The memory of that betrayal still stung.

"Moving doesn't help with the main problem, though," I said. "I simply have too many enemies. We're being attacked from all sides. Hell, if they could manage to coordinate themselves, they could probably overrun us even at Arcadia."

"Well, there's a cheerful thought," Ben said.

Eric folded his hands on the highly polished table top. He had small hands for a man, with neatly filed nails. In fact, everything about him was neat and well groomed. "We need to take out Alicia. Then the proving would be over and Elizabeth would have to call off her dogs."

He was kind of bloodthirsty for a neat freak, but it was a good point.

"We don't know where she's holed up," Garth said.

I waved a hand in irritation. "Details. We could find out."

It took Ben to say what we were probably all thinking. "She has Luce directing her campaign now."

That was the real problem, one we had no answer for yet. But I'd think of something. I had to. I squared my shoulders and made up my mind.

"Okay, first things first. Garth, get the house at Arcadia ready. Once we're a little more secure we can plan an attack."

He nodded and the impromptu meeting broke up. I went to check that Lachie wasn't boring Mac to death, and found them on the floor, heads together, crouched over a Lego house surrounded by a horde of minifigures. It looked like a siege was in progress.

I hoped that wasn't a sign of things to come.

CHAPTER FIFTEEN

Next day Alex and Steve headed out to Arcadia, but Garth wouldn't move when they gave the all-clear. He wanted to wait until nightfall.

"You getting paranoid in your old age?"

He gave me a fierce grin. "Always been paranoid. Why do you think I've lived so long?"

"How old *are* you?" I asked on impulse.

"Older than you."

"Don't forget there's two of us in this body," I joked. "I bet our combined age beats yours."

He rounded on me, his face serious, and poked me in the chest.

"*This body* is only a kid. That's *you*, Kate, whatever weird shit happened with Leandra on New Year's Eve. Don't get so caught up in this dragon crap that you forget you're human too."

Man, he had hard fingers. I rubbed my breastbone. It felt like he'd prodded me with a metal bar.

"You've seen me change. You know I'm as much dragon as human."

"Of course you are. Otherwise we wouldn't be here, would we?" He waved an arm at the foyer, where we stood amongst suitcases and boxes, but I knew he didn't mean our physical surrounds. This whole situation wouldn't exist without Leandra. "But you're more than her, and that's our biggest advantage. Don't you forget it."

Geez. I'd never seen him so serious. "Fine, we'll wait until dark."

And so it was nearly nine o'clock before those suitcases and boxes started to move out to the cars. Having more than one fully furnished home meant we could travel light between them; only clothes and a few personal belongings had to be carted from one to the other, so the two big four-wheel drives had enough room for all of us plus belongings. One was parked right out front, and the other only a few spaces further down, after an afternoon of careful street-watching by Garth, waiting for parking spots to open up. He wanted the move to go as quickly as possible. Alex and Steve had taken their stuff when they'd gone to prepare the house—plus a few boxes' worth of Lego, fortunately, or we might have been in trouble.

Dave stood unobtrusive guard out front while the other guys ferried boxes out. Eric watched the back lane. And Ben stood at the window of the lounge and watched the rapid packing of the cars with frustration on his face.

"It's almost enough to make me wish I was a shifter."

"What is?" There didn't seem anything supernatural about a bunch of guys hurrying up and down the front steps with boxes and bags. Besides, they were all human except Garth and Mac.

He gestured impatiently at Garth with his good arm. "Look at him. I shot him in the chest a week ago. Anyone else would be dead, but there he is, throwing twenty kilos around like it's nothing, while I can't even raise my arm above my shoulder."

"You nearly lost that arm." I leaned into him and trailed a line of kisses down his neck like an apology. He'd been hurt saving me, after all. His skin tasted of salt, though he smelled like a fresh afternoon in a pine forest. "You can't expect it to recover overnight."

But he did. That was the problem. He'd never been badly hurt before; he hardly ever even got sick. Being the one that needed help was a new experience for him, and it didn't sit well with his natural instinct to be busy and useful.

He put his good arm around me where we stood at the lounge room window. I leaned into him and watched the loading in progress. The scene outside was lit by streetlights and the light spilling down the front steps from the open door.

"Maybe I'll get him to bite me come full moon." He sounded only half-joking, his face drawn into a frown as he stared out into the night.

"Sure. That's all we need—you and Garth fighting it out for dominance. Don't even think such things!" I shuddered. "We have enough on our plates without any more complications, thanks very much. Try to be patient."

"I hate being so useless." His dark eyes were so serious. What was wrong with everyone today? So much introspection.

"You need everyone at full strength. How can I help you when I can't even cut up my own goddamn dinner?"

Good Lord. Next thing I knew he'd be trying to get himself turned, out of some misguided sense of duty.

"Benjamin Stevens. You are not some hired muscle. You are far more to me than just a body." Then I grinned and snuggled closer. "Although I'm not saying I have no *use* for your body ..."

I trailed one hand over his chest, let it slip lower. His mouth quirked in a smile in spite of himself.

His good arm held me tight. "True, *parts* of it are still working fine."

I ground my hips against him. "Mmm, so it seems."

He bent his head to mine and I lost myself in sensation as he kissed me—the warmth of his mouth, the heady scent of the cologne he always wore, the feeling of his body against mine.

"Ah—sorry to interrupt ..." Rob hesitated in the door, carefully not looking as we broke apart, awkward as a teenager who's sprung mum and dad making out. A flush spread from his neck up into his cheeks. "Garth says we're ready."

"Great." I crossed the hall to the foot of the stairs, my feet making no noise on the thick carpet, and called for Lachie. "Time to go, Monster."

"Everyone ready?" Garth said as he and Dave came in the front door. "Rob, go get Eric."

Rob nodded and headed down the hall to the big kitchen/family area at the back of the house. He opened the back door as Lachie came pelting down the stairs.

"Slow down!" I moved forward, just in case I had to catch him, but Lachie kept his feet. He offered me an unrepentant grin as he bounded to a stop. Maybe the move would be good for him too—give him space to run around and work off all that excess energy. Being cooped up here wasn't ideal for a ten-year-old, even if the place was bursting with Lego.

I caught movement from the corner of my eye and had just started to turn when Garth shoved me violently. "Get down!"

I sprawled across the bottom of the staircase in a heap with Lachie. Garth landed beside me. Dave and Ben leapt the other way, back toward the lounge, Dave reaching for his gun.

At the back door Rob lay crumpled, his lifeless eyes staring at the ceiling in surprise. It had been him falling that I'd seen in my peripheral vision. A crossbow bolt stood up from his chest, and an ominous red stain slowly crept out from underneath his back and spread across the tiles.

The open doorway behind him showed only darkness. That wasn't right—the lights should have been on outside. No telling who was out there, or how many.

"Still think it was a good idea to wait until dark?" I muttered to Garth.

His eyes had turned yellow and wolfish. "Why haven't the defences been triggered?"

Good question, but not one I could answer right now. We crouched together at the foot of the stairs, out of sight from the back door. I had Lachie shoved against the wall, covering him with my body. His eyes were huge as he looked up at me. I laid a finger on my lips and he nodded.

Dave stood in the lounge room doorway opposite us, his gun trained down the hall.

"What now, boss?" His voice was steady, though his usually cheerful face had paled at the suddenness of Rob's death.

I risked a peek around from the cover of the stairs. Nothing moved at the other end of the hall. Rob's body lay sprawled, the crossbow bolt standing up from his young chest at an obscenely jaunty angle. A black rectangle of night filled the open doorway with menace. We rose to our feet as anxious seconds ticked past.

"Ben! Can you see Thommo and Mac out the front?"

Ben moved out of sight, toward the lounge room window. "They're waiting by the cars. Everything seems quiet out there. Want me to signal them?"

A huge crash of broken glass sounded from the kitchen, out of our line of sight. Pieces of glass skittered into view across the floor. One kissed Rob's outflung hand. Someone had decided a side assault through the window was a safer option than storming the open doorway.

"Cover us!" Garth said to Dave. "Let's go."

I grabbed Lachie's hand and Garth herded us toward the front door. Ben joined us, with Dave bringing up the rear, backing toward the door without taking his eyes off the rear of the house.

Garth opened the front door as Dave started firing. An answering bullet whizzed past my head as I leapt out into the street, dragging Lachie with me. Mac and Thommo looked up in surprise at our sudden dramatic appearance, then Thommo raced up the steps, gun drawn, a fierce expression on his normally placid face. He was a short guy, shorter even than Dave, and generally so laid-back he was almost horizontal, but he shot up those steps as if every dragon in Sydney had just lit a fire under him.

"Go, go, go!" Garth shouted.

Mac leapt into the first car and started the engine. But as our feet hit the pavement the ground suddenly tilted crazily, hurling us into the air.

I landed heavily and tried to scramble up, but only made it to all fours. The concrete footpath had cracked into crazed patterns, and leapt and shuddered like a mad bull at a rodeo. Choking concrete dust billowed into the air. There was no way I could stand.

I looked around desperately for Lachie. He lay at the foot of the stairs, unmoving.

"What the hell is this?" Ben shouted.

The noise was tremendous, as if a giant cement truck was rumbling past. Fresh blood bloomed on Ben's bandages, and his face twisted in pain. Must have landed on his bad arm. I tried to crawl to Lachie, but the ground convulsed under me again and threw me to the side.

The front steps shattered with a deep boom, and chunks of concrete and bits of broken tile rained down. The street lights abruptly went out.

"Lachie!" I screamed.

Someone else screamed too. Dave, I think, tumbling down as the steps disintegrated underneath him.

I heard a growl, and a streak of silver shot from the rocking car. Mac? As she launched herself across the street shots rang out again. Someone was firing at her? I shook my dazed head. No. Thommo, staggering like a drunk but still miraculously on his feet, was firing at three figures in the shadows between two buildings opposite. Another wolf, a big black one, snarled and leapt on the nearest figure. Garth. I hadn't even noticed him change. My dragon-enhanced night vision showed him savaging a tall willowy body that seemed to grow from the pavement.

Leshies.

Last time I'd encountered these wild forest shifters, they'd been on my side. Obviously no longer. It was their command of the earth that kept us thrown around like marbles in a bucket, unable to find our feet and fight back. The silver wolf leapt at one, and he met her with limbs suddenly turned to branches that sprouted vicious thorns half a metre long. The wolf yelped in pain, but her jaws still snapped for his throat.

Anger burned white hot inside me, constricting my throat and sending fire flushing through me. A fine plan, this— frighten us out onto the street, where the leshies waited to knock us down like skittles, then bring on the big guns to finish us off. Easy as shooting fish in a barrel.

Which meant the real assault was still to come.

The silver wolf fought hard, snapping and growling with the black wolf at her side, but she was slowing down. Even from across the street I could see a dark stain matting her bright fur. She fell back and Garth positioned himself in front of her, teeth bared in a savage snarl, fur bristling, ready to spring at the next leshy to attack.

No more! I threw back my head and roared, giving in to the primal urge inside me. The roar deepened, echoing off the blasted street, as I opened myself to oneness. The rest of my self surged back through the channel stone in an ecstatic rush. My body grew to its rightful shape, and I trumpeted defiance at the black sky above and spread my wings with a sound like a thunder clap.

The leshies shrank back into the alley, knowing their earth magic was useless against my fire, and the bleeding wolves dragged themselves out of the way. I leapt into the middle of the rocking street. Alarms sounded a discordant chorus as parked cars bumped into each other, bringing frightened faces to windows, but I didn't care. There was already a price on my head; one more violation of Elizabeth's laws wouldn't make any difference.

I drew in a huge breath, feeling the pressure build deep in my gullet. One leshy still faced me, desperately trying to knock me down with increasing gyrations of the road beneath my clawed feet. It was a fool's game, and his companions knew it. They fled down the alley, but too late.

I breathed out a mighty jet of flame. The leshy in front of me went up like a torch. Ignoring his screams, I thrust my head into the alley and blasted the other two. Dragonfire burned hotter than any other flame, and clung like napalm. It only went out when nothing remained to burn.

In this case, that didn't take long.

Roasted leshy smelled so good I began to salivate. It had been a long time since I'd hunted in trueshape. But now was not the time. Lachie was still in danger.

Lachie!

Thinking of him triggered an involuntary change, as my body instinctively sought the form associated with him: a mother's shape, with arms to hold and protect. Trueshape was too big, trapped in the canyons between buildings. Dragon form rushed away, dissolving back into that other space where it waited till called out again through the channel stone.

I stood naked in the ruined street, surrounded by the rags of my former clothes. Exposed, in every sense of the word. Sudden shifts were hell on wardrobes.

The lights were out in the whole block. The leshies' games must have damaged cables underground. They'd sure as hell busted a few water pipes: a fountain gushed from a deep crack in the gutter, spilling a river across the broken road surface. But there was enough light to see Lachie huddled beside a pile of rubble, his eyes huge with fright.

Garth limped back across the street, supporting Mac, who was bent over like a little old lady. Neither of them had a stitch of clothing left. Dave and Thommo stood back to back, trying to cover every direction with their guns. Ben was on his feet too. All accounted for. I moved toward Lachie.

Before I'd taken three steps a figure leapt down the pile of rubble that had been the front steps and snatched him up. My blood ran cold. I should have known. Who else knew the weaknesses in our security so well?

"Don't move," said Luce. She wore her usual all-black ensemble, hair pulled back in a tight ponytail. She was breathing hard but her face wore its usual impassive expression.

"Let him go." I had trouble speaking. Fear clutched at my throat. Why hadn't I kept trueshape? I knew what this woman was capable of.

"Come any closer and I'll put a bullet through him." She had him over her shoulder in a fireman's lift, and now she held a gun to his side. He kept still but the whimper that escaped him tore at my heart. I didn't doubt she'd do as she said. Trueshape wouldn't have helped. I could hardly blast her with dragonfire while she held my son.

Nobody moved.

"Why are you doing this?"

Her lip curled with something like self-loathing, and her tone was bitter. "Because my lady says I must. You were there; you know I have no choice."

Alicia had bound Luce to her with an ancient ritual that made it physically impossible for Luce to disobey her mistress, or do anything that went against her interests.

"I know that! But he's a child. Leave him out of it. Alicia's problem is with me, not him."

The gun wavered, then shifted to point at me. Garth muttered a protest and stepped forward. She whipped the gun around to cover him.

"I said don't move."

Two men emerged from the house behind her. One carried the crossbow that had killed Rob. What were the chances that Eric had escaped somehow, and was still out the back getting ready to charge them?

I had more chance of winning the lottery. Damn it all. I'd liked Eric, and we could have done with some of his crack shooting right now.

"I'm sorry, Kate," said Luce. I could tell she truly meant it, but that didn't help. She had my son. "I wouldn't choose to do it this way, but Alicia needs you to suffer."

"What the hell for? The crime of saving her sorry ass from Valeria?"

More likely for being a better dragon than her even though I was a half-human hybrid. Bitch. I'd never liked her.

Luce didn't answer. My mind raced, even as my heart pounded in fear. *Lachie.* How to stop her? I couldn't let her take him. But even if I could have compelled a shifter of her power, her binding to Alicia protected her. From the corner of my eye I could see Dave and Thommo looking to me for instruction. They both still held their guns. Could I trust them to shoot Luce and not Lachie? And do it before Luce shot my son?

Not bloody likely. It was too risky. Besides, I didn't want Luce hurt either if I could help it.

But I had to do something fast. Flanked by her two companions, she backed away down the broken street while we stood helpless. *Come on, Kate. Think of something.*

But I couldn't. Frozen in panic, I watched her retreat.

And then I watched the sky fall on her.

At least, that's how it seemed, for one confused moment. Something hurtled from the rooftops, bowling Luce over and knocking her into the crossbow guy. Garth darted forward and snatched Lachie up from the pavement, his big arms cradling my son protectively.

The whirlwind that had dropped from above knocked down the last guy standing with a quick tap to the head, then turned to face Luce and Crossbow Guy, who'd scrambled up. I stared for a moment, amazed at her skill as she disarmed them both with a rapid succession of kicks, always keeping herself between them and us.

Luce shook her head to clear it and squared up to face her new opponent. The woman stood a little taller than Luce herself—most people did; Luce was no giant. Like Luce, she was Asian, but Luce was Chinese and this woman was Japanese, with red streaks through her dark hair. She wore black leathers, as if she'd been riding a motorbike before she decided to jump off a rooftop into the middle of our disagreement.

Luce was a mean martial artist herself, but I soon saw that this woman's skill far exceeded hers. Even the addition of Crossbow Guy to the fight hardly seemed to stretch her.

I suddenly realised I was still standing there gawking.

"Let's go!" I waved everyone toward the cars. Just as well they were four-wheel drives. The new road surface offered a better challenge than any off-road track.

Dave hesitated. "What about them? We just going to leave? I could shoot her."

"Who, Luce? Don't you dare." One day I hoped to free Luce from her bondage to Alicia and welcome her back into the fold. Maybe that was sentimental of me. At the moment she was an enemy, and a dangerous one. But I couldn't bring myself to order her death. "It looks like our new friend has everything under control. Let's get out while we can." Without killing anyone. God, what a mess.

I slid into the back seat of the nearest car and accepted Lachie from Garth. He was crying, little hiccupping sobs that he tried to hold in.

"Shh. It's all right," I soothed, brushing his hair back from his face. Thank God he'd survived. When I'd seen him stretched out on the pavement, so still, it had sent a wave of dread and remembered agony through me. I felt his head for lumps. "Where does it hurt?"

He whimpered and pointed above his right ear. I couldn't find any swelling, though he flinched when I touched the area.

Ben darted across the street and came back with something clutched tight in his good hand. Then he got in the front seat, and Dave slid behind the wheel.

"Wait! Where's Mac?" Lachie cried.

"She's in the other car, mate," said Ben. "With Garth and Thommo. Don't worry."

Fortunately he didn't ask about Rob or Eric. I guess they hadn't played Lego games with him. I swallowed a lump in my throat, dreading the moment when I had to explain what had happened to them. This was no life for a child.

Dave pulled out and we were thrown from side to side as the car bumped over the boulders and rubble that used to be a city street. I glanced back to where our mystery saviour still battled Luce. Crossbow Guy was down and out for the count, like his mate. Only the two women were still on their feet, though Luce was staggering.

The stranger caught my eye and gave me a curious nod, almost like a small bow. She seemed as fresh as when the fight had begun. I hoped she wouldn't kill Luce. Who was she, and why had she come to our aid?

I settled back in the seat as we turned the corner and picked up speed. Thank God she had. I couldn't bear to lose Lachie again. This fighting had to end—but now my situation was even worse than before, with the loss of two good men. I couldn't keep playing by other people's rules.

I had to shake up the game. But how?

CHAPTER SIXTEEN

"Was that her?" Ben asked. "The mystery woman from the ambush?"

"Yep." Who the hell was this woman, and why was she following me around like my own personal white knight? None of our street patrols had seen any sign of her, so either she was very good at concealing herself, or she was psychic.

"Looks pretty fishy that she turns up in the nick of time again." He swivelled in his seat to face me. "What the hell are you doing?"

"Trying to find some clothes, what do you think?" I hung over the back seat, scrabbling through the nearest suitcase in the dark. It turned out to be Mac's, and I grabbed a T-shirt and a pair of shorts. "Stop looking at my butt."

"You shouldn't have taken trueshape." His voice was unexpectedly sharp, and he didn't smile at my attempted humour. "Then you'd still have your own clothes."

"What else was I supposed to do?" I wriggled into the clothes with relief, then clipped my seatbelt on. Lachie snuggled against me gratefully. "Those leshies were crucifying us."

"Are you *trying* to get caught? New Year's Eve was one thing, but this!" He threw up his hands. "Nine o'clock at night in the middle of a city street, where anyone can see you. You've got people out there just itching to start a witch hunt, you've got Elizabeth riding you—plus you've got the police all over you already for Valeria's death—and you think changing into a dragon again is the answer? If anyone got that on film, you are *screwed*. Detective Hartley can close the case. You might as well have signed a confession."

Heat flushed my cheeks, and I had to bite back an angry retort. Lachie had stiffened against me as Ben's voice rose. He was old enough to remember the arguments before Jason left us. No way were we going there again.

"Let's discuss this later. This isn't the time or the place." I looked meaningfully at Lachie and Ben took the hint. He turned back to face front, his shoulders taut with repressed anger.

Well, I had some anger of my own to repress. I'd done the best I could to protect us all. Now I felt like he'd slapped me in the face, hurt and caught by surprise. And underneath that, a purely dragon rage simmered. *How dare he speak to me like that?* I could practically hear Leandra's outraged tone. But I couldn't give in to that feeling. My dragon side had driven a big enough wedge between us already.

And even further down, so deep I had a hard time admitting it even to myself, lurked a tiny worry: was he right? Could I have found a better way? Maybe the wolves had it under control already. Maybe I could have relied on them and Thommo's sharp shooting.

Every time, it got easier, and the dragon called to me more strongly. Did I change because I needed to? Or because I wanted to?

Silence fell as we followed the tail lights of Garth's car down roads that grew more rural the further we went. Handmade signs offering eggs or tomatoes for sale popped up in the headlights as we zoomed past long dusty driveways. Horses and even the occasional cow dreamed in the dark fields, heads nodding sleepily as the cars' lights found them.

Arcadia wasn't a truly rural area. Chicken farms and horse studs lay scattered among rich mansions, churches and the occasional conference centre or restaurant. The only constant was that the size of the properties increased the further we got from the city. Some were rich and some were rundown, but all lay quiet in the light of the waxing moon. Physically it was only an hour from the heart of the city, but culturally it was another world. The only nightlife here was the foxes sniffing around the chicken coops.

We turned down a narrow road and followed Garth around a series of tight bends that switchbacked down a steep hill. Trees hung over the road, and there were no streetlights. It was very dark. When the road straightened out again Garth slowed. In the valley at the bottom, cradled by the surrounding hills, the road ended at a pair of heavy iron gates.

"Are we here?" Lachie sat up straighter and peered at the darkness outside the window. I'd told him we were moving to a bigger house, with a pool for him to swim in, which had met with approval, but there was little for him to see. High brick walls surrounded the property, and the sturdy gates were shut.

Garth pulled into the drive and stopped before the gates. He wound down his window and spoke into the intercom under the watchful eye of the camera mounted in the wall above. In a moment the gates swung open without a sound, and the two cars headed up the drive. Lachie swivelled round in his seat to watch the gates close behind us, but I braced myself for the first view of the house.

It was just as I remembered—a large symmetrical structure, with a two-storeyed central section flanked by single storey wings, now lit up like a Christmas tree with floodlights. The wings were originally guest quarters, but these days they were used as staff quarters for the men. More of it sprawled behind; the bulk of the house couldn't even be seen from here. At the back, also out of sight, was a garage and two separate cottages, a pool house as big as our old home in the suburbs, and an enormous stables complex. Originally the property had been a horse stud, but since Leandra bought it the stables had lain empty. Fields and dressage and training rings stretched out behind that, almost to the base of the hills, invisible in the dark. The whole valley belonged to me.

The house looked as it always had, with no sign of the damage that had ripped through it last year. In spite of myself my gaze was drawn to the window of my old bedroom, where I'd come so close to death, and I looked away with a shudder. One day Jason would pay for that betrayal.

But first I had to find the bastard. None of Garth's contacts, or Trevor's, had heard as much as a whisper of his whereabouts. The last I'd seen of him was when he'd come so close again to damn near killing me on New Year's Eve in the battle at Valeria's house. And then I'd turned dragon and had to forgo the pleasure of stomping his miserable human form into jelly to go save Lachie. Shame I hadn't had the time. A bit of jelly-stomping would have eased the sting I still felt at his numerous betrayals. Being back here made me conscious of them all over again.

Steve came out to meet us, a worried look on his tanned face. I'd rung him on the ride out to give him a brief rundown of events and make sure he was prepared with first aid. He helped Mac from the other car. She hunched over in pain, looking like a child wearing her father's clothes. Wonder whose suitcase she'd raided. Garth got out and came around to take her from Steve. The big werewolf's face was grim but his hands were gentle. She leaned heavily on him as he guided her up the front steps, taking them one at a time.

Ben watched her go. "Bet she'll be bouncing off the walls by tomorrow."

His bitter tone caught my attention. For someone who'd been around shifters his whole life, his resentment seemed a bit over the top. I took a deep breath. "It still hurts, you know. It's not like shifters get off scot-free."

As he well knew. He shrugged and followed them inside without comment. His arm must be on fire after getting thrown around like that, which clearly wasn't improving his mood any. Lachie got out of the car, yawning. I could understand Ben's feelings of impotence. I hated the feeling of helplessness tonight's attack had brought on, and I at least had my dragon powers to fall back on. But even they'd been no use as I stood there, useless as tits on a bull, while Luce threatened my son. Ben had always been such a capable guy too, used to taking the lead. Being forced to rely on others must be doing his head in.

Steve walked beside me, laden with suitcases. "I've got a room set up for Mac in the east wing. Garth says he doesn't think she'll need stitches, just rest. Great to be a werewolf, huh?"

God, not him too. I shot an exasperated look at the big half-Maori. Was everybody jealous of the shifters all of a sudden? "See if you still think so come full moon. Did you pick up anything on police radio?"

"Several units despatched to the house, including ambulance and fire. Someone called in a shooting, and there was a bit of chatter about a dragon. They've got the street blocked off at the moment while they wait for the bomb squad."

"They think it was a bomb?" Better than blaming leshies for the destruction, I guess.

"Just looking for evidence, I think, given the type of damage. How bad was it?"

"Pretty localised. Messy, though. I can see why they might think it was a bomb. Any word on survivors?"

It was a long shot, but even so my heart sank when he shook his head.

"Three charred bodies in the street, one dead in the house and one out back." His tone was unemotional, but his dark eyes reflected my own pain back at me. He and Eric had been friends for a long time.

I sighed. What a night. He left the bags in the grand foyer and went back for more, leaving Lachie and me alone under the glittering chandelier. A wide staircase carpeted in a rich red swept up to the next level. The foyer alone was nearly the size of our old house in the suburbs, and the white-tiled hallway it opened into seemed to stretch off into infinity. Such a big house, with so few of us left. Losing both Eric and Rob in one night was a heavy blow.

I looked down into my son's exhausted face. Life had to go on. "Bed."

"Can't I look at the pool?"

"Tomorrow."

"Can I have a hot chocolate then? It might help me sleep." He put on his best pleading face. Dark circles ringed his eyes, though he'd napped in the car.

"You don't need hot chocolate. You look like you're about to fall asleep on your feet."

His bottom lip quivered ever so slightly. "But my head hurts."

Poor kid. It had been a rough night for him too.

"Okay. But no taking all night to drink it. Ten minutes, and then you're going to bed."

I led him through the foyer, past the majestic staircase and down the hall towards the gleaming steel kitchen at the back of the house. On the way we passed the security room, its door standing open. Alex sat at the desk, surrounded by monitors, his face screwed up in concentration. His blond hair was shaved as short as Garth's, and the long scab on the back of his head was clearly visible.

"Wow." Lachie's eyes grew huge. "What are all those screens for?"

"Camera feeds," said Alex. "To make sure no one sneaks up on us. How's your head, champ? I heard you took a hit. Just like me, eh?" He rubbed ruefully at the healing scar, where he'd been knocked out at the disastrous "meeting" with Carl Davison—was that only two days ago? It felt like forever.

Lachie grinned. "We're twins! Can you show me the cameras?"

"Tomorrow," I said firmly. "Or don't you want that hot chocolate any more?"

The kitchen was big enough to cater a function for a hundred and boasted a bank of commercial-sized ovens, plus enough refrigerators to chill down a dozen bodies. Not that we used them for that, of course. In the daytime the long windows looked out across green fields to the distant tree-covered hills, but now their black rectangles made me feel exposed.

I found hot chocolate and some children's Panadol in the huge walk-in pantry, which the guys had stocked with all the essentials, plus every kind of junk food known to man. Maybe they thought those were essentials too, although Dave might have something to say about that. I shut the door before Lachie could see it and get any ideas. I soon had him sitting at the long kitchen table sipping from a steaming mug.

A couple of minutes later Steve and Dave came in from putting the cars away. Soon Ben joined us, everyone gravitating to the big kitchen, searching for companionship. Though we were all tired, no one was ready to sleep yet.

It seemed as if there should be some kind of rite for our fallen friends, something we could say that would help. Their empty seats left a big gap in our little company.

"Where's Garth?" I asked in an effort to break the gloomy silence.

"With Mac. Still getting her settled," said Ben. "What've you got there, mate? Smells good."

"Hot chocolate," Lachie said. "Want some?"

"Think I might have some coffee." Then he saw the coffee machine, all tubes and dials in gleaming steel. "Or not. Bloody hell. Do you need a licence to drive that thing?"

"Here, get out of the way," said Dave, pushing him aside. "Let the professional handle this."

When the coffee was ready Dave took a cup down the hall for Alex. When he returned he was carrying a laptop, Garth hot on his heels.

"Check this out. It just came up on YouTube."

"How's Mac?" I asked Garth as we shifted so we could all see the screen.

"Sleeping. She'll be fine in a couple of days."

At least that was good news. I sighed and focused on the laptop screen. Dark and blurry footage of the scene outside the house in The Rocks began. Great. Of course someone had filmed it. It was Murphy's bloody law.

"Guess the leshies did us a favour knocking out the power," Garth said.

Unusual for him to find a bright side to anything, but it was true. It was hard to tell what was happening in the dark. I saw myself change and leap across the street, but if I hadn't known what I was looking at it could have been anything. It was nothing but blurred shapes in the gloom. Then flame burst from my mouth, lighting up the scene. The person holding the camera had obviously jumped violently at that point, as the footage wavered and briefly showed the top of a window and part of a ceiling—but there'd been a glimpse of my dragon head first.

Strange, to see myself like that. Part of me knew that was my face. Recognised the glittering golden scales, the flared nostrils on the long reptilian snout. Felt comfortable with the flat, unblinking gaze of those eyes. Another part of me thought it looked like something out of a nightmare, and couldn't get past the teeth. My God, those teeth! As long as your forearm. Such a monster shouldn't exist.

The footage was angled as if it had been shot from a high window further down the street. The burning leshy was on the very edge of the shot. The flames only briefly illuminated the massive dragon body as it stalked past to poke its head down the alley. That was when I'd incinerated the other two leshies, but their deaths were off camera.

Dragonfire rapidly consumed the first leshy. As the flames died darkness fell on the street again, so it wasn't clear what happened to the enormous dragon. One minute it was there, the next gone. Movement in the shadows by the ruined step announced the arrival of Luce, though the scuffle that followed soon after was lost in darkness. Then two cars roared away from the scene, their headlights jiggling wildly as the cars bounced over the broken road. Though the footage lasted a moment more, I couldn't tell what had happened in the fight between Luce and the mysterious stranger. Was it too much to hope the stranger had left Luce alive?

Garth scowled at the screen as the footage finished. "I don't trust that woman."

"Me either," said Ben. "Once could be coincidence, but twice?"

"So she's watching us," I said. It wasn't a crime, and she wouldn't be the only one. "If all she does is save our arses, I'm not going to complain too loudly."

"Why doesn't she join us then, if she wants to help? What's with all the lurking in the shadows crap?" The big werewolf folded his arms. "I don't like having randoms going off half-cocked all over the place."

No, he wouldn't. He didn't like surprises. Worse still, he'd hate the fact that both times he hadn't even known she was there till she chose to reveal herself.

He sighed. "Well, at least the video's better than the New Year's Eve footage. You can't see much. Elizabeth shouldn't be too upset."

I snorted. "Elizabeth is already doing her best to—" I almost said *kill me*, but caught myself in time, aware of Lachie listening to every word. "To shut us down. It can't get any worse."

"Of course it can!" Ben protested. "Detective Hartley—"

"How's that hot chocolate going?" I interrupted.

Lachie looked up guiltily, a chocolate milk moustache decorating his upper lip. Despite being ten years old, he still couldn't seem to eat or drink without leaving traces of his meal all over himself. He tipped the cup to show me it was still a quarter full. He'd been drinking as slowly as possible, trying to stave off bedtime, though his eyelids were drooping. "Not finished yet."

"Drink up, then. Time's up."

Ben clamped his lips on what he wanted to say as I shepherded Lachie toward the door, but his frustration was clear. I paused next to him, urging Lachie ahead with a gentle push.

"Is this still about me taking trueshape?" I kept my voice low.

"It's the last thing you should be doing! You don't need that kind of attention. It's too dangerous."

"So's getting killed in the street. I had no choice."

"There's always another choice."

Garth and the others hung back awkwardly, trying to look as if they weren't listening.

"'Do nothing' isn't a choice, Ben. That's refusing to choose. Sometimes I only get a crap option and a crappier one, but I still have to pick one, because I'm responsible. I might have dragged you all into it, but this is my fight, and I don't get to sit it out."

His eyes glinted with frustration. He would have to learn that he couldn't protect me any more. "I think you just like being a dragon. You *like* taking trueshape. Admit it."

"And I think *you* can't accept what I am." I forced myself to swallow my anger. I couldn't change the fact that I was a dragon, but I refused to let it define me. I could still have a disagreement with someone without wanting to bite their head off. Literally. "But there's no point discussing it now. What's done is done, and plastered all over the Internet already. Let's all get some sleep and deal with the fallout tomorrow."

CHAPTER SEVENTEEN

"You need to see this."

Garth poked his head into the kitchen, where Ben and I were having a late breakfast. A very late, uncomfortable breakfast. Ben had been asleep when I'd finally gone to bed, so late that the sky had taken on the grey light of impending dawn. He hadn't mentioned our argument again and neither had I, but it sat at the table with us like an unwelcome guest.

I felt like something the cat wouldn't even bother dragging in, so tired that not even Dave's superpowered wake-you-up-or-else morning coffee had any effect. I'd been up so late searching for a way out of my rapidly declining situation. I needed a bold stroke to restore my fortunes, but no great genius plan had occurred to me yet. Now the sun streaming in the kitchen windows felt like it was burning my retinas out.

"See what?"

"There's a woman at the front gate who wants to talk to you."

"A herald?"

"No. Says she's the woman from last night."

I pushed my chair back, suddenly more awake. We both followed him to the comms room, where Steve was on duty, surrounded by banks of screens. The quiet hum of computer equipment filled the small room.

The gate camera showed a Japanese woman in leathers astride a motor bike at the closed gates. She'd taken her helmet off to show her face.

"Is that her?" Ben asked. "I didn't get a good look at her last night."

I nodded. Same direct gaze, same red-streaked dark hair. "Yep. That's her."

"What do you want to do? She's probably working for someone."

I remembered another occasion, only a week ago, when an Asian woman had waited at a gate to be admitted. Luce had had her own agenda, sure, but for the time being it had aligned with Alicia's interests, and she'd genuinely been trying to do Alicia a favour. But Alicia's paranoia had refused to let Luce in unless she agreed to undergo the ancient binding ceremony that forced her to submit to Alicia's will. And Luce had been so desperate she'd agreed.

How differently things might have turned out if Alicia had been prepared to compromise a little.

"Yes, she probably is. But she did us a huge favour last night. Who knows? She might be prepared to do more. We need to talk to her. We need all the allies we can get."

Ben frowned. "We shouldn't be letting strangers in. She could be working for Elizabeth, or Alicia. This is why we have heralds. Tell her to use one if she wants to talk."

I stared at the woman on the screen. Her aura was the faintest I'd ever seen, a pale yellow that almost disappeared in the sunlight. If I hadn't been looking hard I might not have noticed it. Even last night in the dark I hadn't seen it. Too busy trying to stay alive. Some kind of earth shifter? I'd never seen an aura that colour before.

She waited with no sign of impatience, the faintest of breezes ruffling the red streaks of her hair, as if it didn't matter to her one way or the other if we let her in. But it mattered to me.

"She could be, but I can't afford to turn anyone away without finding out. Garth, take Steve and get down there. Search her before you let her in."

"I don't trust her."

"Good. Let's all stay on our guard."

They left, and we waited in the humming silence. I slipped my hand into Ben's, and he glanced down at me, his face unreadable. At least he wasn't arguing any more, but he didn't seem happy. What a great way to start a new relationship—constant threats of death, danger and mayhem. Not too many people had fights about whether they should turn into a dragon or not. Most women only had to worry about whether he was going to return your calls or if the third date was too early to sleep with him.

Though I guess if the relationship survived this baptism of fire I'd know it was rock solid. I gave his hand a little squeeze and watched the monitor.

"You didn't come to bed last night," he said.

I looked up into troubled brown eyes. "I didn't want to disturb you. I was trying to come up with a plan, and I couldn't sleep."

"I thought maybe you'd changed your mind. About us."

"Because we had a fight? I'm not that easy to get rid of."

On screen Steve appeared and covered the woman with his gun while Garth patted her down.

"I thought about what you said, about not accepting you as you are. I just feel …"

Our visitor stood still and endured it, but her eyes followed Garth's every move.

"Feel what?" I prompted, when it seemed as if he had run out of words.

He shrugged. "I don't know. As if I've waited for you so long, and now you're even further out of reach than ever."

"What do you mean, you've waited so long?"

"Isn't it obvious? I've been crazy about you almost since the minute we met, but you only had eyes for Jason. Then you guys finally broke up, but I wasn't going to be your rebound guy, so I waited."

Out of the corner of my eye I saw the gate on screen closing, but what was happening in this little room seemed much more compelling all of a sudden. In one corner a little red light blinked in rhythm with my suddenly speeding heart.

"I had no idea." And didn't I feel like an idiot. I'd been so caught up in Jason and our love-hate relationship I'd hardly known which way was up in the first year after our break-up. Now I realised that he'd only married me to get a child, but at the time his actions had made no sense. Probably he'd only stayed with us as long as he had because he was bored with his long life, and marriage was something he hadn't tried. But at the time I'd been so hurt and confused by his infidelities and all the fights and making up I'd thought I could never trust a man again.

Ben hadn't seemed interested, but to be honest, if he had I probably would have run a mile. I'd thought we were just friends.

He laughed. "I know. But when it seemed like you'd finally gotten over Jason, he pulled that trick with the changeling." His expression darkened. "That screwed everything up. You were devastated, and I felt like the world's biggest jerk. How could I even think of you that way when I was hiding the fact that Lachie was still alive from you?"

I shivered, and moved into his arms. "Let's not talk about it. We're together now, and that's all that matters."

"Is it?" He searched my face, brown eyes serious. "But now you're a dragon, and I'm just an ordinary guy."

I kissed him, feeling the familiar surge inside at his touch. He hadn't shaved this morning, and his cheek was warm and bristly under my hand. I loved touching him. There was nothing ordinary about the happiness bubbling inside me as I pressed against him.

"I don't think you're ordinary." I could drown in those dark eyes, lose myself forever in the love I saw there.

"You say that now, but soon you'll have every shifter in the place throwing himself at you."

As if. "First they have to stop trying to kill me."

Over his shoulder I saw Garth and Steve marching the stranger up the drive, one on each side, until they disappeared from the camera's range. Her bike they left standing outside the gate. No quick getaways for our visitor.

In my back pocket, my mobile started to buzz. Reluctantly I let go of Ben. It was a new phone, and hardly anyone had the number.

"Hello?"

"Ms O'Connor?"

"Yes." I stifled a groan. Just what I needed—another conversation with Detective Hartley. "Good morning, Detective."

"Is it? I wasn't sure if you'd be answering. I've been calling you for hours and you didn't pick up. Are you aware of what happened at your address in The Rocks last night?"

Her words were clipped, her tone cool. Not that we'd ever been best buds exactly, but I got the feeling she wasn't pleased with me.

"Yes, I am. We were attacked again."

"I'll need you to come in this morning and make a statement. I have people lining up to talk to you here."

"I don't know if I can—"

"Ms O'Connor," she interrupted, "you are in serious trouble. I would advise you to engage a lawyer immediately. What the bloody hell is going on? There were two dead bodies on your premises, and another three in the street outside. Why in God's name didn't you call the police?"

She was practically shouting down the phone. Ben looked concerned; he probably heard every word. I turned away from the monitors and began pacing in the small space.

"If people are trying to kill you, Detective, you don't stop to call the police. You fight or you run, otherwise you die."

"And which did you do? Did you kill any of those people?"

"No, of course not." I wondered if she'd seen the video yet.

"Then who did?"

"I don't know. I was too busy running."

There was a short pause, then:

"We've had some reports of another dragon sighting."

Right. Guess she *had* seen the video.

"Oh?" I wasn't going to make this easy on her.

"In the street outside your house. Breathing fire, apparently." Her tone held frank disbelief. "I have to ask, are you connected with these supposed dragons in any way?"

"I didn't see any dragons." It was the truth. Kind of.

"Fine. Where are you now? I'll send someone to collect you."

"No, I can't come in today."

"Ms O'Connor, if you don't come in of your own free will, I'll have you arrested."

"On what charges?"

"Suspicion of murder? Public affray? Obstructing a police investigation? Take your pick. You haven't been straight with me. If that's the way you want to play it, we can do this the hard way. In which case you might want to rethink the pack of lies you've been feeding me. It's an offence to knowingly give a false statement to police."

Man, she was really riled up. Maybe having to ask questions about dragons when she so clearly didn't believe in them had gotten under her skin. Or maybe she'd done some digging, and found my name on the concierge's list at Valeria's apartment. Dammit.

I heard the front door open and close as Garth and Steve escorted our mystery woman inside. I'd much rather be talking to her than dealing with irate policewomen.

"You're right, I haven't told you everything." I tried to sound contrite instead of irritated. I had no time for this. "It's my husband, you see—my ex-husband. He's trying to kill me. He says if he can't have me, then nobody will."

There was a short silence on the other end of the line. Did she believe me? Probably not. Detectives were supposed to be suspicious. But maybe she'd go along with it to see where it led.

"Why didn't you tell me this the first time you and Mr Stevens were attacked?"

Good question.

"He—he said if I went to the police he'd kill our son too."

Ben raised his eyebrows at that. Yes, it opened a can of worms. But it certainly made Jason look suspicious. Maybe I could light a fire under his tail for a change and take some of the heat off me.

Time for Lachie to officially come back to life.

"I thought your son was dead?"

Well, she'd obviously done her homework.

"My husband ran a scam, to make everyone think so. He wanted to make sure I didn't get custody. Look, I know it sounds strange. I'll tell you the whole story, but I can't come in today. My son was injured last night, and I don't want to leave him."

Not entirely untrue. Would it convince her?

"I'm afraid this can't wait. I could come and get you, and do the interview somewhere closer. The Hills Local Area Command, perhaps." She sounded slightly less hostile. Maybe she had kids of her own. "Then you could be home with your son again faster. But it has to be today. Soon."

"Okay." If I got her here I could persuade her we didn't need to attend a police station after all. Dragon powers were handy like that. "What time shall I expect you?"

"I'll be there in an hour."

I gave her the address and hung up. Hopefully a compulsion would do the trick. I'd enthral her if I absolutely had to, but that was a last resort. Apart from the fact that people would notice the change in her, the thought of it turned my stomach. She was only doing her job. I didn't want to steal her will. My words to Ben last night came back to me: *Sometimes I only get a crap option and a crappier one, but I still have to pick one, because I'm responsible.* Enthralling the detective would be a truly crappy option, but if there was no other way, I'd have to dragon up and face it. I couldn't keep fighting on so many fronts at once.

Ben and I went to find our guest. Garth met us in the hallway.

"She's in the library. Steve's keeping an eye on her."

The library boasted a huge number of books, most of which Leandra had never read. It had just amused her to have a classic library in the house, complete with glass-fronted bookcases lining every wall and deep leather armchairs scattered around the plush carpet. She'd even put in a fireplace, though no fire had ever been laid in it. If it impressed people, it had done its job. Leandra, like most dragons, was very big on appearances. Substance wasn't quite so important.

When we entered the woman was standing at one of the bay windows tucked between the bookcases, looking out at the view of wide green fields ringed with hills. Or possibly checking security on exits and entrances. Just because I was grateful for her help didn't mean I couldn't be suspicious. Steve stood close by, looking menacing. His gun wasn't out but his hand hovered close to its shoulder holster. His face brightened with relief when we came in.

The woman turned and offered a formal half-bow.

"I am Yamada Kasumi," she said. "I hope you are no worse after your adventures last night."

Her English was excellent, but held a trace of an accent that suggested it wasn't her first language.

"I'm Kate O'Connor. I'm sorry to keep you waiting, Ms Kasumi."

"Apologies." Again she bowed, but this time her formality was tempered with a smile. It lit her whole face, making her look much less severe. "I am forgetting your English conventions. Kasumi is my first name."

I sat down and waved her to the armchair opposite. "What can we do for you, Ms Yamada?"

She sat on the very edge of the chair, hands on knees, and leaned forward. "Please, call me Kasumi. I wish to join you."

CHAPTER EIGHTEEN

"Really?" I sat back in my chair and settled in for a longer interview. She looked hot in her biker's leathers, though the library was air-conditioned, but she'd made no move to take off her jacket. "Would you like some tea?"

"Thank you."

I nodded to Garth and he left the room reluctantly, but I knew Steve had the only gun, and I wasn't ready to let down my guard yet. Bet that would be the fastest pot of tea the big werewolf had ever made. I could tell he didn't trust her from the way his eyes followed her every tiny movement, as if he was ready to leap on her at the slightest provocation.

"Tell me a bit about yourself." Her yellow aura was so faint in the sunlit room I couldn't be a hundred per cent sure it wasn't my imagination. I'd been trying to place it since I saw it on the monitors, but her trueshape eluded me.

"I am kitsune."

Good God. I sat up straighter. One of the fabled foxes of Japan! No wonder I didn't recognise the aura. I'd heard of the kitsune, but I'd never met one before. They rarely travelled outside their own country.

Some of the stories made them out to have nearly godlike powers, particularly the older ones. They were supposed to be able to spit lightning, possess people, fly or take fantastic shapes, maybe even turn invisible. If only half the stories were true, having one on my side could be a huge advantage. It was rumoured they could take on the appearance of anyone at all—imagine what I could do with an ally like that.

"I had heard your people didn't like to leave Japan."

She bent her head in that curious, half-bowing way she had. "That is true, but sometimes there is necessity."

"Did the Japanese queen send you?" If the overseas dragons had decided to take part in the proving, things could turn ugly very quickly. The Japanese queen would be a particularly nasty threat. Not only was she closest geographically, and therefore more likely to have ambitions of widening her territory, but she wasn't Japanese at all. She was the sister of the current Chinese queen, and had stolen the Japanese throne in a coup in the middle of the eighteenth century rather than fight her sister any longer for the Chinese one, so she came with a powerful built-in ally. Not a lady I wanted to come up against.

"No. My business here is purely personal." She could be lying, of course, but her direct gaze suggested sincerity. I found myself drawn to her. Maybe that was just gratitude for yet another rescue last night. "I came in search of my sister."

"And have you found her?"

"Yes." She looked down at the carpet. "She is dead."

Garth came back in with a tea tray. I saw Dave's hand at work there. Garth would never have got out the best china and embroidered napkins. He set it on the big square coffee table and I poured for both of us; Ben refused a cup. He found doing things left-handed awkward, and probably didn't want to look like any more of an invalid than he had to in front of our guest.

"I'm sorry to hear that," I said, as Garth took up a position behind my shoulder, watching the kitsune with a hostile eye. I took a sip of tea, milky and sweet. The cup's shape and colour reminded me of a dove's breast, the white china so delicate it was almost luminous. "What happened to her?"

"She wanted to win favour, so she took a job with your queen Elizabeth. A very simple job, she was told, though the payment was huge."

The hairs on the back of my neck began to prickle. Behind me Garth shifted uneasily.

"Perhaps that should have been a warning to her. I told her not to get involved in the local politics, but she had followed a man here, and the man wanted her to do it."

I swallowed a hot gulp of tea, and it burned all the way down my throat. Carefully I set the delicate cup down on its saucer. I had a very bad feeling about this. A simple job with a large payment: sounded like a bounty. And what would be simpler for a bounty hunter than to attack a man lying helpless in a hospital bed?

Suddenly that strange attack made a lot more sense. If that nurse had really been a kitsune …

Ben sat closer to the kitsune than I would have liked. Steve and his gun were over by the window. I flexed my fingers in my lap. If things got ugly I'd have to protect Ben myself.

"And so she attacked your friend here." She indicated Ben with a tip of her head. There was the tiniest clink of china as she placed her own cup and saucer on the side table by her chair. Her eyes held mine, but they were flat and expressionless; she could have been reciting a grocery list. "And was killed."

By me.

Though she made no threatening move, I rose to my feet. Garth leapt in front of me, a knife appearing in his hand as if by magic. Steve pulled his gun and moved to give himself a clear line of sight. My heart thundered in my chest as the silence lengthened.

She folded her hands in her lap and regarded us all unblinking.

"Why have you come here?" My voice came out in a harsh croak.

"As I said, I wish to join you." She didn't move, yet I felt threatened. It took balls for her to sit there so calmly, hands clasped loosely in her leather-clad lap.

"But you must know ..." I couldn't finish the sentence. *You must know I killed her.* If I said it out loud, surely her unnatural calm would dissolve into violence. Ben was on his feet now too. Every muscle in my body tensed, ready for action. Yet still she sat.

She picked up her cup and took another sip of tea, her dark eyes watching me over the rim of the cup.

"Please sit. I am aware of the circumstances, yes."

Warily I lowered myself back into my chair, though Garth still loomed in front of me, looking as if he'd like nothing better than to sink his knife into her flesh.

"When someone is cut, do you blame the knife or the hand that wielded it?" she asked.

I drank from my own tea, though the clatter of the cup in the saucer betrayed my shaking hands. I didn't know how she could sit there so calmly. I had killed her sister!

"Are you saying I am the knife?"

She nodded. "Precisely. Your queen sent her to kill Mr Stevens without giving her all the information she needed. Without, most importantly, warning her that he was under the protection of the Twiceborn. Elizabeth knew this meant almost certain death for my sister. But she was prepared to throw my sister's life away on the chance that she might succeed."

"The Twiceborn?" I hadn't heard that one before. Guess it beat being called the abomination.

She inclined her head again in that courtly half-bow of hers. "I am determined Elizabeth shall die. Who better to succeed her than one who has already cheated death? So I come to offer my services to you, the Dragon Twiceborn. I believe our goals are aligned."

"Wait." This was crazy. If someone had killed my sister, I wouldn't be so forgiving. She'd already helped us twice, but I couldn't wrap my head around the fact that she wanted to work for me, knowing what I'd done. "You blame Elizabeth for putting your sister in harm's way, but you don't blame me for actually … You'll forgive me for saying that doesn't make a lot of sense."

"It makes perfect sense to a kitsune. Family is everything to us." Well, that I could relate to. "But higher even than family comes honour. I am bound to avenge my sister's death. But you killed her in an honest fight, defending your own family from an unprovoked, even cowardly, attack. It was beneath my sister to accept such a task, but she was blinded by what she thought was love. In fact it was the manipulation of dragons who thought a kitsune would be the ideal tool for their job." She fixed me with a steely glare. For the first time I saw emotion in her dark eyes. "And kitsune hate dragons."

Garth looked from one to the other of us, a wild light in his eyes. I could almost smell the suspicion rolling off him in waves, and his aura flared bright orange.

"You can't seriously believe her, can you? Turn your back and she'll bury a knife in it faster than you can say lying fox bitch."

"Garth. Put your knife away, please." *And leave the talking to those of us with better impulse control.* But I didn't tell Steve to put away his gun. She spun a good story, but I hadn't lasted this long by trusting every stranger that happened along with a convincing line of rhetoric. I'd love to believe she blamed Elizabeth rather than me for her sister's death, but that seemed a little enlightened for a shifter. They were usually more heavily into mindless vengeance.

Garth sheathed his knife with obvious reluctance and took two paces back so he stood beside my chair again instead of in front of it.

"You can't trust her," he warned. He was nothing if not persistent. "If she's telling the truth, why wouldn't she go to Alicia, and destroy you as well as Elizabeth?"

Ben moved to stand behind me on the other side, his good hand resting on my shoulder. A gesture of support, or just giving Steve a better line of sight on the fox woman? None of us were in a trusting mood.

"My friend is outspoken," I said, "but he raises a good point. I am a dragon myself, and you have every reason to hate me. Why would you take my side over Alicia's?"

She leaned forward, red-streaked hair swinging loose by her face. She looked about my age. Thirty-five, tops. Lord knows how old she really was, though. It was notoriously difficult to pick a shifter's real age, and I knew very little about kitsune.

"Because you are something new, something the world hasn't seen before. Yes, you are a dragon, but your spirit is tempered with humanity. You fought for your child, in a way no true dragon would. I have never understood that attitude, as if all responsibility ends once the egg is laid. A woman who understands that, a woman who hasn't been brought up steeped in the belief that the world and every person in it exists to be used, is a woman I would like to see on the throne."

Garth remained unconvinced. "If you hate dragons so much, why do you want any of them on the throne?"

"I don't." She flashed him a tight grin. "But I am only one woman. I cannot change the whole course of shifter history. It will be enough for me to bring down Elizabeth, and see a change for the better."

I cleared my throat. "Not that I'm not grateful for the assistance, but how did you know I would be attacked last night?"

"I didn't. But I have been watching you for some days. When I saw you needed help I decided to step in. You cannot take Elizabeth's throne if you are dead."

Well, she'd certainly been following us the day we went to meet Carl Davison. I recalled the woman in the white car who'd followed us the day we'd collected Lachie's Lego. Could that have been her too?

"And what happened to the woman you were fighting when we left?"

"Lucinda Chan?"

"Yes. You know her?" Not for the first time, I wished she were here. Her long centuries of experience and web of connections would come in pretty handy right now. Leandra knew next to nothing about kitsune.

"She is well known in many places. I disabled her, but she suffered no permanent harm. Kitsune are not so quick to squander lives as dragons. Besides, once you escaped there was no point in prolonging the fight."

Well, that was a relief at least. These were strange times when I was grateful for an enemy's survival.

And when my mother was trying to kill me.

"Tell me more of your abilities," I said. "I'm not familiar with what the kitsune can do."

"I only have three tails," she said, "so I am not very great among our people. But I can shift form more or less at will, and I can appear as a particular person, of any age or gender. I can manipulate the dreams of others if I am very close, but I do not yet have the kitsenubi."

"Which is?"

"The ability to generate lightning. Only the nine-tailed have that power."

She sounded almost apologetic, as if that were a great let-down, but my mind was already turning over schemes for using the other abilities she'd mentioned. I reckoned I could live without nine-tailed lightning power.

"How convincingly can you copy another person?"

"So well not even their own mother could tell the difference."

"Even their voice? Their height? Exactly the same?"

"Exactly."

"And is there anything special you need to perform this transformation?"

"Something personal of theirs. A hair or fingernail clipping is best, but a piece of jewellery can work as long as it is significant to them and they wear it frequently."

A smile threatened to tug at my lips, but I forced myself to remain poker-faced. Oh, but this could be so good!

"In that case I propose a little test. If you can perform a certain service for me, I'll take you on."

Garth shot me a furious look, his aura fizzing like fireworks, but I ignored him. Ben said nothing, which I took for agreement.

"Certainly," Kasumi said. "What is the nature of this test?"

"There is a woman who is causing me problems. A policewoman."

Her brows drew together ever so slightly. "You want me to kill her?"

"No! I want you to become her."

"And then what?"

"One step at a time, Kasumi. She will be here soon. Then you can show me your impression of her."

"It will be flawless," she said. "You won't be able to tell it's not her."

"I hope so." I stood, signifying the end of the interview. "Garth will take you to the kitchen. You can wait there until you're needed." *And he and Dave can keep an eye on you.*

She bowed, and followed Garth from the room.

Ben waited till the heavy oak door shut behind them, then turned to me with a frown. "You're playing with fire." Okay, so maybe he wasn't totally on board after all. But I was sure this would be the answer to at least one of my problems, and then he could stop yelling at me about taking trueshape. "What the hell are you going to do?"

"Detective Hartley's on her way." The big goofy grin I'd been suppressing burst free. "I'm going to rewrite history."

CHAPTER NINETEEN

"I hope you know what you're doing," Ben said.

One hour later, almost to the minute, we stood at the window of the formal lounge room, watching Detective Hartley's car sweep up the long drive. She was certainly punctual. Ben held the heavy curtain back with his good arm; the other was out of its sling today, but he carried it curled against his body as if to protect it. Clearly he refused to play the invalid any longer, despite still being far from comfortable. He was nearly as bad as Garth. God save me from stubborn men.

"Relax," I said, forcing a lightness I didn't feel into my tone. "Kasumi's a godsend. What could possibly go wrong?"

He rolled his eyes and refused to dignify that with an answer. Okay, so there were risks, but I'd done some reading while we waited—Leandra's library had proved useful after all. Kitsune, despite a reputation for slipperiness, had a highly developed sense of personal honour. Their word, once given, was good. Their abilities varied greatly depending on how old they were, but they could all disguise themselves as someone else, which was the skill that most interested me.

Things were looking up for the first time since I'd sent Valeria plunging into the harbour. Kasumi could be the key to success—if I could trust her. The next hour or two would go a long way towards answering that question.

Detective Hartley and her shadow, Detective Franks, got out of their car. One big, one small, proving that size means nothing. I was convinced the small, wiry Hartley was far more dangerous than her larger companion.

Always alert, she looked up as I pulled Ben back from the window, with a gaze that noticed every detail. No doubt she was very good at her job. It was almost a shame to play a trick on her such as the one I had planned.

I heard the front door open and Garth's deep voice rumble in the foyer. No, not a shame. A necessity. My survival, and Lachie's, Ben's—everyone I cared about—depended on this deception. It was the first step in digging my way out from under a suffocating mountain of problems. Sympathy was something the old Kate would have felt. The new one couldn't afford such luxuries.

"Detective Hartley!" I turned to greet her as the door to the lounge opened, a cool smile on my lips. "Thank you for coming all this way."

She nodded. "Ms O'Connor. I hope you're ready to leave." Straight to the point, no polite but fake *you're welcome*. The belligerent tilt to her chin proclaimed her feelings on being dragged out here: she'd gone out of her way to humour me and now she expected full co-operation.

"Not quite. I'll just be a moment. Won't you sit down?"

The two detectives perched together on the antique lounge under the window like a couple of storm crows. Admittedly the furniture in here was built more for looks than comfort, with its hard wooden arms and straight floral-covered backs, but they both sat with the look of people who were eager to be on their way.

I turned in the doorway, as if as an afterthought. "Oh, just one thing …"

Detective Hartley gave me an impatient look. By now she'd probably uncovered my name on the concierge's list at Valeria's apartment building on New Year's Eve. Probably discovered the ambulance had picked Ben up from the Mosman house too. There was a gleam in her eye of the hunter closing in for the kill. She thought she had me. Perhaps she even hoped to frighten a confession out of me, once she'd torn me a new one over the lies I'd told. Clearly she couldn't wait to get me to that police station.

I caught her eye. "I want you to forget everything you thought you knew about this case. What I'm about to tell you will set you on a completely different path."

Frank disbelief met my gaze, but it no longer mattered. I *pushed,* forcing my will on her. Hers was surprisingly strong; her struggle, though brief, lasted longer than most humans' did. Her shoulders sagged as her will snapped, and the look in her eyes changed to one of fervent adoration.

It wouldn't last, of course. This wasn't full enthralment, only its temporary cousin, compulsion. I didn't want a permanent slave. An hour or two of obedience would be enough for my plans.

Her companion waited, his eyes still fixed politely on me. It was over so quickly he wasn't even aware there'd been a battle.

"You're feeling sleepy," I suggested, a grin tugging at the corner of my mouth. An oldie but a goodie. Detective Franks slumped back into the uncomfortable lounge at an awkward angle and began to snore softly. The poor man would have a terrible crick in his neck when he woke.

I turned my attention back to Detective Hartley. This got easier every time. Once I couldn't have looked away to deal with the other detective without losing her, but she still waited, eagerness to serve evident in every taut line of her body. She didn't even look at her slumbering companion.

"What is your password?" Her eyes tracked me as I moved closer, till I was standing right beside her.

"My … password?"

I frowned. Was this resistance? "For the computer system at the station."

Her expression cleared as she rattled it off. Not resistance, just confusion. Being compelled filled your brain with cotton wool, like being enthralled.

I plucked a hair from her head and handed it to Ben.

"For Kasumi."

He nodded and left the room. Detective Hartley's gaze had lost its sharpness. Now it held a dreamy quality that made her look a lot softer than her usual brisk self.

"Could I see your notebook, please?"

She handed it over, and I tore out the page from our last interview, and the two that followed, till I had a nice clean page again.

"Do you normally type these up back at the station?"

She nodded, so I made her tell me where they were filed on the computer system.

"Some of your computer files have become corrupted. You'll have to take some notes so you can re-enter the data."

She nodded again, but before we could begin Ben came in, an odd expression on his face. "Kasumi's ready for you."

"Wait here," I told Detective Hartley.

I left the room and nearly squeaked with shock when I saw who was waiting in the foyer.

"You were right," I said when I found my voice again. "It's flawless."

Detective Hartley grinned back at me and twirled so I could admire her from all angles. At least, I would have sworn on a stack of bibles it was Detective Hartley—if I didn't know that she was waiting in the room I'd just left. This was Kasumi, but so changed I could barely believe it, though she was standing right in front of me.

It was more than an impersonation. Somehow the kitsune magic allowed her to truly *become* Detective Hartley. Height, clothes, facial expressions—everything. Kasumi was right. Even the detective's mother wouldn't have been able to tell the difference. It was truly astonishing.

I gave her the real detective's password. "Make sure you get all the files. I don't want any traces left from that last interview."

"I know what I'm doing," she said, a faint hint of irritation in her voice.

I couldn't help it. As a mother I was so used to micromanaging every last detail. Delegating tasks and relying on others to perform them properly didn't come easily. I heard an echo of Leandra's derision in my head. She'd never had the least problem with delegating—which is why we were so lost now without Luce. Leandra had been all too comfortable with snapping her fingers and having someone else take care of whatever she wanted. That someone now played for the other team.

But maybe Kasumi could replace her? Oh, not in many ways—Luce and I went back too far for that. But there was no denying that Kasumi's kitsune abilities could be a hell of a lot handier than Luce's wyvern ones. In trueshape Luce had poisonous spurs and could spit a toxic mist that dropped enemies in their tracks, but funnily enough there weren't that many opportunities to go round spitting poison at people. Her centuries of experience were her true value.

Kitsune were slippery customers, with many more tricks up their sleeves than the average shifter. Probably only goblins could do more, but their magics weren't inherent; they had to be learned, and your average goblin wasn't the sharpest tool in the box, little more than cannon fodder. Even the mages were a mixed bag—just look at Blue Munroe. Only a few ever became proficient enough to be truly useful.

"Okay. I'll keep them here until you're done. Ring me when you're finished. Good luck."

"Luck isn't necessary."

I watched her leave the house, marvelling at her magic. Even the way she walked had changed, her quick, impatient steps mirroring the detective's usual pace. Shaking my head in wonder, I went back to face the real Detective Hartley.

Kasumi's version was now even more convincing than the real one, who sat where I'd left her with a vacant look in her eyes most unlike her usual alert self. I'd applied the compulsion as lightly as I could. Hopefully it would wear off in a few hours, before any of her colleagues noticed any odd behaviour. It was a delicate balance between the compliance I needed now and her usual independence.

When it did wear off she'd find herself very confused, still able to remember traces of the original interview where I'd shot myself in the foot, but also remembering the new version I was about to implant. The new and improved version would land Jason solidly in the firing line. She'd probably think she was going mad when she checked her files and found no trace of the original "facts", thanks to Kasumi.

Detective Franks was still enjoying his unscheduled nap. A small damp spot had formed on the back of the lounge, where he drooled in his sleep. Nice.

"When you leave here today you'll be convinced of my innocence," I said.

"Of course." She nodded enthusiastically. Her hands gripped her trouser-clad knees as she leaned forward, eager to catch every word.

"You'll concentrate all your efforts on locating my ex-husband Jason Hepburn. He's the one who killed Valeria, and he's been behind all the attacks on me too. He's planted lots of false evidence in an effort to implicate me, but you've realised the truth now. It was him I went to see at Valeria's apartment on New Year's Eve. He tried to kill both of us there, but we escaped to Valeria's house at Mosman, where he attacked us again, and succeeded in killing Valeria, his employer, and wounding my friend Ben. He's a dangerous man. You need to find him before he hurts anyone else."

She nodded again. "A man like that shouldn't be on the streets."

"That's right. There's no telling when he might strike again. You have to stop him."

"Yes." She looked like one of those nodding dogs you see on the parcel shelf of cars sometimes, her head bobbing up and down in agreement. "He's very dangerous. Must be stopped."

Damn, I hoped I hadn't overdone it. She'd be no use to me if she remained an imbecile. I caught her gaze again and eased off a touch, allowing something of her own personality to struggle out from under the compulsion.

She gave me a dazed look, then frowned at her notebook on the table between us. Its reflection gleamed in the polished surface. "I should be writing this down. Wasn't I going to take you to the station so I could record everything properly?"

"It's okay," I soothed. "You don't need to do that any more. You've realised Jason's the one you should be chasing. You just need to ask me some questions about my ex-husband's latest attack. That's why you came today, isn't it?"

"That's right." Still frowning, she leaned forward and picked up the notebook and pen. "That's right." She drew a deep breath. "Please tell me what happened at your residence in The Rocks on Sunday night."

CHAPTER TWENTY

Kasumi arrived back an hour or so after Detective Hartley and a still yawning Detective Franks went on their way, their heads stuffed with new information about Jason the murdering, child-stealing monster. Steve, looming even larger than usual next to the slight Japanese woman, escorted her into the kitchen, where I was killing time while we waited, watching Ben teach Lachie to play double-handed five hundred. There'd been some initial confusion over the left and right bowers, but now he seemed to have hit his stride, and was making outrageous bids. Sunlight streamed in the big windows and fell on the two curly heads, one dark, one light, bent over their cards in concentration.

"Just as well we're not playing for money," Ben muttered as Lachie swiped another winning trick off the table, a huge grin plastered on his face.

"Sit down," I said to Kasumi, and she slipped into the seat next to Lachie and clasped her hands loosely on the warm wooden table top in front of her.

Steve hovered awkwardly, unsure whether to play guide or guard, and I waved him away. I'd said I'd take her on if she succeeded at this task. We couldn't be treating her like a prisoner, always watching her sideways. Garth gave up pacing in front of the windows and drew closer, keen to hear the news. He at least would probably still be watching her sideways, judging by the scowl on his face.

I offered her tea or coffee, but she seemed so horrified when I got up to make it that I let Garth take over. Apparently she had no problem being waited on by werewolves. I stared out at the view of green fields bordered by dusky green bush while he crashed around in the cupboards and boiled the kettle, making his feeling about kitsune known with every violent movement.

When he was done he banged a mug of tea down on the table so hard some of it slopped over the side. She ignored him.

"All is well." She took a sip from the mug, looking like the cat that got the cream—or maybe the fox that got the chicken. "Jason is suspect number one now."

Lachie looked up at the mention of his father's name, but Ben distracted him by laying out another card. Kasumi eyed the cards in Lachie's hand and tapped one without speaking. He set it on top of Ben's and won another trick. Kasumi earned a shy smile in reward.

"Thank you. You've done well. Were there any problems?"

"No. I believe Detective Hartley is not very popular. No one spoke to me. But I did find something that might be of interest to you."

She offered me a folded piece of paper with her customary half-bow. I always found myself wanting to be extra polite around Kasumi, she had such elegant manners.

The paper was a printout of the autopsy report on Valeria. Not all of it, just the summary. Nothing unexpected there, of course. She'd died from being skewered through the heart with a massive object—the blade-like tip of my tail. Cause of death was kind of hard to miss.

The coroner wasn't to know how hard it was to kill a dragon, since the body he was examining looked human in every way. Our powers of regeneration were proof against almost anything. But having your heart obliterated by a massive blade would do it, as would a complete beheading such as Carl Davison had suffered, or blowing us into tiny little pieces, like the way Monique had died. There were a couple of poisons that were fatal to us, like the one that had killed Leandra, but that was pretty much it. Dragonfire would kill us if we were caught in human form, but in trueshape our scales protected us. In trueshape the only thing we had to fear was the teeth and claws of other dragons, since our scales were proof against any blade humans could make. Just as well dragons had a bad habit of fighting each other; otherwise the world would be overrun by entitled overgrown lizards.

At the end of the report was a curious note. *Strange growth noted on subject's left rib. Spherical, 1.6 cm across, black in colour, with silver striations. Substance unknown. Slight electric shock on first contact. Refer to Taskforce Jaeger.*

I looked up from the report and met Kasumi's eyes.

"I have heard of this Taskforce Jaeger," she said. "I believe its purpose is to gather information on the possible existence of supernatural creatures such as dragons."

She smiled. The "possible existence". Right. Our Japanese friend had a dry sense of humour.

I passed the paper to Ben to read. Garth leaned over to scan it too.

"It's your turn, Uncle Ben," Lachie said, impatient with this interruption.

"Sorry, mate." He threw down a careless card, and Lachie trumped it with glee.

"Ha! I still had the king!"

Ben rolled his eyes. "The kid's a card sharp. Save me."

"Lachie, you'll have to take a break. We need to talk to Kasumi. Why don't you go see what the guys in the comms room are up to? You can come back and finish thrashing Uncle Ben later."

Ben laughed. "Thanks for the vote of support."

Kasumi nodded approvingly as Lachie headed for the door. "Your son is very obedient." She grinned, a hint of that humour I'd seen before peeking through. "Good at cards, too."

Garth quirked an eyebrow at me. He and Ben both knew what the black stone was, though Kasumi most likely didn't. Dragons weren't in the habit of sharing the secret of their channel stones. In fact, dragons were just secretive, full stop. "Should we be worried about this taskforce?"

"I don't think so." It wasn't as if we didn't have other things to occupy our minds, without fretting about a bunch of scientists turning up waving dissection tools. "I doubt they'll get any further with that line of investigation. But speaking of investigation …" I turned back to Kasumi, and she sat a little straighter, eyeing me expectantly. "You are aware that Carl Davison's dead?"

Something flickered in those dark eyes. "Yes. I waited outside the day you went to meet him. After you got away safely I went in and saw that someone had beaten me to it."

Whoa. "*You* wanted to kill Carl Davison?"

"He was the man my sister became entangled with. The one who encouraged her to take up Elizabeth's deadly cause."

There was no expression on her face, the words merely a statement of fact, and I felt a chill run down my spine. She was not a person I wanted as an enemy. *But are you sure she's not?* a little voice whispered. *You* did *kill her sister.* If she was ready to kill Carl just for setting her sister up for a fall, how much more must she hate me?

I took a hasty sip of coffee to hide my disquiet, the warmth of its aroma flooding my senses with reassuring pleasure. Give me a good cup of coffee and I could take on fifty murderous kitsune.

Well, maybe not *fifty.*

"He said he had some information about what my sisters were doing."

She waited expectantly.

"I only have one—that I know of. The others are dead. It makes me worried that Elizabeth has held one back."

"Another claimant in the proving? That would be most irregular."

"It would." Which made it odd for the ultra-conservative Elizabeth. I still couldn't understand her reason for favouring one untried daughter over the others. No one could ever accuse our mother of being sentimental. She only ever made decisions based on cold hard logic. "But I need to know for sure. Can you help me?"

She nodded, her expression thoughtful. "I should be able to find something to pattern one of Davison's followers. He may have left papers, or perhaps I can question the staff, if any remain. Someone will know something, I am sure."

"Hang on," said Ben. "Let's look at all the angles here. Carl could have made the whole thing up. Maybe he was trying to lure *you* into an ambush, and he thought hinting about mysterious sisters would be guaranteed to get you to turn up."

"Worst ambush I've ever seen," said Garth.

Ben smiled, and the two shared a rare moment of agreement. "True. It certainly didn't turn out as he planned, if so. But we don't even know what he intended to tell you. It might all have been rumours. We'll never know."

"So what are you saying? That we should wait and see?" I didn't like surprises any more than Garth did. "Why, if Kasumi can find the answers for us?"

He waved his good hand impatiently. "We have plenty of real threats, without going looking for ones that may only be imaginary. I just think Kasumi's skills could be put to better use."

"In what way?" I glanced at Kasumi. She sipped her tea and followed the conversation with polite interest. It didn't seem to bother her that we were talking about her as if she wasn't there.

"Why don't we send her to assassinate Alicia? Then you'd be the heir and Elizabeth would have to call off her bounty hunters. She could impersonate one of Alicia's people perfectly and get close before Alicia realised anything was wrong." He turned to Kasumi. "You could do that, couldn't you?"

She shrugged. "Certainly, if I had something to pattern one of them with."

"Yes, but how would we get that?" We'd had this conversation before, only then it had been Garth suggesting using a goblin seeming to get close to Alicia. Kasumi's impersonation might be flawless, but the original problem was no easier to solve: how to get something to work the magic with in the first place.

"Actually, I think we've already got it." He looked at me. "Those leshies you killed in the street—I grabbed a handful of ash before we left."

I remembered him running across the road just before we left. In the chaos I hadn't noticed what he did.

"You picked up the ashes of a dead leshy? What the hell for?"

"Because I thought we might be able to use them in a goblin spell." Enthusiasm gleamed in his eyes as he turned back to Kasumi. "But this would be even better. That would work, wouldn't it? You said you could do it with hair or fingernails, and they're just dead tissue."

"But not *burnt* tissue," I objected.

Kasumi shook her head regretfully. "I am sorry. It is possible to assume the form of a dead person, but only if their body has not begun to decompose. I'm afraid in this case I would only be able to transform into a pile of ashes."

"Damn." Ben looked crestfallen.

"It wouldn't work anyway," Garth said. "Imagine Luce if someone she thought was dead turned up alive after two days. 'Suspicious' wouldn't even begin to cover it."

True. Luce hadn't lived as long as she had by being trusting. If only she was still on my side. I shuddered to think what new plan of attack she'd be coming up with. I needed a way to remove her from the equation.

"Back to Plan A, then."

Kasumi nodded and rose from the table. "I will find Davison's people and see what I can discover about this mysterious sister."

She gave me one of her little half-bows and left the room.

Garth watched her leave with his usual scowl.

"I don't trust her," he grumbled. "She smells wrong."

I rolled my eyes. Werewolves and their delicate noses. "Maybe she just smells like fox, and you want to chase her."

"I'm not a dog." He gave me a flat stare, but I was long past being cowed by Garth.

"I'm heading out to the stables," I said to Ben. "Want to come?"

That earned me a raised eyebrow. "Why? Are you planning a roll in the hay?"

I grinned. "Tempting, but no. Come out and I'll show you."

We went outside, followed by Garth, who mumbled dire warnings about exposing ourselves outside the protection of the house. I ignored him. It was a beautiful day, warm and sunny but with enough breeze to cut the heat—a day to lift the spirits and make you glad to be alive. Yes, there were a lot of people trying to kill me, and some of them had magical abilities, but a short walk between buildings wasn't much of a risk. No one could even sneeze within earshot of the estate without being caught on camera.

Besides which, I needed room for what I had planned.

A row of stalls opened onto the outside of the stables. In days past they would have housed a whole herd of happy horses checking out the view across the fields and the training ring, but now they stood empty. Leandra's only interest in horses had been in eating them.

The inside of the building had once been divided into more stalls, tack rooms and other essentials, but Leandra had hollowed it out, and now it was a great empty shell, dark and cool.

"See? No hay." I flicked on the lights, then waved my hand at the vast empty space. The weak bulbs did little to chase away the dimness. It smelled of horse, and hay, and honest sweat and leather, together with the not-altogether-unpleasant aroma of old horse dung.

"You could hold a ball in here," Ben said, his footsteps echoing as he moved into the centre of the emptiness.

"Or a soccer game," said Garth, pulling the big sliding door closed behind us with a crash.

"Why so much space?" Ben asked. "What did Leandra use this for?"

"Let me show you. Garth, face the wall."

He did as he was told, and I pulled off my T-shirt and stepped out of my shorts. Ben's eyebrows climbed into his hair and disappeared.

"What are you doing?" He threw a mischievous glance at Garth's broad back. "You want to try it *without* hay?"

"Life isn't *all* about sex, you know." I peeled off my underwear, feeling a little of the old Kate's self-consciousness, despite my best attempt at shifter pragmatism. He was a very new partner, after all.

His gaze roamed appreciatively over my body.

"Of course it is. What fool told you that?"

Garth snorted, but didn't turn around.

I stepped into the middle of the concrete floor to give myself plenty of room, its rough surface cool beneath my bare feet. Then I closed my eyes and gave in to the urge for union that always nagged at the back of my brain. I felt the familiar rush of warmth and elation as the barrier between the two parts of myself dropped away. Dimly I was aware of my body expanding and changing as I revelled in the sweet release of oneness.

When I opened my eyes my vision was different, sharper. I could see every speck of dirt on the floor, every tiny mote of dust that floated in the beams of sunlight from the high windows. Colours were brighter. Garth's aura blazed orange, outlining him in fire. He'd turned around—hopefully *after* I'd taken dragon shape.

Ben's face was a different, bleaker, picture. I bent to bring my massive head closer to his.

"What's wrong?" My voice echoed in the empty building, deep and powerful. He stepped back as my breath huffed across his face, lifting his hair.

He shook his head. "This is just hard to get used to. Every time I see you like this I remember how much I hate dragons. I couldn't bear it if you became like one of them."

He looked away, and some of the pleasure I felt in being in my trueshape leaked away. This was me, just as much as my human form. If he couldn't even look at me in this form, we had a problem.

"I'm still Kate. I'm not going to change."

He shrugged, as if to say I already had, which was kind of hard to argue with, considering I was currently the size of a bus and armoured in scales. But inside, where it counted—I was still the same person, wasn't I?

It was too much to deal with right now. I spread my wings and reared up on my hind legs, enjoying the chance to stretch muscles that rarely got a workout these days. Most dragons had a place like this—a warehouse, a remote clearing, a barn— where they could take trueshape unseen. It felt so good.

And sometimes it had a purpose. I lowered my head to my front leg and nuzzled at it, trying to hook a tooth under the edge of a scale. Humans didn't know how lucky they were to have hands. Clever little monkeys.

"What are you doing?" Garth asked. His expression was one of childlike wonder; he'd only seen me change a couple of times before. Shame Ben didn't see my trueshape the way Garth did.

I didn't reply. Proceedings were at a delicate stage. I tugged with a quick jerk of the head, and succeeded in prying a scale loose. It lay on the floor, catching the light from the windows like a piece of shimmering golden glass. I rested one taloned foot on it.

"What does it look like?" Again my voice boomed, filling the emptiness. Some dirt shook loose from the rafters above and pattered down onto the concrete floor.

"You're sending a message to someone?" Smart wolf. "Who?"

"Alicia." This time I remembered to keep my voice down.

Ben frowned. "A death threat? Really?"

Something dark stirred in me at the doubt in his tone. Did he think I was weak? Powerless? Dragon thoughts came more easily in dragon shape, and no dragon liked to be questioned. I drew in a deep breath. It took an effort to remember that this was Ben, and I loved him. His human doubts were only realistic, given my current circumstances.

"Yes. Really. Summon a herald."

I placed a talon on the glittering scale just so, then leaned my weight on it. It snapped with a distinct crack. Satisfied, I regarded the broken halves. This was a most ancient threat, one that no dragon could misunderstand. *I will break you as easily as I broke this scale, and all your mighty armour will be no protection.* Once Alicia received this, she would be looking over her shoulder every minute, waiting for my shadow to fall on her. Nothing Luce could say would prod her into action.

Meanwhile, I would be moving in a different direction entirely.

CHAPTER TWENTY-ONE

"Is Uncle Ben a dragon too?" Lachie bobbed up out of the pool again, wet curls slicked down against his head, and hurled another question at me. He shook his head and water sprayed across me where I sat on the edge, dangling my feet in the clear blue depths. The rippling water cast dancing reflections on the glass walls of the pool house, long shimmering streamers of light. We were in our own little chlorine-scented world, just the two of us again, at least for an hour or two, and he'd been peppering me with questions the whole time.

I guess he hadn't seen a lot of me since we moved out here. I'd been busy, and had left him to amuse himself a lot, or spend time with one or other of the men, or Mac. Hard to believe that only a week ago I'd thought him dead, and would have given anything to spend another moment with him. Now I had him back, and already I was taking him for granted.

"No, why?"

Not taking him for granted. Trying to keep him alive.

"I was just wondering. Dad's a dragon, you're a dragon, Garth and Mac are wolves ... everyone seems to be something special."

"Not everyone, Monster. Steve and Dave and the other guys are all regular humans, same as you and Ben."

He trod water, big brown eyes solemn. "I wish I was special. Do you think I might turn into a dragon one day too?"

God forbid. I wouldn't wish the way I'd done it on anyone. Fortunately it wasn't likely to start a trend, since it required a dying dragon to transfer their consciousness to their channel stone and make sure their target body swallowed the thing while they still had the strength to form a connection. And then came the whole fighting-for-control-of-the-body part. Fun times. "You don't have to be a shifter to be special, honey. You are the specialest, most fantasmagorical kid that ever lived as far as I'm concerned."

He gave me a sceptical look. "But you're my mum. You're supposed to think that."

"Oh, right, so my opinion doesn't matter, huh?"

"You know what I mean, Mum. It's different. You can turn into a dragon any time you want, and do all this cool stuff." I saw a new thought clamour for attention. He was so easy to read. "Don't dragons like swimming? Is that why you're not getting in?"

I laughed, and eased my way down into the water, the cold shock of it rising up my body. "No, I'm just a wuss. I don't know. I hadn't thought about it. I guess … not? Not many creatures swim for pleasure—unless they're meant to be aquatic, like otters, or dolphins or whatever."

"Did you know elephants are the only mammals that can't even swim?" He was like a kitten, chasing every bright shiny new idea that rolled past.

"Where did you hear that? That doesn't sound right."

"Don't know. I read it somewhere, I think." He tipped his head to one side and frowned. "But maybe I'm getting mixed up. Maybe they're the only animal that can't jump." He eyed me consideringly. "Do you reckon you could heat this whole pool if you breathed fire into it?"

I snorted. The things that went through the mind of a ten-year-old boy. "No idea."

"Why don't you try? I'll get out if you like."

So thoughtful. "No, that's fine. I think I'll just float here and relax for a while."

I lay on my back, tipping my head right back so the cool water reached its wet fingers into my hair. The ceiling of the pool house was painted a dark blue and strung with fairy lights, giving the effect of looking up at the stars in the night sky. With my ears underwater, Lachie's splashing made strange muffled noises, like listening to a heartbeat through an ultrasound. I felt shut off from the world, floating in my own little cocoon.

It made me sad that my baby didn't feel special enough in this strange new world we'd entered. Being his own unique wonderful self should be enough, yet in his own childish way he'd hit on a problem I hadn't considered before. What would his place be if I did pull off the enormous task before me and become queen of the shifters? He'd be fawned on by people trying to curry favour with me, or perhaps endangered by others plotting against me. He'd never know whether his shifter "friends" were true or not. Most of them would secretly look down on him, since he was merely a human. As if there were anything "mere" about being a human. The old Kate bristled at the thought, though the new one, with access to all Leandra's memories, knew too well how shifters thought. They were all full of themselves, and dragons were the worst—they even looked down on other shifters. Humans barely rated above animals, as far as they were concerned.

I scudded along with my hands, watching the fake stars swirl above me. And what about Ben? Where did he fit in?

Dragons often took human playmates—but "play" was the all-important word there. How could a dragon queen take a human for a true mate? They didn't even form lasting partnerships with other dragons.

And yet there'd have to be some kind of partnership, with at least one male dragon, or there'd be no dragon queenlings to fight over my throne one day. God, why was I even thinking about this now? Plenty of time to worry about succession planning later—first I had to win the damn throne.

Ben wouldn't live forever anyway. I stood up, suddenly too agitated for floating. What if we had kids? Would I have to watch them all die? Would I have to watch Lachie grow old and die, and his children and grandchildren after that, while I stayed the same?

I swallowed abruptly, feeling sick. Water swirled around me as Lachie splashed past, but I hardly noticed. No wonder dragons grew so bitter and selfish. I'd already seen Lachie die once. I didn't think I could do it again.

"Uncle Ben!" Lachie called, his voice alive with welcome. "Come and have a swim with us!"

I looked up, jolted out of my dark thoughts. Ben stood at the edge of the pool. His feet were bare but he wasn't dressed for swimming.

"No, thanks, mate. Better to keep this arm out of the water, I think."

"It might help," he said, his face serious. "Tanya went in the pool all the time when she had her sore knee. She said it was hydro—hydro-thingy."

"Hydrotherapy. Yeah, maybe next week. It's a bit sore today."

Probably because he was using it too much, in an effort to prove how much better he felt. Another one who was convinced he couldn't be special enough without being a shifter. He sat on the edge, legs in the water. I swam over and heaved myself out to sit next to him, spraying him with droplets.

"Nice in?" he asked.

"Very refreshing." Refreshing, my arse. The weight of the world bowed my shoulders. *Stop feeling sorry for yourself. You have a beautiful son and a loving partner right now. Yeah, so life is fleeting. Get over it.*

"You sent the herald off?" I asked, in an effort to distract myself.

He nodded. "I also asked him, if I had a message for Jason, whether he'd be able to deliver it."

"That was good thinking." Not knowing where Jason was, or what he was doing—because he was undoubtedly doing something that would bite me in the arse the minute I least expected it—only added to my stress levels. And God knows they were high enough. "What did he say?"

"Sadly, no deal. He thought he might be overseas. Says no one's seen him since New Year's Eve. Obviously didn't have a clue."

"That's a shame." I sighed. "I guess that would have been too easy. And nothing's ever easy lately, right?"

"Oh, I don't know." He took my wet hand and raised it to his lips. "Some things aren't too difficult."

"Like what?"

He still held my hand captive. "Like loving you."

I drew in a sudden breath, startled out of my glum mood. I squeezed his hand, my heart thumping, as warmth flooded me.

"I love you too." My voice came out in a whisper, tinged with emotion.

"Good God, woman, don't *cry*. It's meant to be a happy thing."

"I *am* happy." I swiped at my brimming eyes. "And I'm not crying. It's water from the pool."

"Right. And I'm a monkey's uncle."

"Hey!" Lachie splashed us both. "I heard that! You're *my* uncle. Well, sort of. Are you calling me a monkey?"

"I don't know." Ben considered him, grinning. "At the moment you're more of a drowned rat. You need to eat more, mate. You look like a strong wind could blow you away."

I laughed, and felt a tight knot ease in my chest. After all, no one's life came with a guarantee. We should all live for the moment; it was all we were sure of. The future would bring whatever it brought, and worrying about it now made no difference. For the moment I was happy.

He leaned in for a kiss. His mouth burned hot against my lips, still cool from my swim. "You know, maybe we should put Lachie to bed early tonight."

I glanced at the sky beyond the glass walls of the pool house. Only the faintest tinge of pink hinted at the coming of night. "It's not even dark yet."

"But he's had a very tiring day. All that swimming, you know. Come have a shower and I'll help you wash all those hard-to-get-at places."

"Such a noble sacrifice!" I shoved him affectionately and clambered to my feet. He certainly knew how to tempt a girl. I still tingled from his kiss. At least he seemed to be over his moodiness about me taking trueshape. His earlier words echoed uncomfortably in my mind. *I couldn't bear it if you became like one of them.* Would he be so keen to get me naked if I were covered in scales? I pushed the thought away. We were all stressed. It was no surprise if he was having trouble adjusting.

"Come on, Lachie. It's nearly dinner time. Time to get out."

"Ohhh! Five more minutes? Please, Mum?"

"All right."

I stood there dripping, watching him splashing about. He swam much better than last time I'd seen him in the water, ducking and diving like an otter, all sleek and gleaming brown skin. I guess that happened when you missed a whole chunk of someone's life. Must have had good swimming teachers at that ritzy boarding school of his.

I grabbed a towel and attacked my wet hair. Mustn't get maudlin again. I heard footsteps on the tiled floor, and came out from under the towel as Garth approached. He wore jeans despite the heat, and a plain white T-shirt that clung to his muscled chest. For once there were no Star Wars characters on it. Beads of sweat clung to his upper lip, and sparkled on the tips of his short, greying hair.

"You look like you could use a swim," I said.

His gaze swept over my body, and for a moment I felt naked. Then he bared his teeth in the most feral grin I'd ever seen. "I've got something much better in mind. Mac and I are heading off now."

I wrapped the towel around myself, suddenly self-conscious. Full moon tonight. The pair of them were going bush, disappearing into the national park around Berowra. It wasn't far from here.

"Are you sure you don't want to stay? We could lock you in the stables."

I'd made this argument before, reluctant to risk them to the wide open spaces. What if someone saw them? What if they attacked some poor hiker? Full moon was the one time when werewolves couldn't control their change. Other nights they could choose to change or not, but at full moon it was forced on them, and the strength of the compulsion sent them wild. All except the oldest and most experienced lost any trace of their humanity.

As a result they either spent the night locked safely away, or found some remote location far from accidental contact with humans. I worried about what might happen to them outside the safety of these walls.

"No thanks. I need a run." With an effort, he dragged his gaze back to my face. "It'll clear my head."

He walked away, something of the predator's prowl already in the way he moved. Should I have insisted? The back door of the house opened and Kasumi came out. Garth angled his steps more toward the garage so he wouldn't have to pass too close. She also gave him a wide berth. No love lost there.

Ben followed my gaze. "Don't worry so much. He's big enough and ugly enough to look after himself."

"Maybe." What was wrong with me today? I saw doom everywhere. "But what about Mac?"

"I wouldn't want to meet either of them in the dark tonight." He watched Kasumi approach. "Let's hope this is good news."

I felt even more awkward than usual having Kasumi bow at me while I stood dripping in my bikini.

"You really don't need to do that. We're pretty laid-back round here. How did you go?"

"Not well. None of his thralls survived his death. All mind-wiped. I found a human servant, but she knew nothing of any sixth sister."

"What about his shifter servants? Those three wyvern brothers?"

"It was one of them whose form I used to question the servant. She didn't know where they'd gone, but I couldn't press her too hard without it looking odd. The goblins have disappeared too, perhaps back to their clans. Not surprising, in the circumstances."

True. Everyone would be ducking for cover after the murder of their master, afraid they might be next.

"So basically we're no better off than before," said Ben. "We should find Blue and see if he can do something with those leshy ashes."

God, was he still on about that? "You know that's not going to work. Lachie, get out now."

Lachie dragged himself up the ladder in slow motion, reluctance in every movement.

"Why wouldn't it work? Just because Kasumi can't use them doesn't mean Blue couldn't."

I sighed, exasperated. "Blue is unco-operative, and a drunk. Plus now he'll be hiding even more carefully than before. He made his opinion on helping us again quite clear."

"Well, what other options do we have?" He looked as exasperated as I felt.

I had an idea in mind, but I wasn't ready to share it yet.

While we bickered, Kasumi retrieved Lachie's towel and held it out to him. He accepted it with a polite "thank you", then looked up at her.

"Could you turn into me?"

"Yes."

His eyes grew round. "Wish I could turn into you."

She studied him gravely. "It takes years of practice. My own children play a version of hide and seek where they must hide in another form, and see if their friends can pick them out."

"And can they?" He swiped ineffectively at the water on his skinny arms.

"Usually. A pine tree with a fox's tail tends to stand out." She smiled, and her whole face softened. "For some reason the tail is the hardest part to change. I had terrible trouble with it when I was your age. It was forever peeking out from under my clothes."

"That sounds like fun."

She shot me a look at the wistfulness in his voice, half-guilty, half-apologetic. Then she answered him in a brisk, no-nonsense tone. "Not at all. It's a lot of work. No more exciting than doing homework is for you. And my children are so busy practising they don't have time to play with Lego."

"Lachie, you're dripping on Kasumi's foot," I said, a little more sharply than I'd intended. The yearning was still plain on his wet face. Ben took one look at me then removed the towel from Lachie's unresisting hands.

"Bet they don't play cards either." He flicked him playfully with the towel. Lachie squeaked and jumped out of the way. "When are we going to have a rematch? I reckon I'm going to thrash you this time."

"Not a chance. Race you!"

He hurtled out of the pool house, his bare feet leaving a trail of little wet footprints all the way back to the house.

"Thanks, Ben."

He nodded and followed Lachie more slowly. So, still annoyed with me, but prepared to help out by distracting my son. Guess it really was love. My exasperation with him eased a little, and I turned back to Kasumi.

"I didn't know you had children."

"Two. A boy and a girl, back in Tokyo."

We walked side by side back to the house. The sun sat just above the trees, a white-hot orb. "Do you miss them?"

"Of course. But they have their father, and their uncles. They are probably too busy to miss me."

"You all live together?"

"We are a close-knit family."

Ah. And I had killed her sister. Probably not the best direction to take the conversation.

"I should not have spoken of my children to your son," Kasumi said, a little hesitantly. "I can see he wishes …"

She paused, and I filled in the silence. "Lachie's obsessed with shifters at the moment. Understandable, I guess. So's most of the rest of the world."

She nodded. "He longs for what he cannot have."

"Don't we all?"

A little house in the suburbs, filled with laughter and the sounds of two male voices, one deep and one high and piping. Just the three of us, living a regular life.

We paused at the back door. Pink tinged the high clouds to the west. The sun was going down, and soon the moon would rise.

"Where are the wolves spending the night?"

I sighed. "Running around the bush."

"You wish they had stayed here?"

"You've very perceptive."

"I have to be. Kitsune are trained from an early age to study people. You cannot imitate something you do not understand." She held the door open for me. "Why did you not command them to stay if that was your wish?"

I met her searching gaze. "They wanted to go. This isn't a prison. I'm not going to hold people against their will. You said it yourself: I'm not like other dragons."

CHAPTER TWENTY-TWO

A terrible grinding crash jerked me awake. What the hell was that? I sat up, still groggy from sleep. Last thing I remembered was falling asleep curled up against Ben's back. That felt like hours ago. The room was dark, but moonlight crept in the window, enough to show me that his side of the bed lay empty now. The clock said 3:09.

I staggered up. Somewhere a car engine roared, accompanied by the squeal of metal. I ran to the door, snatching up a dressing gown as I went, and out into the hall.

"What's going on?" I shoved my arms into the sleeves and tied a hasty knot around my waist. An alarm shrilled from the control room.

"Someone just rammed the gates!" Steve's deep voice, from his station at the monitors.

I took the stairs two at a time. Down the corridor to the east wing, doors slammed as Thommo and Dave turned out in answer to the alarm's shrill summons. Both wore shorts and had obviously been asleep. Thommo's hair stood up like a broom. Dave looked more alert, and was buckling a shoulder holster as he ran.

We'd need more than handguns. "Break out the assault rifles," I told him, and he ran back down the corridor to the armoury.

I heard the squeal of tyres, then the roar of a high-powered engine as I arrived at the comms room. I was just in time to see the gates explode off their hinges onscreen as a dark van rammed them again. Momentum carried it through the gateway and halfway up the drive. Sparks fountained as it dragged one gate with it, entangled in the wreckage of its front bumper. It listed drunkenly off the driveway onto the grass, and rolled to a stop. Dark figures spilled out of the back doors and sprinted towards the house, bent low over their guns.

"Steve, Thommo, take the front." They ran, collecting guns from Dave as they passed. "Dave, you're on the roof with me."

I pelted back up the stairs, meeting Alex on the way down.

"Where do you want me?"

"Stay with Lachie. Have you seen Ben? Or Kasumi?"

He shook his head and took off toward Lachie's room, while Dave and I sprinted down the hall to the door that opened out to the rooftop garden. Snuggled between the peak of the main house's roof and the western wing, it looked out over the back of the estate, with a view across the surrounding bushland. Tonight I wasn't interested in the view, and I scrambled up the slope of the roof to the ridgeline so I could see what was happening at the front of the house.

Dave dropped beside me and rested his gun on the ridge. The sharp rat-tat-tat of rapid fire sounded already from below us, as Steve and Thommo opened fire from the house. Some of the invaders threw themselves down and returned fire, while others kept running. Still more poured in through the open gateway.

Of course they picked full moon to attack, when Garth and Mac were out of action. I scanned the darkness. Where the hell were Ben and Kasumi?

"Where did they all come from?" breathed Dave. Then, in a very different tone: "What the hell are *those*?"

Creatures erupted from the grass all around the invaders. Someone had shot out the floodlights, but the full moon, riding high in the sky, provided plenty of light for my shifter vision. Dave's gun rained death down on the invaders, but it was like shooting fish in a barrel, because suddenly all those figures on the lawn were fighting for their lives against a new threat.

Half a dozen were pulled down into the earth before they even realised they were under attack. Then the screaming started. Guns had no effect on the shadowy creatures. Bullets passed right through them as they faded to mist. Next minute they were all too solid as their claws slashed the throat of a slow-moving invader.

"Dragons' teeth," I said, with grim satisfaction. It was nice to know Leandra's money had been well spent. And it had been an exorbitant amount. Looked like Blue wasn't a bad mage when he tried. Ironic that his spell was now being used against fellow goblins, for that was what our unexpected guests were, judging by their murky auras. Not that Blue would have cared.

Dave spared me an incredulous look as he paused to reload. "Dragon's *teeth*? They look like scarecrows."

Particularly vicious scarecrows, but yes, they did have that rather thrown-together look about them, and their movements were jerky and unnatural. Effective though. I watched another skewer a goblin through the guts. The goblin folded forward around the fatal blow, vomiting blood that looked black in the moonlight.

"Well, these were made from scales, actually. 'Dragons' teeth' is just a nickname, from the Greek legend." He looked confused. "You know, the field sown with dragons' teeth, and they all sprouted into warriors? No? Well, never mind. They're just constructs. A good enough goblin mage can transform almost anything into something else." Like sticks and vegetables into a copy of a boy so exact even his own mother had been fooled. A precious boy, who I'd mourned after Jason had "killed" the changeling in a car accident. "These pieces of Leandra's scales have been lying dormant underground. Any attack on her triggers the magic."

I stood up on the ridgeline to get a better view of the carnage below, a fierce joy in my heart. If only all my enemies would die so easily. Shame the dragons' teeth didn't last a bit longer. They were already fading, falling back into the earth, though a handful of enemies remained.

A massive blow slammed me in the back. I went cartwheeling off the roof, screaming as the sky spun about me. No time! Quick! I reached for union as the ground loomed, but I was caught mid-change. Agony stabbed through me as the bones in my legs shattered on impact.

I whimpered, pinned in place by blinding pain. A figure loomed over me, a goblin, snarling in triumph as he levelled his gun at my face. Stupid goblin. That was no way to kill a dragon.

Then another appeared beside him, armed with a chainsaw, of all things. Yes, that would do it. I shut my eyes and *pulled* as the machine roared into life.

Just in time. I surged to my four enormous feet and bit the chainsaw-wielding goblin in half with a contemptuous snap of my teeth. His companion screamed and turned to run, his useless gun hurled away in panic. I leapt on him too, then spat to the side. Ugh. Something about goblins just didn't taste right.

A bright form streaked down from above. Then another and another. Moonlight glinted off perfect red-gold scales. Wyverns. I guess that explained where Carl Davison's followers had disappeared to. These must be his goblins too, out for revenge—or more likely, the bounty on my head.

Except for Luce, the only good wyvern was a dead one, though you couldn't even eat the corpses; they were full of poison. Poisonous spurs on their feet, poisonous fangs in their snakelike mouths—even their skin oozed poison like some kind of vicious flying cane toad.

I leapt into the air to meet them. Their poison wouldn't kill me but the effects wouldn't be pleasant if the three of them got within spitting range and coordinated their efforts.

But they weren't trying to. I spiralled higher, chasing the elusive creatures. I'd almost have one, then another would dart in from the side and in avoiding that one I would lose the first.

I belched flame, but they were so quick, zipping all over the sky, that my flames went wide.

We'd climbed some distance from the house when I realised I'd been hearing gunfire again—more and more of it. I looked down and saw creatures streaming toward the back of the house from the bush behind. This triggered another wave of dragons' teeth.

But some of the gunfire was single shots, and it came from inside.

I folded my wings and dived, consumed by sudden fear. Those damn wyverns had been leading me on, drawing me away as new enemies arrived. Like an idiot I'd fallen for it.

I swooped low behind the house, my fire carving a deadly path through the enemies I found there. Goblins screamed and died, engulfed in dragonfire. The pool house went up like a torch as I sent gouts of fire raging across the lawn.

The wyverns joined the fight too, now I refused to be lured away any more, their slashing claws more effective against the dragons' teeth constructs than the bullets of the goblins. They were clever, timing their attacks to strike the constructs as they formed out of the shadows into something solid.

I landed amid the devastation, blasting a group of goblins who huddled together in futile resistance. Their bullets bounced harmlessly off my scales. Two others escaped into the house. I had to let them go for fear of firing the house itself. Once dragonfire took hold nothing would put it out.

The night was alive with the crackle of flame, its light dancing on the buildings, sending shadows flickering everywhere. A wyvern dived to buzz me and I turned my head and caught it full in the face with dragonfire. It fell like a flaming meteor to earth and crashed through the roof of the burning pool house. Its two companions darted away, giving up the fight now their goblin allies were all down.

Heat from the blaze behind me licked against my back as I stalked toward the main house, pushing some of my mass back through the link so that by the time I reached the door I could squeeze through it. I wasn't much bigger than a wyvern myself now, and I wouldn't be as effective at this size, but I didn't dare relinquish trueshape yet. A naked human form would be useless, and there were precious lives at risk inside the house.

I found Thommo dead in the hallway outside the comms room, his body ripped open by a hail of bullets. I startled a goblin inside the room and leapt on it, spraying the monitors with its blood. A moment later it fell limp under my slashing claws.

Upstairs. Lachie! Dread sunk vicious claws into my heart. I ripped apart two more goblins who stood in my way, then bounded up the stairs. At the top I found Steve, slumped against the wall, but still alive.

Faster! I rushed along the hallway towards Lachie's room, following sounds of a struggle. Something crashed into the wall. Someone grunted.

And someone screamed, a high-pitched wail torn from the throat of a terrified child.

I hurled myself through the doorway with a roar of anguish. Kasumi fought two goblins, holding them off from Lachie, who cowered behind her. She'd disarmed them both, but her whole right arm ran with blood from a bullet wound to the shoulder, and she didn't move with her usual smoothness. The goblins turned as I entered, and I leapt on the one closest and tore his head from his shoulders.

The other froze for a brief, shocked second, and Kasumi stepped in and dropped him with a smart blow to the temple.

"Kasumi! You're hurt." Though the shoulder obviously pained her, it clearly hadn't been a silver bullet, which suggested that whoever planned this attack hadn't known I had a new shifter in my camp. With the wolves away for full moon, they'd assumed there'd be no point bringing silver to a gunfight against humans and a lone dragon.

I looked past her to Lachie, huddled against the wall, and trueshape rushed away, leaving me naked and staggering. He was curled into a tight ball with his arms wrapped around his skinny frame, eyes squeezed shut. Was he hurt?

In front of him a familiar body lay unmoving. Alex. I dropped to my knees. The carpet squelched with his blood. Too much blood. His blond hair ran red with it. My heart sank as I reached out to turn him over.

Kasumi bent over, hands on knees, heaving in air. "Don't," she gasped as my hand touched Alex's still shoulder. "The boy …"

The boy would see.

The boy *had* seen. I lay a hand on Alex's arm. His skin was already cooling. Lachie had seen Alex die right in front of him. Trying to protect him, as I'd asked. Tears stung at my eyes, and I turned away and gathered Lachie's shivering little body into my arms. This was a nightmare I couldn't wake up from. How many more people had to die?

Kasumi pulled a blanket from the bed and covered Alex's body. Lachie wound himself tightly around me and sobbed into my shoulder. I rocked him as Kasumi retrieved a gun from the floor and limped to the door.

"I'll make sure we got them all."

"Steve's in the hallway. He's hurt." I forced each word past the lump in my throat.

"Dave?"

"I don't know." He'd been on the roof with me when the wyverns struck. He was probably dead too. So many dead. "I haven't seen Ben either." Worry for him gnawed at me.

Kasumi frowned. "I saw him drive out about an hour ago when I was doing a tour of the perimeter. I don't believe he came back before the attack."

Thank God for that. I dropped my head to Lachie's hair, grateful beyond all telling for the warm, live weight of him in my lap. Alex had given his life for this precious bundle of humanity. Somehow I had to find a way out of this mess and make that sacrifice mean something.

CHAPTER TWENTY-THREE

Eventually I rose and carried Lachie to my room. He'd cried himself to sleep in my arms, but woke again with the movement and started crying again.

"Where are you going?" he asked as I set him down on my bed. He grabbed at me, desperation in his panicked grip. "Don't leave me!"

"Shh." I stroked his hair, but he kept crying. "There are things I have to do."

I tried to pull away, but his panic mounted, so I caught his chin and forced him to meet my eyes. "Be calm. You will go to sleep."

At once he sagged like a rag doll, and I laid him down and covered him with the sheet. It was only a light compulsion, and I felt absolutely no compunction about using it. Sleep would be the best thing for him.

An envelope lay on Ben's pillow. My name was scrawled on the front in his messy handwriting. If I hadn't been in such a panic when the attack began I would have seen it before.

The message inside was terse.

Gone to find Blue. I can't sit around doing nothing any more. Back when I can. Ben.

Oh, for God's sake. I screwed it up, shrugged on a pair of shorts and a T-shirt, and went downstairs.

I found Dave in the comms room.

"You escaped the wyverns?" I should feel glad, but my emotions were in such a turmoil already. Ben was alive—thank God—but he'd taken off on his own to find a goblin I didn't even want, which made me crazy. Half of me was giddy with relief that he was alive, and the other half wanted to punch his stupid face the minute I saw him again. The wolves were safe, but at the same time I couldn't help feeling I'd made a big mistake in letting them go. Alex and Thommo might still be alive if I'd put my foot down. What kind of leader was I if no one listened to me? Leandra would never have tolerated people running off and doing their own thing.

"Luckily for me they were more interested in you. Gave me time to duck back inside." He looked ten years older than normal, his face drawn and deathly pale, with none of his usual good humour. Probably shock. "Kasumi's out patrolling the grounds. I said I'd watch from in here."

"Good." With only two of them, there was little else they could do. And whose fault was it that half our strength was gone when we needed them? I was so busy trying to be consultative and not your typical dragon that I'd brought us to the brink of ruin. "Steve?"

"Concussed, but not too bad. He went out to dig a firebreak around the pool house."

Something I should have thought of. Dragonfire would burn till it ran out of fuel, and we didn't want it anywhere near the house. At least the night was still, with no wind. Hopefully that, and our location in the bottom of a secluded valley, meant that the fire brigade wouldn't be arriving on our doorstep any minute. Our nearest neighbours, tucked on the other side of the hills, wouldn't be able to see the flames, so as long as there was no wind to spread the smell of smoke, we should be safe from having to answer awkward questions.

"I'll go check on him."

Outside it was still dark, though the blazing pool house provided plenty of light to see by. It couldn't be more than four o'clock in the morning, and the sun wouldn't be up for a couple of hours. The moon hung low in the sky. Not long till Garth and Mac returned.

I found Steve in the barn, putting the tractor away. He'd used it to gouge a wide circle out of the ground all around the fire, leaving nothing but bare dirt, not even a blade of grass for the fire to feed on.

"How's the head?" Someone had tied a bandage around his head, which showed a small bloodstain.

"Not too bad. Feeling a bit sick."

I didn't tell him he shouldn't be working, though it was true. Tasks needed doing, and there was no one else to do them. I looked at the goblin bodies scattered across the yard and clenched my fists. What would Detective Hartley have to say about this?

Screw Detective Hartley.

I was done with playing by the human rules. No more police investigations, no more awkward questions. No more letting everyone steer their own course. I was the captain. If I was a dragon, it was time to act like one, and Ben could take it or leave it.

I removed my clothes and handed them to Steve. He didn't blink an eyelid, just stood there holding them like some old-time valet. Smears of ash and blood decorated his dark face.

Lit by flames, I eased back into trueshape and felt some relief from the storm of anger and regret raging inside me. I always felt different in this form—still me, but better. Different parts of me came to the fore in trueshape. More decisive, more commanding. Less tangled in painful emotions. Choices became clearer.

I scooped up the nearest pile of goblins and took to the sky. I saw Kasumi in the shadows at the front of the house. And where had *she* been when the attack began? Out checking the perimeter, she'd said. Another one wandering round doing her own thing. Her upturned face was a white oval in the dark as she watched me fly over. Nothing moved anywhere else. It seemed we had been lucky—in this form I could consider it lucky—and beaten back the attack at the cost of only two lives. No one had called the police or the fire brigade. Our neighbours were all too far away to notice any disturbance in our hidden valley. Probably tucked up safely in their beds. I flew a circuit of the boundaries of the property, then wheeled back toward the fire. Even up here I could feel its heat, though the flames burned lower now, barely the height of a man.

When I was right above it I dropped the goblins, and watched their bodies disappear into the flames.

The pool house was nearly consumed by now, and the fire was dying down. I fed it every goblin I could find with a grim satisfaction. There would be nothing left of them when the fire died out, no inconvenient evidence left lying around for Detective Hartley to harass me with.

I went inside, shrinking down again to fit through the door, and brought out the goblins who'd died there and added their bodies to the fire. And then I made two more trips, first for Thommo and then Alex. Steve said nothing as he watched me drop Thommo into the blaze, as aware as me that we'd reached crisis point. All or nothing now.

I felt a pang as I leapt skyward with Alex's body hanging limp in my claws. I lifted him and nuzzled his cold face, his blood-soaked blond hair, but he smelled like any other piece of dead meat. The man who'd given his life for my son was gone, and this was only his shell. Only humans bothered about what happened to the shell once the life within had fled. I was a dragon.

I consigned his body to the fire too, then flew down to join Steve. He handed me my clothes in silence once I'd transformed, then we stood and watched the flames together. Kasumi came out to join us. She'd changed clothes and cleaned up, so only the edge of a bandage peeking out from her top showed where her shoulder had been hurt.

"They died bravely," she said.

I answered through gritted teeth. "They died *needlessly*."

Maybe there was a reason dragons were such autocratic arseholes. At least they didn't have to deal with people wandering off on their own like I did. I could cheerfully have strangled Ben at that moment, and my feelings for Garth and Mac weren't much kinder. But my strongest loathing was reserved for myself. I should have been firmer, should have handled my people better.

The moon had slipped below the horizon as I worked, and now the sky to the east began to glow with the faint promise of dawn. We stood there as the fire dwindled and the sky blushed pink and then orange. We stood there as the sun lifted over the horizon, and the fire sank into glowing embers. The snap and crackle of flame faded away, replaced by the sound of currawongs warbling in the trees.

"Do not worry for your son," Kasumi said. "Children are remarkably resilient. He will recover." The first pale light of day lit her face. She turned a frank gaze on me, sympathy in her eyes. "My own children have seen atrocities you would not believe. But still they laugh and play."

I nodded. Time would tell, I guess. The sound of a car coming up the drive broke the stillness. Steve twitched nervously, but I laid a hand on his arm.

"It's Garth and Mac."

The four-wheel drive rounded the corner of the house but stopped short of the garage. The two werewolves leapt out and rushed over to us.

"What happened?" Garth's gaze took in Steve's bandage and the bloodstains on the paving out here, then flicked to the smouldering ruin of the pool house. "The gate—?"

"Rammed. We were attacked."

His eyes blazed. He looked as if he'd like to pat me down and check for injuries. "Who?"

I shrugged. "Goblins and wyverns. I imagine they were Carl Davison's. No one else has three wyverns on staff, and they probably thought revenge would be all the sweeter with a bounty as reward."

"Any injuries?" Mac cut to the heart of it. *Any losses?* she meant. Her eyes still showed the pain of losing Jerry.

"Thommo and Alex are dead. Steve's concussed. Ben's buggered off somewhere. The rest of us are fine." For certain definitions of fine, of course.

Garth sucked in a shocked breath. "I should have been here. You were right. We should have stayed."

"Yes." My voice was bleak. "You should have."

"I would have enjoyed killing a few goblins." His lip curled in a snarl.

"The mistress barely needed our help," said Steve.

Odd. It had been a long time since he'd called me "mistress". Not since his thrall days. Had he seen the change in me?

"How is Lachie?" asked Mac, her blue eyes hard with repressed anger.

"Sleeping. He's frightened. He saw things he shouldn't have."

"But not hurt?"

"No." Not in any way you could see. The memory of his sobs tore at me, that frightened way he'd curled into a ball as if to shut out the horror happening right in front of him.

I sighed, and scrubbed wearily at the dirt and ash on my own face. I might never get the stink of smoke out of my nostrils. God knows the damage that had been done tonight to the poor kid's psyche. I hoped Kasumi was right.

No matter. I couldn't allow myself to be distracted by such thoughts. At least he still had a psyche to be damaged, and wasn't ashes in a fire. My only goal now was to keep him from the flames that were eating up my world.

"Come inside. Once I'm cleaned up we need to talk."

"And see about getting that gate fixed," Garth said.

"No need," I said. "We're moving on."

CHAPTER TWENTY-FOUR

Dave passed around coffees and plates heaped with bacon and eggs. The smell of the food turned my stomach, but I forced myself to take a serving. Then he left to relieve Steve in the comms room. Having a concussed man watch the screens was hardly ideal.

We made a subdued group around the large pine table. Early morning sunlight streamed in the kitchen windows, sparkling on the steel bench tops, but it did nothing to lighten the mood. Only five of us sat around the table now—me, Steve, Kasumi and the two werewolves—and the empty spaces felt huge.

While we ate I filled the wolves in on what had happened while they were gone.

"I want everyone packed and ready to go in half an hour," I finished. The bacon tasted like ash in my mouth. I washed it down with coffee, black and bitter. Despite the shower, I still didn't feel clean.

"Where are we going?" Garth asked. His cheeks bulged with food like a chipmunk. He and Mac had probably spent all night running. They were the only ones with much appetite this morning.

"You three and Dave are taking Lachie into hiding. Kasumi and I are going to visit my mother."

Garth choked and nearly spat bacon. "What?"

Kasumi said nothing, merely laid down her knife and fork and waited expectantly.

"We're out of time," I said. "We can't keep facing these attacks, being whittled away little by little. Every time they hit us we lose someone else. If we don't do something bold, *right now*, while they think we're still licking our wounds, the next attack could kill us all. We have to take the fight to them."

"But … *Elizabeth*? How can six of us take on the queen?"

She had the resources of all Oceania at her fingertips. He didn't need to say it; we all knew.

"Not six. Just me and Kasumi. The rest of you will keep Lachie safe."

"Just her?" He looked at Kasumi, his gaze full of hostility. "Why her? She's been with us all of five minutes. How do you even know you can trust her?"

"This is not a democracy, Garth." I challenged his glare with one of my own. No more arguments. "She could have killed us all several times over last night. Why shouldn't I trust her? She kept Lachie alive for me while you were off chasing rabbits in the bush."

Garth looked down at his plate. Okay, that was a low blow, but I was past caring.

"What is your plan?" Kasumi asked. Her stillness spoke of a coiled spring, ready for action. Garth shot her a resentful glare, but her attention never wavered from me. There might have been no one else in the room.

"I've sent Alicia a broken scale. She doesn't cope well with death threats. She'll most likely sit tight and hope that one of the bounty hunters can take me out without her having to risk anything. So that removes one enemy from the equation, at least until Luce can coax her into action again. Elizabeth won't move overtly against me—but she doesn't need to, having set every bounty hunter in Sydney onto me."

Kasumi's mouth curved into an approving smile, though Garth still looked confused.

"So what are you going to do? Beg Elizabeth to call them off?" His expression showed exactly what he thought of *that* idea.

"No, of course not. I'm going to kill her." I locked eyes with the kitsune. "Or rather, we are."

Kasumi gave me an approving nod, as if she'd expected no less. There was a stunned silence from the others.

"But she's the queen," Steve said at last in his deep rumble. No one was eating any more, not even the werewolves.

"Exactly. And if I kill her, *I* will be queen, and the bounty hunters will have no reason to kill me. Or Ben. There'll be no more bounty."

Problem solved. A neat solution, if I said so myself. And one that I hoped would save Ben's exasperating arse before he managed to get himself killed. Every time I thought of him running around out there, alone and all but defenceless, anxiety closed its fist on my heart.

"How in the hell are you going to do that?" Garth said.

I ignored him and focused on the kitsune. She didn't seem bothered at being asked to assist in a regicide, though if it went wrong her death would be horrible. In fact, she hadn't seemed bothered by anything I asked of her. She truly was a godsend. With her unique abilities, I might actually be able to pull this off.

"Davison's dead and Jason's disappeared, which means Elizabeth herself and Gideon Thorne are probably the only two dragons at court at the moment."

"Davison's servant said her master had spent a lot of time recently with Gideon Thorne," Kasumi commented.

I shrugged. There could be any number of innocent explanations. It didn't matter now what Davison had been up to.

"Who's Gideon Thorne?" Mac asked.

"A very influential dragon in Elizabeth's court," I said.

"I've never heard of him."

"He likes to keep a low profile. Prefers to work in the shadows."

"He's her spymaster," Kasumi said.

"Really?" Mac looked as surprised as if she'd just discovered the Easter Bunny was real. Maybe it did sound old-fashioned, but such things were necessary, especially in a paranoid world like the shifters'. Even human governments had spies, though they didn't like to call them that any more. "Agents" sounded so much more appealing.

Kasumi turned to me. "She also told me that the bounty on your head has gone up to two million, with a bonus if they bring you in alive. Elizabeth hankers for a good old-fashioned execution."

"A ritual beheading for the abomination, eh?" I smiled for the first time today. "Perfect."

Garth eyed me as if I'd run mad. "How is that a good thing?"

"Because Kasumi can impersonate anyone she likes. Even a bounty hunter. If she assumes the identity of Carl Davison's wyvern again she can bring me in to Elizabeth. I will be *this* close to her." I held my thumb and forefinger a centimetre apart. "She'll think I'm finished. And then I can strike."

"Bit hard to strike when you're wrapped up in chains," he objected.

"Silver chains." Silver prevented a shifter from taking trueshape. Whenever the hunters were required to deliver a live captive they bound the unfortunate shifter in silver, so they couldn't access their powers. "And I seem to be immune to silver's effects now. Remember the silver bullet?"

He glanced sideways at Mac. Yes, she probably remembered the silver bullet more than any of us, but that was no reason not to speak of it. People tried so hard not to say things that might remind you of your loss, but I knew from my own bitter experience that you didn't stop mourning a person just because no one mentioned them.

She nodded, her gaze firm. "You weren't affected by silver poisoning at all."

Yet Jerry had died in agony. If she thought that unfair she said nothing. But I'd paid a high price for my new immunity. I wouldn't wish the events of the past months on anybody. Well, maybe Valeria, but she was already dead.

Garth pushed his chair back with a violent motion. That man couldn't bear to sit still. He stalked to the window, then turned abruptly and regarded me, arms folded across his massive chest.

"So you're going to let her chain you up and deliver you to the one person who wants you dead more than anyone else, in the middle of her court, surrounded by security and probably a dozen other shifters."

"That's the plan," I agreed.

Garth would never make a poker player. His face darkened, that monobrow drawing into a furious scowl.

"I won't allow it."

Red-hot rage flooded my body, spreading fire through my veins. He wouldn't *allow* it? Who the hell did he think he was?

"I don't remember asking your permission."

Goddammit, why couldn't I surround myself with thralls? Unquestioning obedience looked a lot more appealing all of a sudden. How dare he? He was only a wolf.

Listen to yourself. That's dragon thinking. Rage disappeared as suddenly as it had come, leaving me chilled. Ben would be horrified if he knew I'd felt like that, even for a moment. I took a deep breath and reminded myself of all the things that were wrong with taking thralls. I refused to become like the other dragons. I wouldn't lose my humanity, but I *would* have obedience.

"I'm the head of your security," he burst out. If looks could kill Kasumi would have dropped dead on the spot. His aura flickered with the violence of his feelings. "This is suicide!"

"It's risky—"

"Risky? It's bloody ridiculous."

"—but *we can't keep going the way we are*." I held his gaze in challenge until he looked away. "We can't take any more hits like last night. It's worth taking a risk to *win*, and have this damn proving over with."

"Then why not have one of us take you in? I'll do it. I can pretend I'm after the money."

"Now who's being ridiculous? As if Elizabeth would fall for that. She'd be on her guard from the minute we walked in, and we'd both be dead."

"But what's to stop your precious kitsune from handing you over for real? Maybe that's been her plan all along, and that's why she joined us."

"For God's sake, Garth! That would be a bloody convoluted plan. What's wrong with you?"

He clenched his fists. "I need to keep you safe."

"Perhaps I can provide some peace of mind for the wolf," Kasumi said. She always called him that; I'd never heard her use his name. He certainly wasn't her favourite person, but she didn't seem offended by his open distrust. "He may hold my hoshi no tama as surety while we are gone."

"What the hell does that mean?" he growled.

She reached into her pocket and pulled out something that looked like a large pearl, though to my dragon-enhanced sight it glowed with a strong yellow aura. It was the same colour as

Kasumi's own aura, but much brighter, as if the aura that normally showed around a person had in her case been concentrated in this one tiny object instead. No wonder her aura was so hard to pick out. Her power resided here instead, in this glowing pearl. She hardly even looked like a shifter to my dragon sight.

"This is my hoshi no tama." I could tell from the expression on Garth's face that he wasn't impressed. To him it would look like a normal pearl—a biggish one, sure, but nothing special. "They are sometimes called star balls. Every kitsune has one; it is the heart of our powers. Some say it is our soul made visible."

It sounded rather like a dragon channel stone to me, though the functions it fulfilled were different. Interesting that it was outside her body. That must be awkward sometimes. What did she do with it when she took fox form? Carry it round in her mouth?

"If a kitsune is without her hoshi no tama for long," she continued, "she will wither and die. You must guard it carefully while I am gone."

She placed the pearl on the table and he stepped forward and took it. I thought she flinched slightly as his big fingers closed on it, but that could have been my imagination

"You'd better look after her, then," said Garth, a world of menace in his voice, "or I'll crush this thing to dust."

She nodded.

"Satisfied now?" I took my plate to the sink. As far as I was concerned that was the end of it, though I knew Garth. They could have put his name in the dictionary for the definition of the word "stubborn". He probably wouldn't be satisfied if she promised him her firstborn child. I turned the tap on hard and blasted smears of egg yolk and toast crumbs off the plate and watched them swirl in the sink.

"I still don't see why I couldn't come too." Yep. Stubborn. "I could pretend to be a captive."

"In silver chains? It wouldn't work." The hissing jet of water carried away every trace of breakfast. Wish it was so easy to get rid of my other problems. "Give it up, Garth. I need you guys to keep Lachie safe for me. And if I don't come back …"

He glared at me. "That's not an option."

CHAPTER TWENTY-FIVE

Garth was still arguing as we prepared to leave.

"I'll need my hoshi no tama to make the transformation," Kasumi said. "Just for a moment. You can have it back."

He dropped it into her open palm. "Why couldn't you turn into Gideon Thorne, or the head of Elizabeth's security—someone she trusts—and go in there on your own and kill her?" He turned eager eyes on me. "Then we wouldn't have to risk you."

"And what do you think would happen to Kasumi if she managed to kill the queen without me there to take power?" Swift and bloody vengeance, that's what. Garth would probably see that as a feature, though, not a bug. His dislike of the fox woman was as intense as it was illogical. "Thorne would finish her off and call Alicia to tell her the crown was hers. We'd be no better off."

He opened his mouth to argue.

"Garth! No more. I've made my decision."

He closed his mouth and looked away in reluctant submission. Kasumi drew a tiny silk bag from her pocket. She opened it and extracted a single short hair.

"I will use Carl Davison's servant again," she said. "I have one more of his hairs."

Right. The wyvern whose form she'd worn yesterday on her little fact-finding mission. Fascinated, I lingered on the bottom step of the sweeping staircase, watching as she placed the hair on top of her head, then brought the hoshi no tama to her lips. For a minute I thought she was going to put it in her mouth, but then she inhaled deeply, and the yellow glow surrounding it rushed from the pearl into her nostrils. She drew in so much her face began to glow softly, like a child's night light. To my dazzled gaze each crystal of the elaborate chandelier overhead caught and reflected the light back on her where she stood by the front door. I blinked in the bright light, and then her features started to slip.

It was a little like watching a werewolf transformation, only without the horrendous bone-crunching sound effects. The whole thing seemed much more peaceful, almost Zen-like. Her nose lengthened and her wide, rather flat face narrowed and developed pronounced cheekbones. A man's strong jaw appeared, dotted with stubble, and her dark hair lightened and shrank away, till a man stood before us.

Taller than Kasumi, he looked even older than Garth. I knew his face, though I doubt I'd ever known his name; he was just one of the guards I'd seen hanging around Carl Davison at my rare appearances at court. It was astonishing, but even more impressive to me was the fact that a sky-blue aura glowed around his form. The man was a wyvern, and now Kasumi's aura reflected that. This made a goblin seeming look like amateur hour.

"That's freaky," Garth muttered. And he couldn't even see the aura.

She handed the hoshi no tama back to him without commenting or even looking at him. Their hands were now the same size. Amazing.

"What happened to the hair?" I asked as she put the little silk pouch away.

"The one I used in the transformation?" Her new voice was deep, and it caught me by surprise. "Burned up by the change."

"Oh." So there were some limits to the superhero-type powers of the kitsune. "So it's a one-time thing?"

"Yes."

"And how long does it last?"

"That depends on many factors: the age and strength of the kitsune, their familiarity with the subject, the power of the source. It will last long enough for our purposes."

A little evasive, but that was shifters for you. They didn't give up their secrets readily.

Before we left I ran upstairs to Lachie's room to kiss him goodbye. He still slept, and didn't stir as my lips brushed his soft cheek. I eased gently into his sleeping mind to check the strength of the compulsion: fading now but still strong enough to keep him calm till I could return.

I refused to consider not returning.

I turned to find Garth watching from the doorway.

"It's all right," he said softly. "I'll make sure he's okay."

"I know." Funny how quickly trusting Garth had become second nature. Now there wasn't a safer pair of hands in the world to trust my son to, but it wasn't that long since he'd been trying to kill me in my own kitchen. Ben had saved me then.

Thinking of Ben brought a rush of anxiety. This was no time for a one-armed man with a bounty on his head to be wandering around unprotected. Not that there was ever a great time for that, I guess. Stupid, stubborn man. All because he wanted so desperately to be useful. He wasn't answering his phone. Not surprising, since he must know I'd only yell at him if he did. Steve hadn't even been able to track it. He'd probably dumped it.

I watched Lachie, reluctant to leave. He slept hard, his small body splayed across the bed, the sheet dragging on the floor, half kicked-off. He looked younger asleep. I could glimpse the cute curly-headed preschooler he used to be in the curve of his cheek and the way his arms were flung above his head in sleep, though it was a long time since those scrawny arms had carried any baby fat.

"He might be a bit out of it when he wakes. Get some food into him and he'll probably go right back to sleep."

"What if he asks about you, or … or anything else?"

He meant Alex, of course, and all that Lachie had seen.

"I doubt he'll be that lucid. Just tell him I'll be back soon."

"I bloody hope so."

He looked so miserable I gave him a quick, hard hug on impulse. It felt like hugging a rock. The guy was solid muscle. "Cheer up. What's the worst thing that could happen?"

"We could all die?"

"Okay, the second-worst." He still didn't even crack a smile, and he hugged me back with a firmness that bordered on desperation, as if he thought he'd never see me again. I felt his lips brush my hair. "Oh, come on, Garth. Have a little faith."

Not that I had much to spare. Hope was in pretty short supply too, but I wouldn't give up as long as I could see any glimmer of it. Whatever it took to keep Lachie safe.

"It'll take more than faith—we need a bloody miracle."

"Then it's lucky we have Kasumi to work one for us."

"I don't like how much you're relying on her. It's dangerous."

"Being alive is dangerous." But the alternative was unthinkable. I thumped him hard on the shoulder. "You just concentrate on staying that way, and I will too, okay?"

His gaze softened. "Okay."

I left him there and hurried back downstairs. Kasumi waited in the foyer.

"Ready?" she asked, her deep voice catching me by surprise again.

What had I been expecting? That she'd still sound like herself? That wouldn't be at all obvious, would it? Of course she'd take on her new persona's voice as well as his looks. But knowing there was a woman inside that body felt so weird.

She wound a length of silver chain around my body several times and padlocked it shut. Not that that would hold me. The chain would snap like string, padlock and all, once I took trueshape.

Despite the heat I wore a long-sleeved shirt, to disguise the fact that the silver wasn't raising the usual welts on my skin. Apart from the heaviness and the occasional clanking as I moved, I felt quite comfortable. Though I'd expected that, it was hard to forget a lifetime's aversion to silver. It seemed like a miracle. I decided that was a good sign. This was meant to be.

We went out to the car.

"I'm sorry," Kasumi said as she opened the hatch, "but you'll have to ride in here. It wouldn't look right otherwise."

"No problem."

Kasumi laid the back row of seats flat to make room for her "prisoner". She helped me in, and I lay down awkwardly, the carpet tickling my face. The slam of the hatch closing reverberated through my skull. As the car moved off I watched treetops and sky swing past from my odd vantage point. I had to brace my feet against the side wall as we took the first corner.

The upside-down trees rushing past made me queasy, so I shut my eyes and focused on the plan. Elizabeth would be keen to make a spectacle of me; she'd probably have me dragged into the throne room as soon as we arrived, to ensure the greatest number of people witnessed my downfall. A crowd could certainly work to my advantage once the fighting started, with so many people shocked and panicking.

The big flaw in the plan was weapons, since Kasumi wouldn't be allowed to bring any with her, and if they found one on me our cover would be blown. Of course, not finding welts on my skin would do that too.

I should probably do something about that. I opened myself to a trickle of power and urged my body into a new shape. Unlike Kasumi the chameleon, I only had two to choose from: my regular human and dragon shapes. But I knew that each could be adapted slightly, and one form could bleed into the other, like my dragon claws appearing when the rest of me wore human form.

I focused on the areas where I could feel the chain digging into me, and pushed for something ridged like scales, but still made of soft human flesh. I wouldn't know how successful I'd been till later, but hopefully it looked enough like welts to pass a cursory inspection.

At last the car turned and slowed to a stop. I knew it wasn't just another red light when I heard Kasumi's assumed voice, deep and gravelly.

"Bill Watson to see the queen."

"Haven't seen you in a while, Bill," another voice, presumably the gate guard, replied. Well, that was a relief. We would have been screwed if Bill was already here. I lay still, eyes closed, as if I were unconscious. If I hadn't had dragon hearing I wouldn't have been able to hear the guy over the rumble of the engine. It sounded like he stood a good distance from the car. Perhaps he hadn't left the gatehouse. "Sorry to hear about your lord. You been laying low?"

"Something like that. You know how it is when a dragon dies. Everyone's looking for someone to blame."

"Do you have an appointment?"

"No. But I guarantee she'll want to see me. I've brought her the abomination."

"You're kidding."

"No."

"Seriously?" A new note of respect entered the guard's voice. "Show me."

"Sure."

The car door slammed and footsteps approached the rear of the car. Then the hatch opened. Through slitted eyelids I saw the gate guard leap back as if bitten.

"She's not gagged! Are you crazy?"

"Relax. Those chains are made of silver. She couldn't even compel you into taking a cruise to Hawaii."

The guard chuckled a little nervously, then stepped forward and laid a tentative finger against the chain. He snatched his hand back and inspected the blister forming on his fingertip with satisfaction.

"Well done." He slammed the hatch and walked away. "You'll have to tell me how you managed it some time. I'll buy you a beer. I bet it's quite a story."

Kasumi laughed. "Sure is."

Then she got back into the car for the short trip up the driveway.

Next time the hatch opened I was more prepared. Kasumi's strange male face grinned down at me. A familiar mansion bulked behind her, and I could smell the tang of salt on the air.

"Show time," she said.

CHAPTER TWENTY-SIX

Like a stone dropped into a pond, ripples spread out from us. The moment we stepped into the cool of Elizabeth's foyer the whispers started. It was as if the blast of air-conditioned air that greeted us carried the rumour of our presence around the house. I heard doors, not slammed exactly, but closed with a sharp sound that spoke of haste, and voices passing on the news with various degrees of excitement.

The abomination was here! Captured and brought before the queen for punishment. People found reason to be in my path to sneak a peek, and I heard footsteps tapping down the tiled hallways before me, everyone rushing to get to the throne room in time for the big showdown.

Too bad I looked so ordinary—much more soccer mum than Satan. If they expected horns they were in for a disappointment, though hopefully the show I had in mind would be worth staying for. Butterflies fluttered in my stomach. I took a deep breath and forced them away. Now was the time for Leandra's steel, not Kate's feelings.

Kasumi glanced sideways at me as we strode through the halls, flanked by two guardsmen. The gate guard must have phoned ahead with the news, as they'd been waiting for us at the door, all guns and attitude. No doubt the guns were loaded with silver. They'd already inspected the chains before letting us in. My fake welts had drawn smiles of satisfaction, so they must have been convincing. Suspicion was a healthy thing when dealing with dragons. They were a bunch of backstabbing bastards.

I didn't look at her, keeping up my act of beaten-down captive. To be honest it was easier if I didn't look. I found her ability to be absolutely anyone fascinating, and could easily forget to stop staring once I started. As far as I could recall, she was a perfect replica of this Bill Watson guy, from his short grey hair right down to his chewed-off fingernails. Her new aura still astonished me, glowing that soft wyvern blue as if she were born to it. Auras were fundamental to a shifter's essence; that her magic could affect this as well seemed more amazing than the rest of the transformation. Would she actually be able to shift into his trueshape? I had no idea how far the kitsune's abilities went. I was prepared to believe her capable of anything by this point. As long as the real Bill Watson didn't turn up no one should be any the wiser.

I stared at the intricate patterns of the tiled floors until we stopped before double doors, and one of our guards disappeared inside. Last time I'd waited at these doors had been the night of the Presentation Ball. Someone had died that time too—my sister Monique, dead before the proving was more than a few hours old. I'd narrowly escaped sharing her fate. Let's hope my dodging skills were up to the challenge today too.

The guard beckoned us in, and we entered the enormous throne room. Long and narrow, with bifold doors all down one side standing open onto an even larger paved terrace, the room offered a magnificent view of a golden sweep of sand below, and blue water stretching to the horizon. A cooling sea breeze brought the scent of salt and the faint sound of children's piping voices from the beach below. With a location like this, the place must be worth a fortune. Nothing but the best for the dragon queen of Oceania.

At the far end of the room my dearest mother sat on a carved chair that was unashamedly throne-like, raised above the crowd on a marble dais. Very old-fashioned. I suppose that shouldn't be a surprise, given she was one of the oldest queens still living.

Though not for much longer. We paced the length of the long room, and the closer we got, the more clearly the signs of her great age showed. I'd last seen her less than a year ago, and the change in her was shocking. Even if my plan today failed, it was clear she'd be lucky to see out the year.

Her hands clutched the arms of her chair like claws, the flesh wasted away. You could have cut glass with her cheekbones, they were so sharp, and veins showed clearly through paper-thin skin. Her eyes were a fierce but faded blue, and pink scalp gleamed through the snowy strands of what had once been a chic bob. She didn't look old as a human looks old, all wrinkles and age spots and shaking limbs, but old like a dragon, burned out by the inner fire, fading to transparency.

That was how it worked with dragons; our decline, when at last it came, was sudden. I guess it beat lingering in a nursing home, gumming mushy food while you slowly lost your mobility and your marbles.

A short, rotund man stood beside the throne: Gideon Thorne, the spymaster. Sadly he showed no signs of age yet. Oceania would be a better place without his forked tongue whispering in the queen's ear. Was he frightened by Elizabeth's decline? He should be. There'd be no place for him at court when I took the throne.

There were perhaps twenty other people in the room, though judging by their auras he was the only other dragon. Thank God for that. Most were humans or goblins, though I saw one leshy and a couple of sea people in the crowd. Thorne bent to murmur in Elizabeth's ear as we approached, his flat, expressionless gaze never leaving my face.

"Halt." Her voice, at least, was still commanding. "That's close enough, Mr Watson. I can't abide her filthy human stench in my nostrils."

"That's a little harsh, Mother. I'm sure even you wouldn't smell like a bed of roses chained up in this heat."

Her eyes flashed. "I am *not* your mother, abomination."

"What, you only want to claim the winners? You're running awfully short of daughters in that case, with Valeria gone, and Monique and Ingrid too. Just me and Alicia left now."

"You will not speak, filth."

Damn. I'd been hoping for some gloating revelation about the rumoured sixth sister. If only this were a James Bond movie, where the baddie laid out his whole evil plan in the moment of his triumph. Instead the compulsion in her voice rocked me where I stood, as I tried to stand tall in the teeth of a mental gale. Her power was still immense.

But not strong enough to cow me. Whatever she chose to believe, I *was* her daughter, after all.

"You'll have to do better than that, Mother." I lifted my chin and glared at her, ranging my own mental forces against her. Surprise flickered in her eyes at my resistance. "You're breaking your own law, you know, interfering in the proving like this. Not very sporting to send bounty hunters after me. What do you think the penalty should be?"

The portly little man at her side stirred restlessly.

"You're right, Gideon," she said, though he hadn't spoken. "This creature is beneath our notice."

"Shall I dispatch it, Your Majesty?"

She inclined her head, and he stepped down from the dais and strode across to the wall where an array of weapons hung. Swords of every length, some curved, some straight, spears, maces—but nothing since the invention of gunpowder. It was like a shrine to the good old days, when dragons ruled the earth and peasants could be mowed down without consequence by every jumped-up lordling. A murmur whispered through the crowd like a wind sighing through leaves as he took down a massive axe.

A headsman's axe, not a battle axe.

I held myself still, though my pulse quickened as he made a theatrical swing with the great axe. I was confident, but hell, confidence only goes so far. Kasumi stood like a rock by my side, holding the end of my chain as if I were some dog on a leash. She hadn't moved a muscle. I drew a deep breath and tried to emulate her calm.

"Don't be afraid." Thorne followed the direction of my gaze with a smirk. "It's very sharp. Your head will be rolling across the floor before you even realise you're dead."

He swished the damn thing through the air a couple more times, his grin growing wider. Elizabeth hunched forward on her throne like a vulture anticipating a feast.

"Your Majesty." Kasumi stepped forward and bowed deeply. "A favour, I beg of you."

"Yes, Mr Watson?"

"She killed my late master." She shot me a look of hatred so convincing it sent chills down my spine. All of Garth's gloomy warnings echoed in my ears. "I invoke the Right of Retribution. May I be the one to wield the axe, in his name?"

A long moment passed while Elizabeth deliberated. Carl Davison had been dead before I even arrived at the rendezvous, and I had no idea who'd killed him, or why. Perhaps someone had wanted to stop him telling me whatever he'd been going to tell me. But his death could have been completely unrelated. It wasn't as if most dragons were short of enemies. If Elizabeth had asked for proof that I really had been responsible, Kasumi would be on shaky ground.

Fortunately Elizabeth wasn't interested in justice, only in seeing me dead. Even if she'd ordered Carl killed herself— which was entirely possible—she was happy to accept Kasumi's version of events.

She studied Kasumi's borrowed face. "That seems fitting. Dear Carl would be proud of your loyalty, I'm sure. Perhaps you would like to gather all his former staff, so that they may see justice done. We could wait."

"Begging your pardon, my queen, but the Right of Retribution allows me to claim immediate justice." Kasumi glared at me. "And I do."

Fingers of fear crept up my spine again. Either she was a brilliant actress, or I'd been well and truly played. What was my Option B? But a glance around the room showed that even Option A would be a struggle. Too many people. Two dragons. Kasumi herself. I shifted uncomfortably, feeling the weight of my chains. But their silver had no power over me any more. I still had that element of surprise.

And Kasumi knew that. Surely if she planned to betray me she wouldn't be going through with this charade. She would have done it as soon as we walked in. *Relax. You said you trusted her. So trust her.*

"Very well. Give the axe to Mr Watson, please, Gideon."

Kasumi left me with the two guards and strode forward to receive the axe. Thorne relinquished it with bad grace. He must have really been looking forward to lopping my head off. Well, he'd just have to cry into his Dom Perignon later, if he lived so long. My heart began to thud in anticipation.

The two men bowed very formally to each other as Thorne handed the weapon across. So polite. Elizabeth nodded approvingly.

Then Kasumi leapt onto the dais, whirling the axe above her head. She moved so fast the blade was a gleaming blur.

Elizabeth's mouth had barely begun to form an "O" of surprise before the axe bit into her neck and her head went bouncing across the floor.

Thorne was right. That sucker *was* sharp.

Time seemed to stand still as the headless body folded gently forward and toppled from its seat. As if in slow motion the guards at my side, and the two behind the throne, also collapsed, like puppets whose strings had been cut—thralls, shocked senseless by the sudden severing of their bond with their mistress.

Thorne leapt forward with a roar of fury, exploding into dragon form. Black, and monstrous, he was the biggest dragon I'd ever seen. If he'd caught Kasumi in those massive jaws she would have been crushed like matchsticks, but she was already gone, dancing among the screaming onlookers with her bloody axe.

I answered his roar with one of my own, *pulling* myself into trueshape and bursting free of my chains. My claws bit deep into the floor as I launched myself across the room, putting my golden body between Kasumi and the black dragon's fury.

"Stop!" I bellowed, pouring every drop of compulsion I possessed into the command.

Every creature in the crowd froze, some even caught mid-change. The leshy I'd noticed earlier now wore a bear's head on top of his business suit. Foul blue goblin blood spattered the suit, and the goblin who'd been standing next to him lay at his feet, his head some distance away. Kasumi looked enquiringly over her shoulder, axe trembling at the high point of its swing. Even the black dragon paused, his yellow eyes drawn unwillingly to mine.

"The queen is dead." The rumble of my voice filled the room as I paced forward, claws clicking loudly in the silence. I stepped over Elizabeth's feeble human form and up onto the dais. No one moved as I set my right foot on the tiny chair that stood there. "The throne is mine by right of conquest and inheritance. Swear fealty to me now and I'll spare your lives."

The black dragon's tail lashed angrily as he circled. "The proving is not over! You are not queen till all other claimants are dead." His eyes narrowed, filled with hate. "And not even then, if I have anything to do with it."

"You'd rather one of the overseas queens took the throne? They circle the proving like vultures. You want us to lose Oceania like Elizabeth lost England?"

Smoke rose from his nostrils. I watched carefully for the first hint of attack. Blue sky beckoned beyond the open doors to the terrace. If I had to fight I'd rather do it out there where I had room to manoeuvre—but it would be better not to fight at all. He had a huge size advantage on me. Kasumi circled round behind him, but he took no notice. In this form she mattered less than a buzzing insect to him. All his attention was fixed on me.

"I would rather a dragon sat the throne," he hissed. "Not an abomination like you."

I gave a dragon version of a shrug, half opening my wings. "Well, you know what they say—if it walks like a dragon and breathes fire like a dragon … it's probably a dragon. I think you're getting caught up on technicalities here."

Kasumi had discarded the axe and now crouched by one of his massive back feet. He could crush her without even knowing she was there. What the hell was she doing?

He growled, a sound like a jackhammer starting up, and I tensed, ready to leap for the relative safety of the open sky. Kasumi would have to take her chances with the handful of shifters who remained functional. Pretty good odds for her. I had faith.

Thorne's tail lashed back and forth. I watched his eyes, waiting for his spring, and so I saw the moment when he lost focus. The growling stopped, and he sat back on his haunches with the look of someone who'd accidentally swallowed a bug.

Kasumi! For one horrible moment I thought she'd been crushed by a giant dragon butt. But there was no sign of her at all, just a faint wisp of yellow mist that swirled around the dragon's foot and disappeared.

"Twiceborn, I've got him."

The words came from Thorne's mouth, but certainly not from Thorne's consciousness.

"Kasumi?" I could hardly believe it. Was there no end to the miracles this kitsune could perform? "Is that you?"

"Yes." Thorne panted, and his great head jerked from side to side. "He's strong … wait … let me try—"

The black dragon dissolved into a naked man sitting on the tiles, his scrawny legs splayed wide. Thorne was no oil painting at the best of times, but without his clothes he was enough to turn even a dragon off sex for life. With his beer gut sitting in his lap he looked nine months pregnant, and the dazed look on his face made him seem a few sandwiches short of a picnic.

I stepped forward and nuzzled at him. He made no move to resist me. He certainly smelled like Thorne.

"But where is—where's Bill?" No sign of Kasumi's previous form remained, nor of her own petite Japanese self.

Thorne staggered to his feet, reeling like a drunkard. "He's too … strong. I'm losing him!" He clutched at his head, then fell against my leg, hands scrabbling at my scales. "Get my hoshi no tama! I can't hold him. Suggest you … knock me out … now!"

Expressions chased themselves across his face: pleading, rage, cunning, back to pleading. Curiouser and curiouser. Still, this was no time to start ignoring Kasumi's always-excellent advice.

I raised a foot and knocked Thorne halfway across the room. He skidded across the tiles and his head met the wall with an audible thump. Following orders had never been so satisfying.

CHAPTER TWENTY-SEVEN

The leshy had subsided back into human form, though the vibrant green of his skin showed he was still unsettled. He huddled with two goblins and a selkie against the far wall, watching me as if expecting every minute to be his last.

If I was any other dragon it probably would have been.

Dragons weren't big on clemency. Where was the sense in leaving the supporters of your rivals alive to plot against you? Better to kill and move on than leave your back exposed. Thralls were different, of course—you could turn them to your own use, if the death of their previous master or mistress hadn't sent them insane or killed them. But shifters …

"I don't remember you," I said to the leshy. He quailed visibly at being singled out, and the selkie took a very unsubtle step away, as if the green man's bad luck might rub off on her. "What's your name?"

"Robert Macadam, ma'am." He swallowed convulsively. "But most—most people call me Bear."

"Bear." I moved closer, looming over the little group. Goblins were a dime a dozen, but it was a shame to waste a leshy. I'd seen what they were capable of in the battle at Alicia's bush property, where a handful of leshies had held off Valeria's troops, at least until Valeria herself had joined the fight. They couldn't stand against dragonfire, though they were brave and versatile in form. Unlike most shifters, who only had one trueshape, they could shift at will between many options, which made them hard to fight. No prize for guessing why this one was known as "Bear". It was one of their favourite forms. "How long have you worked for my mother, Bear?"

"All my life." He stared at a point somewhere on my shoulder, avoiding my gaze. As if that would make any difference. I might not be able to enthral a fellow shifter permanently, but I could certainly bend one to my will long enough for most purposes, whether or not they looked into my eyes.

His human form looked to be in his late fifties, with a shock of grey hair receding up his green forehead. Odd that I didn't recognise him, then, if he'd worked for Elizabeth all his life. Maybe he was one of Gideon's spies.

"I thought all the local leshies supported Alicia."

"Not all. Some of us remained loyal to the queen."

"Your queen is dead. What will you do now?"

"I could—" He gulped and tried again. "I could be loyal to a new queen."

I smiled, though I was aware the effect wasn't terribly reassuring in dragon form. No one liked to see such big teeth on display.

The selkie beside him nodded so vigorously her brown curls bounced. "Yes, my lady! We'll support you."

A drop of sweat trickled from her temple down her cheek. It was a hot day, but not that hot. I leaned closer, the breath from my nostrils ruffling her hair, and she cringed away in terror.

"I know you will. The four of you will be my first and most loyal subjects."

I caught them all in my gaze till they nodded stupidly. The compulsion wouldn't last long, but for a few hours at least I could trust them not to stab me in the back. By the time it wore off Garth and the others would be here, and these would be safely locked away behind silver bars.

Once they were secured, I ordered Bear to bind Thorne in my discarded silver chains. Maybe that would harm Kasumi— I hoped not—but I couldn't risk leaving him unbound when her grip on him was so weak. With that done I felt safe enough to shift back to human form. While the selkie went running for some clothes for me I moved among Elizabeth's shattered thralls, catching them all in my web and enthralling them to me. It sickened me to have to do it, but the alternative was a slow, lingering death. Their bodies were no longer capable of functioning without the bond. Once I'd woven my strands into their minds they returned to their senses, all except one. Either he'd been enthralled too long to make the switch or he was particularly weak-minded, but I couldn't call his mind back from where it wandered. I tried for some time, knowing the alternative, but by the time I gave up I was exhausted, and he was close to death.

I accepted a simple shift dress from the selkie and shrugged it on. The four shifters watched me closely, eager for some way to serve, while the new thralls waited impassively for orders. I hated that mindless obedience. Ten new thralls. Sickening.

Judging from their reaction when Elizabeth died, they must have been enthralled for years. Not that it made me feel any better. I slumped down on my mother's throne and stared at her headless body, collapsed in a graceless heap at my feet, still sluggishly leaking blood. A normal person would feel bad about that. Mostly I felt relief.

Like it or lump it, I was a dragon now. This *was* normal.

Bloody hell. How could anyone live like this? I closed my eyes and let my head flop against the padded back of the seat. I should just tell Alicia she could have it all and run away to some tropical island with Lachie.

Yeah, right. And the first thing she'd do would be send assassins after me, just to be sure. Dragons didn't like loose ends.

"All or nothing," I reminded myself.

"Pardon, my lady?" Bear asked, coming forward eagerly. His skin had faded to a respectably human brown now, and he looked much happier.

"How many others are in the house?" Probably should have asked that earlier. God, I was tired.

He did a quick scan of the bodies in the room. "Ah ... there's usually two thralls in the comms room at all times ... another one, maybe two, in the kitchen ..."

"Bring them to me."

He nodded at the two goblins and they ran off.

"Any other shifters?"

Again his eyes roamed the bodies. Kasumi had killed four before I stopped her, all shifters. Smart woman. She knew the fewer hostile shifters I had to deal with the better.

"Only the gate guard."

I nodded. He could wait. I beckoned two thralls forward. "You know how to work the comms room?" When they said yes I sent them off to man the monitors. The last thing I needed now was any surprise visitors crashing my party.

I held out a hand to Bear. "Phone."

Hastily he pulled out a mobile and gave it to me. I dialled Garth's number and felt my whole body sag with relief when his gruff voice answered.

"It's me. We did it."

"Halle-friggin-lujah. You okay?"

"I'm fine." He didn't ask after Kasumi, though. "I need you guys to come in. Make sure you bring the hoshi no tama with you."

"You sure you want to give it back to her?"

"Don't be a jerk. She was brilliant—and now we need it again."

"If you say so." He didn't bother hiding the doubt in his voice. I'd never have to worry about my ego with Garth around. He was more than capable of telling me, in great detail, whenever he disapproved of my choices.

"How's Lachie?"

"Having a ball. Mac's been playing some game with him. He keeps killing all her ninjas. There's Lego shit everywhere. You want me to leave him here with her?"

I hesitated. I purposely didn't know where they were, so that if things had gone wrong on this end I couldn't have given away his location. Would he be safer holed up somewhere with Mac, or here where I could protect him?

"Bring him." I needed him here, needed to know he was safe. And if I couldn't protect him here, in the heart of Elizabeth's stronghold, there wasn't a safe place in all the world. "I'll tell the gate guard to expect you."

The goblins returned, each supporting a shuffling, blank-faced man. Was this where the legend of zombies had come from? Thralls who'd been mind-wiped by the death of their master or mistress?

I sent two of the more recovered thralls down to the gate to subdue the shifter there and watch for Garth and the others. Then I forced myself to enthral these, and the next two as well, though by now I felt about as compelling as three-day-old fish. All I wanted to do was sleep, and leave the world and its problems behind.

So long I'd dreamed of this moment, imagining the triumph I'd feel. I glared at Elizabeth's body. I had nothing left but hate and exhaustion. Stupid bloody dragons and their medieval bloodfest of a proving. And all for what? A dragon crown I didn't even want.

Thorne started to stir, and I had the selkie woman prop him up. She leaned him against the wall, careful not to touch the silver chains that bound him. I knew he'd been born before Australia was even settled by Europeans, and he'd been one of Elizabeth's inner circle for most of the last century, but he looked no more than forty. A comfortable, well-padded forty, like somebody's favourite uncle. He wasn't a tall man, and looked even shorter slumped awkwardly against the wall, his fat belly resting in his lap, like a particularly ugly puppet whose strings had been cut.

He'd been the only dragon apart from my mother I'd known through my long, isolated childhood. He looked no different now than he had the night he'd brought me home in disgrace from my failed attempt to see my sisters, and told me I was a disappointment as a dragon. The silver chains must have been hurting him, but he watched me calmly. That probably meant Kasumi was still in charge.

"Garth's on his way," I said, and he—or she?—nodded.

I went outside and paced the terrace, anxious for Garth and the others to arrive. The view was spectacular and the day perfect, but I was in no mood for either. What did Kasumi need the hoshi no tama for? Was she all right in there? And what the hell had happened to her body? My knowledge of kitsune only covered the basics. Could she be trapped in Thorne's body forever?

Two of the thralls brought me the gate guard, another goblin, and I laid a compulsion on him almost without breaking stride, still caught up in my worries. I set some of the thralls to disposing of the bodies and cleaning up the throne room, but then there was nothing to do but wait. A long half-hour passed before I heard Garth's voice in the hallway and Lachie's piping tones replying.

My son burst through the door with his usual energy, Garth and Mac hard on his heels, and his eyes widened at the size of the room, then practically fell out of his head when he saw the array of weapons displayed on the wall.

"Nice house, Mum. Are we going to be staying here now?"

He hurried toward me, eyeing the little group of shifters and thralls warily.

"Probably." I'd given up making promises. If the last week had taught me anything, it was how quickly plans could change. I hugged him tight and breathed in a lungful of that unique Lachie-smell, all apple shampoo and little-boy sweat. His curls were plastered to his forehead in the heat.

I expected the next question to be *Is there a pool?* but he caught sight of Thorne and changed tack.

"Who's that?"

"Kasumi, I hope." I greeted Garth and the others. "Where's the hoshi no tama?"

"Here." Garth handed it over. "Where's Kasumi?"

I indicated Thorne and he frowned. "Why's she chained up?"

"Things got a little crazy. I think she's possessing him."

"So that's actually Thorne? I thought she was playing dress-up again."

Thorne shot him a cold look. Now *that* looked like Kasumi.

"I do not play dress-up, wolf."

He shrugged. "Whatever."

I crouched down beside her. "How do we get you out of there? What happened to your body?"

"You'll have to unchain me. I have him contained for the moment, but be ready. As soon as I leave his body you must chain him again."

Or else we'd have a rampaging dragon on our hands. Definitely not something I needed to see again so soon. Or ever, really.

"You should have time. He'll be disoriented when I release control."

I nodded. "The rest of you stand back."

Garth ignored me, of course, but Steve and Dave drew back, forming a protective shield with Mac around Lachie. Lachie leaned against her like a dog looking for reassurance, and she slipped an arm around his thin shoulders. With her huge childlike eyes and demented haircut, she could have been his big sister.

I unwound the chain, alert for any sign of Thorne's ascendance. If it was anything like my own experience with Leandra, control of the body could change hands in a heartbeat. Kasumi might not even know it till he'd already beaten her down. But Thorne's face remained calm, his movements slow and deliberate as he took the hoshi no tama and raised it to his face.

He breathed in deeply, and yellow tendrils of mist curled up from the luminous pearl and disappeared into his nostrils.

"Can you see that?" I asked Garth, without looking away.

"See what?"

"Never mind." So it was definitely her aura I saw, that strange magical essence that every shifter possessed but only dragons could see. Thorne's eyes closed, and the mist billowed as he breathed in and out, its glow intensifying till it seemed impossible that no one else could see it. I had to squint against the glare.

So it took a moment to realise his face was glowing too. For a second Thorne's rough features took on an angelic shine, before all the light rushed away. I blinked.

Then it exploded out of the shared body, flooding the hoshi no tama with radiance. The pearl fell from Thorne's hand and his eyes rolled back in his head. I leapt forward and wrapped him in the silver chain before he could recover himself, so I missed what happened next, but I heard the collective gasp.

When I turned my head, a fox stood next to me, its pointed face lifted enquiringly. Its white-tipped tail curled above its back like a question mark. At first I thought it was especially bushy, then I realised there were actually three of them.

Good God. She'd said she had three tails, but I thought that was a metaphorical thing, signifying rank—not that she actually had three physical tails. It was the weirdest-looking bloody fox I'd ever seen.

Before I'd had a chance to do more than gape at her tails, the fox shimmered. Yellow light fountained and the fox grew into Kasumi's familiar shape.

"Hot damn!" Garth's voice dripped with envy. "You get clothes too?"

I hadn't even registered it but yes, Kasumi was fully clothed in her normal all-black ensemble. Now *that* would be a neat ability. No more running around naked or borrowing other people's clothes. I'd never heard of a shifter who could do that.

"You're a bigger fool than I thought." A new voice intruded—Thorne, chained but no longer voiceless. "You're mad if you think you can ever come out ahead in dealing with a kitsune. Unless you hold their damn star ball there's no power on earth that will stop them."

Reflexively I looked at the hoshi no tama. Kasumi slipped it into her pocket.

"I seem to be doing all right so far," I said.

Kasumi, a relative stranger, had been more loyal to me than I'd had any right to expect, while my family and all their associates did nothing but try to kill me. I knew which one I preferred.

I ordered two of the thralls to take him away and lock him in the dungeons. They'd originally been wine cellars, but Elizabeth had had them converted years ago with shifters in mind. Silver-coated bars and goblin spells made it impossible for even a dragon to escape. At least he'd have Bear and the other surviving shifters for company soon—I couldn't trust my compulsion to hold them much longer.

When the door closed behind them I let out a relieved breath and regarded my little band of supporters.

"So. Here we are, then," said Garth. "What next?"

I shrugged. "Somehow we have to find and destroy Alicia."

Before Luce destroys us.

Kasumi cleared her throat. "I have an idea that might help."

CHAPTER TWENTY-EIGHT

"She'd never fall for that." Garth, of course, was instantly dismissive, just because it was Kasumi's idea. Despite everything she'd done for me, he still didn't like her. He stood at the kitchen window, looking out at the raised herb garden, as if he couldn't even bear to look at Kasumi while we spoke.

I wasn't so quick to jump to conclusions. Okay, it was ambitious, but we'd already pulled the same stunt on Elizabeth. Why shouldn't it work again?

"I don't know," I said, turning the idea over in my mind, looking for flaws. Alicia was the most cautious of the sisters, which was why she was still alive, but she did love a good gloat. Someone else's downfall? Yep, she'd be all over it. "No one knows what's happened here except us. No one's left the building. Everyone with access to a phone is under our control. As long as we can keep word from getting out, she's got no reason to suspect anything."

Kasumi remained silent. She sat at the kitchen table, an island of calm as people moved around her. She'd said her piece; now she merely awaited instructions. I got the impression she thought I shouldn't tolerate argument from the underlings. Guess they did things differently in Japan. It was enough to make me want to emigrate.

"Well, where are we going to get one of Elizabeth's scales?" He was determined to find fault with the plan.

True, that could be an issue. If we'd been the same colour, I could have used my own, but mine were golden where Elizabeth's were black. Like Gideon Thorne's. Maybe we could take one of his if we got desperate.

Good God, what a hideous thought. Imagine trying to control him once he'd taken trueshape again! "Desperate" didn't begin to describe it.

But if we were lucky …

"Some dragons keep a stash, so they don't have to keep changing every time they want one." Particularly if they were like Elizabeth, who always seemed more comfortable in her human shape. I sent one of the thralls for Bear.

He scurried in, eager to please. Obviously the compulsion hadn't worn off yet.

"Did Elizabeth keep a supply of her scales on hand?" I asked.

"Yes, my lady."

Well, that was good news. "Where?"

"In the safe in her office."

"Do you know the combination?"

"No, my lady. Only the queen herself and Gideon Thorne had the combination."

Dammit. There was always a catch.

But Bear wasn't finished. "If my lady wishes, I could try to get it out of him."

"Oh yeah?" Garth cocked a sceptical eyebrow at him. "You and whose army?"

Like most leshies, Bear was tall and slim almost to the point of scrawniness. He certainly didn't look capable of beating a secret out of anyone, if that was what he meant.

Bear drew himself up to his full willowy height and shot Garth a disgusted look. "Thorne has no access to his powers. I do."

Leshy magic was earth magic. Though it was more effective outdoors where the leshy was in touch with his natural element, they were still strong shifters. I'd seen a leshy turn into a grizzly and rip a man apart. I had no doubt Bear could prove very persuasive if he wished. He hadn't earned that nickname for nothing.

"Take a thrall with you."

It never hurt to have backup, and they were all armed. Even though a silver bullet wouldn't kill Thorne, no one liked being shot. Bear nodded and gestured for the thrall who'd fetched him to follow him out.

After he'd left the only sounds in the kitchen came from Dave clattering around with pots and pans. Dave was a firm believer in the ability of food to make everyone feel better, and he'd wasted no time in firing up the oven. The most delicious smell of meat slow-cooking in red wine now filled the room.

Elizabeth's kitchen was smaller and more old-fashioned than the ones our crew was used to. One smallish window by the back door looked out onto a raised herb garden. A glance showed mint, parsley, coriander, dill, rosemary and many others I didn't recognise, enough to provide a chef's every need. But that seemed to be its best feature. There was only one commercial-sized oven, four hotplates and a preparation area not much bigger than the one I'd had at home in my modest suburban kitchen. Her cooks must have had a hell of a time catering for such a big household from such a small and poorly thought-out space. Not that Elizabeth would have cared.

Even with only a handful of us in it it felt crowded. Still, we always seemed to gravitate to the kitchen when there were decisions to be made. I'd poked my head into her dining room on the way past. Though it boasted a dining table long enough to seat thirty its formality made it unwelcoming. Give me a scratched and battered kitchen table any time. It made a place feel like home. This one certainly fit the bill, covered in dents and marked with coffee rings and other, less identifiable stains.

Mac and Lachie came in. Lachie sniffed appreciatively.

"Something smells good!"

"That's your lunch, mate," said Dave.

"Can I have something to eat now? I'm starving."

"You'll have to ask your mum about that."

He gave me his best imploring look.

"Have a piece of fruit. You don't want to spoil your appetite."

I looked around at the others as I spoke. Did anyone else find this surreal? This kind of conversation was probably going on in hundreds of other households around Sydney right now.

But none of *them* were waiting on the results of a leshy torturing a dragon in their dungeon.

Apparently not. Steve was in the comms room, but the others were here, looking as if they did this every day. Garth paced, as usual, and Kasumi and I sat at the table, while Mac and Lachie scrounged for snacks in the kitchen cupboards.

And Dave looked the picture of domestic bliss standing at the stove, chatting with Lachie like the perfect househusband.

Except he wasn't my husband. My real ex-husband was a dragon, and my new partner had disappeared on a wild goose chase somewhere. He could even be dead, for all I knew, since the bloody man wouldn't turn on his phone. How did shifters stand this life?

Life was so much simpler back when I was plain old Kate. Happily divorced and living with my beautiful son in the suburbs, working at a preschool, my biggest worry how to be both father and mother to Lachie. I shoved my chair back, impatient with myself. I had no time for self-pity—or any kind of pity. That was why I'd just sent someone to torture a man.

We were so close now, it was killing me. But the ordeal wouldn't be over until Alicia was dead.

Garth looked up, alert to my mood. "You all right?"

"Fine." I got up and joined him at the window. Some of the herbs sagged in the heat, their limp green heads nodding above the dried-out dirt. "You haven't heard from Ben, have you?"

"Nope. Could be anywhere by now."

He certainly could, damn him. I checked my watch. Over two hours since Elizabeth died, and no time to fret about missing boyfriends. Time was not on our side here. "We need that combination."

"You want me to go check on that leshy guy?"

"No. I'm just … impatient." Among other things. Worried, stressed, exhausted. If Alicia had been standing in front of me I could have torn her apart with my bare hands, just to have it over with.

Garth laid a warm hand on my shoulder.

"It'll be all right. Your problem is you think too much. You're all knotted up." His fingers began working at my shoulders, loosening the tension there. A thrill shot through me. Oh, Lord. Add "oversexed" to that list. I stepped out from under his hands. When was Ben coming home? My dragon blood was up, and I needed action—of one sort or another.

"It's not the thinking that's the problem. It's the feeling."

His face softened. "Well, you need to become a heartless bastard like me, then. Solves everything."

I snorted. I'd seen the way he watched over Lachie, fretted over me and watched the backs of Mac and the others. There were plenty of uncomplimentary words to describe him, but "heartless" wasn't one of them. I sat back down, determined to keep my cool while we waited for Bear. But if he didn't come back soon, I'd have to crash the party in the dungeon and hurry things along.

Thankfully he was only a few minutes more. His speed surprised me, though I was hardly an expert on the usual length of torture sessions. All eyes turned to him as he entered the kitchen, and his beaming smile left us in no doubt that he'd succeeded.

I stood, nearly knocking the chair over in my haste. "You've got it?"

He shot a victorious glance at Garth. "Told you I would."

He led the way to Elizabeth's office. Another unwelcoming room, furnished in austere style. If I was going to live here there'd have to be some big changes. Her desk chair looked so uncomfortable it was hard to believe anyone ever sat in it.

Perhaps they didn't. Elizabeth was big on leaving work for the minions, while dragonkind wallowed in the fruits of others' labour. This whole room could be all for show—or perhaps Thorne parked his pampered butt in that chair. He had enough padding to make it bearable, and someone had to oversee the workings of the empire, after all.

Bear had written the combination down for me, but I got him to open it, in case of goblin booby traps. Garth placed his body between mine and the safe in a seemingly casual way that fooled nobody, but our precautions were unnecessary. The safe unlocked with a satisfying click when Bear punched the numbers into the keypad, and he swung the heavy door open without any fatal effects.

Inside were stacks of money in various currencies, including a thick wad of Australian hundred-dollar notes, and an even thicker one of greenbacks. A pile of documents and several jewellery cases sat neatly beside them.

Bear pulled out the largest, a red velvet number of the kind that usually housed a necklace or a string of pearls. He opened it to show the three black discs resting inside.

Thank God for that. Kasumi's plan wouldn't get very far without one of these babies. I took the top one and waited while Bear put the others away and closed the safe again.

"Thank you, Bear. You may go."

He bowed and left, not without a last triumphant glance at Garth.

"I see you've made another fan there."

He shrugged. "I'm not in the business of making friends."

"Really? I hadn't noticed."

"What are you going to do with that now?" he asked, ignoring my weak attempt at humour. "You need to take trueshape?"

"I think I can manage."

There was plenty of space in the throne room for a dragon, as Thorne and I had already demonstrated, but it was always good to practise new skills, and I was becoming adept at this one. I reached for my essence—the barest trickle—and willed my forefinger to a new shape. The tip of a dragon claw sprouted: not my usual slashing blade, but something much more subtle. Control was difficult and it wavered in size before settling into the form I wanted.

Then I laid the claw to Elizabeth's scale. Garth watched, no doubt curious to see if I could pull it off in this hybrid form. Dragon claws weren't designed as writing implements. It wasn't a physical act that put words on our scales but a mental effort, similar to a compulsion. Words were a dragon's best weapons, though flame came a close second. I probably could have done it without changing my finger's essence, but something about the tap of claw on scale just felt right.

I reached for my will and urged the words to appear, holding Alicia's image in my mind as I did so. As I moved my claw across the scale fiery letters blazed into life. Garth leaned forward to read them before they faded. They wouldn't reappear until Alicia's touch brought them back to life.

I have the abomination in chains. I feel sure that you would wish to administer the coup de grâce yourself. Come to me at once.

CHAPTER TWENTY-NINE

We crowded around Steve's chair in the comms room, Garth, Mac and I. Lachie was still in the kitchen with Dave, who was probably seizing the opportunity to stuff him with treats. Dave looked set to become his new best friend, though Mac's willingness to play games of make-believe with Lego was hard to beat.

The monitor that held our interest showed Elizabeth's study, with Elizabeth herself seated in that uncomfortable chair behind the desk. Or so it seemed. Kasumi's abilities were uncanny. I could hardly bear to look at her. Mommy Dearest had come back to life, and I wanted to kill her all over again.

There was no sound, but we saw the door open as one of the thralls ushered a herald into her presence. In true Elizabeth style she continued to read the document in front of her and ignored him for several minutes. He stood perfectly still in the middle of the carpet, staring at the drab brown wall as he awaited Her Majesty's pleasure. Bear had called in the herald who did most of Elizabeth's jobs, so he was probably used to it.

At last Kasumi looked up and spoke, though we couldn't hear anything. Elizabeth wouldn't have wanted anyone eavesdropping on her private conversations.

"I wish we could hear what she was saying," Garth said.

"Probably 'Why aren't you bowing, slave?'" said Mac.

I shot her a surprised look, but she was still watching the screen. Guess nobody liked my mother much.

"She could be telling him anything," Garth persisted.

"Garth." I injected a warning note into my voice. I was sick of his suspicion of the kitsune. Yes, her ability was freaky. Yes, her power in the wrong hands would be a nightmare. But she'd proven herself loyal time and again. "It's a simple enough job. All she has to do is give him the damn message."

On screen Kasumi handed the scale in its wax-sealed envelope across to the herald and waved him away. He bowed, but she was no longer looking, absorbed once more in her reading.

"She really looks like her," Mac said, brushing her shaggy fringe out of her eyes with a slim hand. "It gives me the heebie-jeebies."

Me too, though I wasn't going to say so. And it was more than the physical appearance. Kasumi captured the way each subject moved, their habitual gestures, even the way they spoke. Her own speech was formal and rather clipped, but as someone else she could sound relaxed and colloquial or haughty and long-winded. Every imitation was an Academy Award-winning performance. How she could get all that from one little hair was beyond me. Kitsune gave new meaning to the word "magic".

We waited until the monitors showed the herald leaving the house, then left the comms room.

"What if he can't find her?" Garth said. "You know what Alicia's like. She's probably cowering in a hole somewhere waiting for the fighting to be over."

"Or she might even be on high alert because of Ben stumbling around out there looking for Blue. Who knows? We still have to try. Do you think you could possibly bring yourself to stop questioning every single decision I make?"

"I'm not—"

"Yes, you are. You and Ben are as bad as each other, always arguing and thinking you know better. I get that you don't like Kasumi, really I do. You've made that perfectly clear. Can we move on now?"

"Okay, okay." He held up his hands and backed away. "Just trying to help."

"Well, don't. I trust Kasumi, and I have no idea why you can't seem to." My turn to hold up a hand. "No, don't tell me. Between you and Ben, I've had plenty of your kind of help. I just hope Ben's latest effort hasn't stuffed up our chances now of luring Alicia."

He scowled down at his feet. "Ten to one he hasn't even found Blue. He's probably crawling round a lot of empty caves finding nothing but bat shit."

"Maybe. But he's a herald. They have their own ways of finding people."

"Do you want me to go look for him? Then you could stop worrying."

Coming from Garth that was a peace offering. "Why should I worry about a defenceless one-armed man with a price on his head wandering around out there on his own?"

Garth grinned in a sudden change of mood. "Young he is. Reckless is he."

He was a different man when he smiled. Far more attractive. The way his smile lit those blue-grey eyes …

"The herald says he can deliver the message," Kasumi said.

I jumped. Even with my dragon-enhanced hearing I hadn't noticed her coming up behind us in the long tiled corridor. From the scowl on Garth's face he hadn't either. I sighed to see that grumpy look back in place. He hadn't been happy since Kasumi joined us. It'd been nice to hear his Yoda voice again.

At least Kasumi wore her own form. Having my dead mother sneak up on me would be too much.

"That's good. You looked great in there."

A rare smile lit Kasumi's usually serious face. "He didn't suspect a thing."

She fell into step beside me, while Garth stalked on ahead, anger in the rigid set of his shoulders and neck. I was almost tempted to send him out looking for Ben, just to be rid of the storm cloud of resentment that poisoned the atmosphere whenever he and Kasumi were in the same room. And maybe to give me room to focus without my hormones getting in the way.

"We will have you on the throne before the day is over," Kasumi said.

"Let's hope so." That was the plan, anyway. I eyed her speculatively. "What will you do then? Would you consider staying on with me?"

Garth made a choking sound, but I ignored him.

"I would like that," she said, "but I've been away too long already. My children will be missing me." Her dark eyes softened. "Almost as much as I am missing them."

I would be the last person to stand between a mother and her children, much as I might regret the loss of such an ally. "I understand."

My own child shoved something behind his back as we entered the kitchen.

"I can tell from the way your cheeks are bulging you've got something there, buddy. Don't bother trying to hide it."

He gave me a crumb-spattered grin and held up half a homemade chocolate muffin. "Dave said I should try one to make sure the batch was all right."

"Oh, did he?" I gave Dave a mock-glare and he grinned back, as unrepentant as his co-conspirator.

"Lunch is nearly ready," he said. "Have you got time now?"

"Sounds great," I said, though I was too keyed up to have much appetite. This was it: the end of the road, one way or another. After all this time, the proving would finally reach its bloody conclusion. How could I think about food? But if we were facing Alicia in a couple of hours, it made sense to refuel. We needed every advantage we could get. Besides, it gave Garth something to do besides pace and scowl at Kasumi. We were all on edge.

Dave's cooking was a marvel. Even Lachie liked it, and ten-year-old boys are notoriously hard to please. I picked at some and pushed the rest round my plate while the others ate. Garth and Mac, predictably, went back for seconds.

"I want to be there too when she comes," Garth said, shoving his plate away at last.

"Well, you can't."

"Why not? You could put me in chains too."

"No one would believe Elizabeth would go to the trouble of a formal execution for you," Mac said. "Wolves are no better than animals as far as she's concerned. She'd put a silver bullet through your head and be done with it."

Garth glared at her. She continued mopping up her gravy with a piece of bread, totally unconcerned.

"Don't pull that face, you know she's right," I said.

"But Luce will be here." A note of desperation crept into his voice.

"And? You're no match for Luce anyway, even if I wanted you to take her on—which I don't." I made my voice coaxing, the way I had when Lachie was little and I was trying to get him to drink the yucky red medicine. "Come on, Garth, just a little longer. With Alicia dead, Luce will be back with us and you can finally relax."

The last couple of weeks had been hard on him. He was used to having Luce take charge, and bearing all the responsibility for my safety without her had taken its toll. He certainly used to smile more in the days when Leandra was Leandra and he'd never heard of Kate O'Connor.

Not that the last couple of weeks had been easy on any of us. Even Lachie, poor baby. He had his mum back, but he'd seen Alex die in front of him. At the tender age of ten, he'd been thrust into the dangerous world of the shifters, and found himself surrounded by monsters.

I glanced across at him, busy collecting dirty plates under Dave's direction. How would he feel knowing his mother was planning to murder someone in cold blood? For that matter, how did his mother feel about it?

Not as calm as Leandra would have. I hated being forced into this position, loathed the proving for setting up this whole hateful bloodbath. Kill or be killed. In millennia of so-called civilisation, this primitive hack and slash was the best dragon culture could come up with? Hadn't they ever heard of elections, for God's sake?

The whole shifter world was rotten to the core, with its violence and its feudal hierarchies. It was everything a human in a free democratic society abhorred. Yet even those at the top of the heap weren't safe. You want to be queen? Fine, just kill off your whole family.

Was any amount of power worth that much?

Now Dave had Lachie at the sink, drying dishes. He'd always tried to wriggle out of that job at home. I wondered what Dave had promised him for his help. Or maybe he'd learned to do his share of chores living in a boarding school.

That was one family member I'd do anything for. Even kill. Alicia's life didn't even budge the scales when weighed against his. It was more than kill or be killed. It was kill or see Lachie die, and that made all the difference.

CHAPTER THIRTY

In the end Garth accepted the inevitable. When the thrall on the gate called in to say Alicia's party had arrived, he and Mac and Steve retired to the comms room.

"Don't forget to search them before you let them in," he told the guards in the foyer as he passed. "No weapons of any kind."

"Garth. They know what to do. Get to your position." I shook my head. "You worry too much. I thought I was bad but you make me look reckless."

"You *are* friggin reckless."

I laid a hand on his cheek, by now rough with stubble. It had been a long day, and there was still a huge hurdle to leap before it was over. He scowled down at me, but I was used to his scowls by now, and I could see the fear that lurked behind his surly front. It shone in the yellow wolfish glint in his grey eyes. Fear for me.

He reminded me of Ben in many ways. Maybe that was what drew me to him. And it probably explained why they didn't always get on so well. They were both a little too alpha and determined to have their way.

"Cheer up. It's nearly over."

He caught my wrist in his big hand. "Well, excuse me if I don't start partying yet."

"Just stay out of sight. Kasumi and I will handle it."

I tugged on my hand but he didn't let go.

"Be careful."

"Always."

I pulled harder and he released me. Geez, why did I always seem to surround myself with control freaks? First Ben, then Luce, now Garth. Kasumi was the only one that took orders without arguing.

Thank God for Kasumi. Together we headed for the throne room. The thralls all had their orders: two would meet Alicia's party and guide them here. The rest were already spaced around the walls on guard duty, with two more ready to play the role of Elizabeth's personal bodyguards and two to be my captors.

Bear and his selkie companion, together with the remaining goblins, stood ready to play spectators. I'd taken a few moments to strengthen my earlier compulsions. It would be more than awkward if they wore off in the middle of the big showdown.

The only ones missing were Dave and Lachie. Since I didn't want Lachie seeing what was about to happen, I'd given Dave the job of keeping him amused in the kitchen. With all that junk food on hand, he had the easiest role of all.

Kasumi settled on the throne, looking every inch the ageing queen, the huge executioner's axe laid across her bony knees. Elizabeth's blood had been cleaned off it and its sharp edge glinted in the afternoon light from the open doors onto the terrace. She looked like some ancient goddess of war, one thin white hand clenched on the axe haft, a blood-red aura shimmering around her. Her likeness to the dead queen sent an uncomfortable shiver down my spine. Déjà vu, and not in a good way.

But this time the outcome would make it all worth it. One more death and I would be free. Well, relatively free. Not free to live the life I truly wanted. I stared at the ancient woman on the throne. One day Lachie would be that old, and I would have to see it. I'd have to see him die. See Ben die.

No, it wasn't the life I wanted. But it seemed it was the only one left to me now. And I would seize it with both hands if it meant Lachie did get to live to be an old man.

A heavy silence settled on the massive room as we all waited. The seconds ticked by. Why were they taking so long? Had something gone wrong?

I shifted uneasily, my silver chains clanking. One of the thralls held the end of my chain. It was only loosely connected to the main chain so he could use the length as a weapon in the fight to come. I was about to send him to check what was happening when I heard footsteps approaching in the hall outside.

Alicia entered, with Luce at her side. Luce looked the same as ever, her dark hair pulled into a no-nonsense ponytail, her clothes loose enough to permit easy movement. Luce was always ready for anything. Though she was still my enemy, my heart rose at the sight of her. She looked once at me, her gaze taking in the chains wrapped round my body, then turned her attention to Kasumi.

Two leshies followed them in and took up positions flanking Alicia. Though they bore no weapons, they too seemed ready for action.

Alicia was the only one who looked happy to be here. In fact she positively lit up when she saw me. Any fear she might have had melted away as she stalked toward me on her designer heels. She made a full circuit around me, her heels tapping on the marble floor, admiring the chains from every angle. They were looser this time, and I was holding my arms a little out from my body to keep them tightly secured. The game would be up if they slithered to the floor ahead of schedule. I stared straight ahead, trying to portray stoic resignation. My acting skills weren't anywhere near as good as Kasumi's.

"Satisfied?" that lady said finally, her tone icy.

Alicia tore her eyes away from me at last and gave her mother a perfunctory nod. "Where's Thorne? I thought he'd want to see this."

"Unavoidably detained, I'm afraid."

Kasumi's hands shifted on the axe, drawing Alicia's gaze like a magnet.

"Should we wait?" Alicia glanced around at the sparse crowd. "Somehow I'd pictured a more … elaborate occasion."

"If you'd prefer a full gala celebration, that could of course be arranged." Kasumi's tone was acerbic. "But I, for one, feel this proving has dragged on long enough." She held the axe out to Alicia. "It's up to you."

I held my breath. If Alicia chose to wait we were up shit creek and no mistake. There'd be no hiding what was really going on here, and we'd be relying on luck and improvisation, our carefully crafted plan in ruins.

But my sister didn't disappoint. "You're right. Time to end this."

Her gaze never left the axe as she all but skipped forward to take it. So much for Garth's worries. He'd been unsure of this part of the plan, concerned she might make Luce do her dirty work for her.

But Leandra knew her sister well enough for me to feel confident she wouldn't be able to resist the DIY approach. Alicia was a coward, true, but as long as there was no danger to her precious person she was only too happy to kill someone who couldn't fight back.

Axe in hand, she approached me and struck a pose like some avenging warrior maiden. It might have looked more impressive if she hadn't been wearing a tight pencil skirt with a silk blouse. As it was she looked like a rampaging accountant.

She laid a cautious finger on the chain that wrapped me, just to check. Dragons were such a suspicious lot. She pulled it back and observed with satisfaction the blister that formed and was then reabsorbed into her body.

"Wait." I spoke softly, though obviously there was no hope of a truly private conversation surrounded by all these shifter ears.

She shouldered the axe, a vicious delight twisting her pretty features into something ugly.

"Yes? You wish to plead for your life, perhaps? Oh, this should be amusing."

"You don't have to do this."

"I don't?" She stepped in, the chains making her bold, and shoved her face into mine. "What could you possibly offer me that would tempt me to let you live? You have nothing. You are a worm. Worse than that, you are a worm that's standing between me and the throne. Frankly, my dear, your situation could hardly be worse."

I was so sick of blood. She was probably beyond saving, but I made the effort, feeling like an idiot. I could just imagine Garth's reaction as he watched this from the comms room. It would be far safer for us all to kill this woman.

"Take the throne. I never wanted it anyway." Not strictly true—there was a time when Leandra very much desired the power that came with the throne, but now? Now it made me sick. "Just give me back Luce, and me and mine will never bother you again."

From the corner of my eye I saw Luce start. Alicia turned to her.

"Hear that, Luce? You're worth a whole domain. My sister here thinks highly of you indeed."

Alicia's mocking laughter filled the room, and Luce's eyes blazed. Alicia could force her loyalty, but not her love.

Kasumi cut in, still perfectly in character. "Must we listen to any more of this? Stop playing with the creature and kill it."

She, at least, felt no conflicting desires, no last-minute regrets.

"Yes, Mother." Alicia turned back to me with a sneer. "Never has obeying an order given me so much pleasure."

"It's on your head, then," I said.

She raised the axe. "No, I think it's on yours."

The glittering axe head swept through an arc as she took a back swing. The thralls on either side of me exploded into action. One drove his shoulder into Alicia's exposed midriff. The other attacked Luce with a length of silver chain jerked free from my bonds.

Alicia crashed to the floor and the axe went flying. I threw off my chains and lunged for it, but Luce got there first. As she snatched it up her eyes met mine.

"Help me," she whispered.

I punched her hard in the face and her eyes rolled back in her head. Then I pulled the axe from her unresisting hands and leapt across to where my thrall was scrambling away from Alicia as her form shimmered. No one wanted to be underfoot when an enraged dragon materialised.

She saw me coming and her eyes went wide with terror. I swung the axe with power born of desperation. Damn, but that blade was sharp. It sliced through her neck like a hot knife through butter.

Blood sprayed. I dropped the axe, panting hard from the adrenalin rush. Thank God Lachie didn't see *that*.

The door flew open and Garth burst in, Mac and Steve hard on his heels. He ran straight to me, careless of the spreading pool of blood underfoot.

"Are you hurt? Are you okay?"

"I'm fine. Check Luce."

Obedient for once, he knelt over Luce. She groaned, and he helped her into a sitting position. I watched, heart pounding. Alicia's death should have severed the binding between them.

Blood dripped from her nose. Oops. Maybe I should have pulled that punch a little. I'd probably broken it. Just as well she was a shifter. She felt it gingerly, then grinned up at me.

"What kept you?"

I grinned back, then burst into tears.

CHAPTER THIRTY-ONE

Garth shook his head. "You cry *now*? When it's all over? Women."

But he was smiling too, as glad to have Luce back as I was. I pulled her into a hug, and she stiffened in surprise. Leandra hadn't been the hugging type. Then she squeezed me tight. Garth patted us both on the shoulder awkwardly, so I dragged him into the hug too. For a moment we were our own little pack of three, drawing comfort from each other's nearness.

"I'm getting blood on your clothes," Luce protested, and she pulled away, still wiping at her nose. The blood was already drying. Anyone else would be sporting a black eye after a punch like that, but super healing came with the gig for shifters. No shiners for us.

Kasumi came down off the dais to join us, wearing her own form again.

Luce raised one delicately arched eyebrow. "And who is this?"

I made the introductions, and Kasumi offered one of her formal little half-bows.

"It's rare to meet a kitsune outside Japan," Luce said.

"I am the first in a generation. After a moon cycle we begin to sicken and must return. In fact—" She turned to me and bowed again more deeply, red-streaked hair swinging loose. "I'll go now and make the arrangements to have my sister's body returned to Japan."

"Must you go so soon?" I couldn't help the disappointment that coloured my voice. I'd grown fond of Kasumi, even apart from her undeniable usefulness as an ally. "It's Friday night. Nothing will be open now anyway. Stay and celebrate with us."

She laid a hand on my arm; a rare intimacy from her. "I don't begrudge you your celebration. You will make a much better queen than any of these others."

She cast a scornful glance at Alicia's headless body, sprawled messily on the pale marble floor.

I squeezed her hand, surprised to find a lump in my throat at the thought of saying goodbye to my newest friend. "I couldn't have done it without you."

She bared her teeth in a quick, savage grin. "Perhaps not, although you will never get the wolf to admit that. But I have done what I came to do, and my time is running out. The people who will help me do not keep office hours. I must go."

"I'll miss you."

"And I you. May your rule be long, Twiceborn."

And just like that, she spun on her heel and strode out. Garth watched her leave with undisguised delight. When he caught me watching him he quickly rearranged his expression into something less gloating.

"Strange," said Luce. "I've never heard that business about moon cycles and sickness before."

"Such a shame," I said. "She's amazing."

"I'm heartbroken," Garth said.

I punched him.

He barked at the two nearest thralls to remove Alicia's body. He, at least, was eager to start the clean-up and move on without Kasumi. Alicia's leshies had stood quietly as we spoke, surrounded by my thralls, who had them covered with guns loaded with silver. Now they watched her corpse leave the room with despair on their faces.

"What about us?" one asked. "Will you kill us too?"

"They could be useful," Luce said in an undertone.

That wall of weapons was coming down first chance I got. I was sick of killing. Sick of hard decisions too. I would be a new sort of queen. The adrenalin rush had worn off, leaving me feeling limper than a wet rag.

"Take them to the dungeons," I said to Garth. "You'd better take Bear and the other shifters too." My compulsions wouldn't last forever, and I wanted them safely under lock and key—not to mention silver—before they wore off. "I'll decide tomorrow. Oh, and give Thorne the good news while you're there."

Was there any hope of gaining Thorne's support now I was the last one standing? Probably not, given his views on "abominations". Something else to think about tomorrow.

"Sure." He detailed a couple of thralls to help and left the room with a procession of shifters.

"This calls for a drink," Luce said, watching them go with a smile. "I can't believe you did it."

"And cake!" said Mac. Trust a werewolf to think of food. "We should celebrate."

Personally I felt more like hitting the sack, exhausted from the stress, but Mac was trying, so I nodded and tried to look enthusiastic. She probably had no more real desire to celebrate than I did. Jerry had only been dead a week.

"Have you got the old crew back together?" Luce asked as we headed, inevitably, for the kitchen. "Steve and Thommo? What about Eric?"

"We've lost a lot of people." All the bad news I'd have to deliver sat like a weight on my chest, suffocating me.

As we entered the kitchen a small form streaked across the room and wrapped his arms around me. "You won! Good job, Mum."

His little face glowed, reminding me of the good news. My spirits lifted. "And we gained one, too. This is my son, Lachie. Lachie, this is Luce. She's a wyvern."

Her eyes widened. Nope, definitely not the Leandra she was used to. "I didn't know you had a son! Hello, Lachie."

"What's a wyvern?" he asked.

I had to laugh. "Don't answer too many of his questions. He's got a million."

Dave popped a bottle of champagne and offered me the first glass.

"Not to be a party pooper, but if I don't get a coffee in the next thirty seconds I'm going to fall asleep on the floor."

"Whatever Her Majesty commands." He bowed in a very over-the-top way, unable to keep the grin off his face. Glad to see someone was happy, at least. I flopped into the nearest chair. Wonder where Ben was now? If only he would walk in I could stop worrying. And then we could go to bed and sleep for at least a week. Among other things.

So ... I was queen. Finally. For me it had only been a couple of weeks, but Leandra had been working towards this day her whole life. And no, it didn't feel anywhere near as good as she'd expected. The price was too high.

Mac snagged my champagne and sat down next to me. "If you're not going to drink that ..."

"Be my guest."

She stared at the stream of bubbles rising through the glass, then tossed it off in one gulp. "I think I'll dye my hair pink. In honour of Jerry."

What did you say to that? Dave set a steaming coffee in front of me, and refilled Mac's glass. I raised my coffee in a toast.

"To Jerry."

Mac lifted her glass, her blue eyes meeting mine. "To all our absent friends."

I could drink to that.

The coffee burned my lips, strong and hot. I inhaled that glorious coffee smell and waited for the blessed caffeine to hit.

Garth stormed in, his eyes sparking yellow and his aura roiling like a thundercloud, dragging Bear by the arm. "Thorne has escaped!"

"What?" I slammed my cup down in the saucer. Coffee sloshed over the sides. "How?"

He'd been chained in silver. Escape wasn't possible—unless he'd had outside help. And why had Garth dragged Bear back here? My tired brain took a long moment to put it together.

"Ask this piece of scum. That thrall he took with him when he got the combination from Thorne was chained up in Thorne's place. Dead."

A contemptuous shove sent the leshy sprawling across the tiles at my feet, narrowly missing bashing his head on the solid wooden legs of the table. He gazed adoringly up at me, but made no move to rise.

"How did that thrall end up chained in Thorne's cell?"

"I put him there, my lady."

"Did you kill him?"

He nodded eagerly. "Yes, my lady."

How the hell did that work? I scrubbed at my face wearily. "You'd better start at the beginning. What happened when you went to get the combination from Thorne?"

"I sent the thrall in before me. I told him to check the chains were still secure. While he had his back turned I killed him."

Poor bastard. I didn't even know his name. I could barely remember what he looked like. Was he the tall guy with blond hair, or the shorter muscly one?

"Then I freed Thorne and asked him for the combination."

"But you were under a compulsion." I frowned down into that eager face. In this condition he'd do almost anything for me. It ought to be physically impossible to actively work against me.

"No, I wasn't. It had worn off by then, only I pretended it hadn't, and waited for an opportunity. I could hardly believe my luck when you sent me to the dungeon."

And then I'd renewed his compulsion just before Alicia arrived, leaving him all puppy-dog eager to serve again. Or I thought I'd been renewing it. Actually I'd been setting it afresh, which I might have noticed if only I hadn't been so damn tired and distracted. I looked into his smiling face and had to fight the urge to drive my fist into it. Stupid, stupid, stupid. Why hadn't I locked the little bastard up earlier? I knew the damn compulsion wouldn't last forever. I looked up at Garth. His aura flared bright with anger.

"What about the selkie and the goblins? Didn't their compulsions wear off too?"

He nodded happily. "Yes, but I told them to play along. Mr Thorne was very pleased with me."

I bet he was.

"But why did he give you the combination?" Mac looked as puzzled as I felt.

"Oh, he didn't want to at first. But when I told him you needed it to defeat Alicia he realised what a good idea it was."

"I don't understand," said Luce.

Well, that made two of us.

"If he didn't want me to be queen, why on earth would he want me to defeat Alicia? Shouldn't he be supporting her?"

"It appealed to his sense of fun to let you kill her and think you'd won. It made your defeat even more crushing when it came." His sense of fun. Right. Sick dragon bastard. "And he needed her dead anyway."

"But then there'd be *no* queen," said Luce.

"Oh, no," said the leshy. "The first proving would be over, but the second could begin."

"The second proving?" I must be more tired than I thought. I was having trouble following.

"Yes. Elizabeth's little insurance policy. She's kept it very secret over the years; only a handful of us know."

Were the rumours of a sixth sister true after all? But who would she be fighting if I killed Alicia and Thorne killed me? I rubbed my forehead, where the mother of all headaches loomed.

"Five years after she laid the first queen clutch, she laid another." He smiled at me as if he'd just given me a great gift. "You have seven other sisters."

Holy crap. That was *not* what I was expecting. Judging by the stunned looks on the faces around the room, nobody else was either.

My heart sank. Seven more sisters to kill.

"Of course," he went on, in that jaunty tone that made me want to punch him, "if a legitimate daughter had won the proving, they would all have been killed. She always thought Valeria would win. The second clutch was only a back-up plan. She and Mr Thorne were arguing about it only a few days ago. She would still have accepted Alicia, but he wanted her to initiate the second proving. He has his own favourite he's hoping to see on the throne."

Of course he did. "And where is he now?"

"With the young candidates. Whichever one of them manages to kill you will gain a great advantage in the second proving. They'll all be coming for you, and they won't stop until you're dead."

Lachie burst into tears. Bloody hell. I'd forgotten he was here. What a mess.

I went to him and gathered him into my arms. His little body shook with sobs. I stared out the window at the herb garden, where a perfect summer's day was fading into a perfect evening. A lone cricket chirped somewhere nearby. How come every time I thought I was getting somewhere, things just got worse?

"It's all right, Monster. I won't let anybody kill me."

"I thought we'd *won*," he sniffed.

Yeah, me too.

"We have. I'm queen now, and nobody's going to take that away from me." I gestured at the grovelling leshy. "Garth, lock him up. Luce, I need a proclamation to go out tonight. Call in every herald you can find. Tell the world that the Twiceborn Queen claims the throne."

If nothing else, that might shake the bounty hunters off Ben's tail, wherever he was.

CHAPTER THIRTY-TWO

Several weary hours later I climbed the stairs to kiss Lachie goodnight. Guards were posted, the house secure. The heralds had been and gone and the prisoners were safely locked away in their silver-barred cells. Tomorrow I'd have to decide what to do with them. Elizabeth's leshy would probably have to spend a considerable length of time in my dungeon, but Luce seemed to think Alicia's two could be trusted. I hoped she was right. It would be handy to have two such powerful shifters on staff. I missed Kasumi already.

I sat on the edge of Lachie's bed and picked pieces of Lego out of his sheets, moving them to the bedside table. "Time for sleep."

"Can't I read for five more minutes?"

"Honey, your eyes are nearly falling out of your head already. It's late."

He didn't argue, which meant he really was tired. He put the book next to the Lego and snuggled down into the pillow. He seemed calm again.

It was good to be a kid. If the grown-ups told you everything would work out it must be true. How nice to have that faith.

"Where'd you get the book?"

"From Mac." He yawned fit to crack his jaw. "She's nice."

"She certainly is." I looked up at movement in the doorway. "And speak of the devil—here she is. Come to say goodnight too, Mac?"

I stood up to get out of her way.

"Yes." She gave me a strange look. "Goodnight."

Then she plunged a dagger into my heart.

I staggered, then fell heavily, striking my head on the corner of the bedside table. Lachie's shrill screams pierced the air as Lego and books scattered. My head exploded with pain. I should get up. I should protect him … from *Mac*? What the hell? The room spun and my vision darkened.

No! Get up, get up! I tried, but my legs were jelly and I couldn't draw a breath. My chest burned like fire. I expected every moment to feel the bite of the knife again.

"Mum! Mum!" I felt, a long way away, Lachie's hands tugging at me. "You killed her!"

His voice was shrill and panicked. I struggled to move, to reassure him. I'd be all right. My body could recover even from a blow like that, given time. I opened my mouth, but no sound came out.

"Mum! Wake up!" Little hands pulled, desperate. "Don't die!"

Then bigger hands replaced them, and I heard Garth's voice, hoarse with shock.

"What the hell happened?"

He lifted me onto the bed and shoved something against the pulsing wound in my breast.

"She killed her, she killed her," Lachie shrieked.

"Mac, what's going on?"

"It was Kasumi. She attacked and then escaped out the window before I could stop her. She said ... she said it was bane leaf."

"Oh, God. Kate! Kate, can you hear me?"

I could barely hear anything over Lachie's hysterical screams. I'd missed a piece of Lego; I could feel it digging into my back.

"Get the kid out of here," he snarled at Mac.

No! It wasn't Mac. I groped for his hand, tried to explain, but my voice came out in a croak. I could barely make out his shape looming over me. His big hand caught mine.

"Easy, Kate. I've got you."

"Mum! Muuum!"

Don't let her take him.

The door slammed and Lachie's shrieks cut off abruptly. Had she killed him? I struggled to get off the bed, but Garth's heavy hands held me down.

"Don't move."

"Lachie ..."

"He's all right. Mac'll look after him."

"Wasn't ... Mac."

"What?" He bent closer.

My vision was clearing. I could make out his face hovering over me. Were those tears? I tried again.

"Not … Mac." My breath was coming a little easier. The pain in my chest eased as the edges of the wound slowly began to knit. "Kasumi. Betrayed us."

"I know. She stabbed you."

As he dashed a tear away Luce burst in. "What's all the screa—oh, my God."

"It's bane leaf," he said, a catch in his voice.

Luce's hand flew to her mouth. Bane leaf poisoning had killed Leandra once before, and started this whole thing. The agonising stomach cramps, the spastic tremors, the gradual collapse of the whole system, starting with the extremities—been there, done that. I knew exactly what it felt like.

And this wasn't it.

I squeezed Garth's hand. *Come on, Garth, focus.*

"Kasumi disguised as Mac." I gazed up at him imploringly. "Save Lachie."

I knew the minute he caught on—his face was a picture of horror when he realised he'd just sent Lachie away in the care of an enemy.

"Shit! Luce, that wasn't Mac, it was Kasumi. Get after her!"

"Bloody kitsune." Luce skidded out of the room.

"Go," I urged him.

"No." He tightened his grip on my hand. His grey eyes were bright with tears. "I'm not leaving you here alone."

He thought I was dying. I tried to push him, but he wouldn't budge. I may as well have pushed a brick wall.

"Not dying."

He rocked back, a cautious hope dawning in his eyes. "But … bane leaf."

I felt much stronger. "She must've been lying."

He picked up the dagger from where it had fallen and gave it a cautious sniff. All I could smell was the iron tang of my blood, but werewolves specialised in scent. To anyone else the infamous poison was odourless, but his sensitive nose wrinkled in distaste.

"Sure smells like it."

I tried to sit up, but I wasn't strong enough yet. I'd stopped leaking blood, but my chest still felt like I'd been kicked by a Clydesdale. He helped me to a sitting position. Well, half sitting, half leaning on him. I felt a hundred years old, my body shaking with the effort of healing that vicious stab wound.

"Then it's good to ... be an abomination. Bane leaf's not fatal any more."

Maybe sitting hadn't been such a good idea. My stomach started to churn in an ominous way.

"What does bane leaf do to humans?" he asked.

"Makes them ... throw up."

And then I leaned over the side of the bed and demonstrated.

CHAPTER THIRTY-THREE

How had I not seen it? Like they say, if something seems too good to be true, it probably is. Kasumi had seemed like an answer to my prayers, so I'd refused to see the truth, in spite of all Garth's efforts. She'd even told me she wanted revenge for her sister's death.

And I had killed her. I had no one to blame but myself.

It had taken me a good half hour to stop throwing up. I still felt nauseous, but I couldn't tell if that was the after-effects of the poisoning or nerves. My insides were a roiling mass of barely controlled panic. Kasumi had my son.

Kasumi had my *son*.

She could be doing anything to him right now, while I hunched in a chair in the comms room reviewing video footage. He could be dead already.

No, I mustn't think like that. It would paralyse me, and I had to stay strong. Surely if she meant to kill him she would have done it on the spot. Why take him if she only meant to kill him? There must be some other plan.

I'd questioned that fool Bear. My compulsion still held and he was only too happy to answer, but he knew nothing. No, he'd never heard of a kitsune being involved with Elizabeth's secret daughters. No, he'd never seen her before. Gideon Thorne might know more, but he wasn't privy to everything that Thorne knew. Bear had spent most of the past twenty years supervising the upbringing of my seven unwanted sisters, and had only recently arrived at court, which explained why I had never seen him before today.

So. If I couldn't find Kasumi, I would hunt down Thorne. The minute I'd been able to string two words together again without vomiting in between, I'd ordered Garth to call in Trevor and the pack. For a hunt I needed hunters.

Luce and Mac came in, Mac sporting newly pink hair. While Kasumi had been parading around impersonating her, she'd been in her bathroom with her head stuck under the tap.

"You even told me you were going to dye your hair," I said now. "Why didn't I realise something was wrong the minute she walked in with brown hair?"

"You weren't to know I was going to do it straight away," she said. "You had no reason to be suspicious."

I shook my head. Kasumi had proved over and over what a consummate actress she was, but I should have known, shouldn't I? It was a mother's job to protect her child. Where were my motherly instincts when I needed them?

"Did you find the car?" I asked Luce.

Luce had contacts in the police force. She'd passed on the registration of the car Kasumi had left in. I'd watched the security tape of her exit three times already. The black sedan rolled down the drive, waited while the guard opened the gate, then turned right onto the street. Easy.

"Nothing yet."

She didn't say the chances of them ever finding it were slim. She didn't have to. Four and a half million people lived in Sydney; there were a lot of cars.

I didn't care. I would try everything I could think of. I'd tear the city apart if I had to.

I hauled myself out of the chair, pain shooting from my chest right through my body. I may not have died, but that didn't mean I felt great. Even a dragon takes a while to get over a knife to the chest.

I leaned on the back of Steve's chair till the dizziness passed. "Keep looking."

He nodded, not taking his eyes from the screen. Kasumi's face whizzed past. In the foyer, in the kitchen, in the throne room. We were looking for anything out of the ordinary.

Clutching at straws.

Garth followed me out into the hallway. "You should lie down."

"I can rest when I'm dead." I sagged against the wall and shut my eyes. Bitterness overwhelmed me. "That shouldn't be long. Seven other sisters. Can you believe that? Seven."

Just when I'd thought I was home free. I'd beaten the odds! What a joke.

He leaned against the wall next to me. I opened my eyes to find him watching me, his usual scowl tempered with sympathy. He'd been right all along about Kasumi, but he hadn't even said I told you so, which under the circumstances seemed like a superhuman restraint.

"You know what the stupid part is? I don't even want the friggin throne. I just want to be left alone to live my life with Lachie." And Ben. Just the three of us. "A normal life."

He snorted. "Normal kind of went out the window the minute you met Leandra. This is it now. It's not so bad once you get used to it."

"I just want him back, Garth." My voice shook. "I need him back."

He pulled me into a hug. He smelled of wolf: of hot blood and dark moonlit nights, of fresh air and moist earth. I buried my face in his brawny shoulder.

"Uh … Kate?"

Mac's voice. I wiped my eyes, sniffing. She held her mobile phone out to me.

"What? Is it Trevor?" The pack leader should have been here by now.

"It's Lachie."

"*What*?" I snatched the phone. "Lachie?"

"Mum?" He whispered into the phone, as if he was trying to hide the call from someone.

"Oh, my God, I was so worried. Are you all right? Are you hurt?"

"I'm fine."

"Where *are* you?" I could hardly get the words out, my heart was hammering so hard. "Can we trace this?" I whispered to Garth.

He dragged me back into the comms room and began a whispered conversation with Steve, who skidded his wheeled chair across to another computer and began typing furiously.

"I don't know," Lachie said. "Some hotel."

"Is there a name? On a menu, or a notepad or something?" *Come on, baby, tell me where you are so I can come and get you.*

"I'm in the bathroom," he whispered.

"Good thinking. How did you get Kasumi's phone?"

"It's not hers. It's Dad's."

I froze. Jason's?

"You're with *Dad?*" Every face in the room turned to me. I felt for a chair, and sank into it, my knees suddenly weak. Last I'd heard Jason was overseas. Had he been in Sydney the whole time? Had he somehow discovered Lachie had been kidnapped and rescued him?

No, that was ridiculous.

"Is Kasumi there too?"

"No, she left to go back to Japan." In the background I heard a man's voice. "Mum? I've got to go—"

There was a crashing sound on the other end of the line, like a door being thrown back against the wall.

"Lachie?"

No reply, just muffled noises, then a voice raised in disbelief. "Your *mother?*"

"Kate?"

I knew that voice. I was tempted to hang up, but Steve was gesturing at me to keep the conversation going.

"What are you doing with my son, arsehole?"

"I can't believe it." He sounded genuinely shocked. "What does it take to kill you, for God's sake? That bitch told me you were dead."

"Hope you didn't pay her much for the job, then. Guess you can't trust anyone these days. Don't tell me you killed one of her sisters too?"

"What are you talking about? She doesn't have any sisters." *What the hell?* "She did a good job though, getting rid of Elizabeth and Alicia. Such a shame she didn't finish the job properly. My lady won't be pleased."

"Oh? And who are you brown-nosing these days?" My new sisters must be fools if they trusted this guy, after what he'd done to me.

"My new queen. Kasumi's gone to bring her over. I'd offer to introduce you, but she really will be very disappointed if you're not dead when she gets here. So I guess I'll be seeing you soon."

"Give me back my son, you worm, and I might let you live."

"Sorry, no can do. And now I bet you've almost got this call traced, haven't you? Shame about that."

He hung up.

I turned to Steve, heart in my mouth. "Did you find him?"

Steve shook his head. "I needed another few seconds."

I threw the phone across the room. There was a distinct cracking sound as it hit the wall. No one said a word.

Then I remembered it wasn't my phone. "Sorry. I'll get you a new one."

"No problem," said Mac, her big eyes wide. With that new pink hair she looked even more like an anime character than ever.

I swivelled the chair back and forth as I thought. At least my immediate fear for Lachie had eased. Jason was a dirt bag, but he loved his son in his own twisted dragon way. Lachie should be safe for a little while at least.

Garth came and perched on the desk beside me, but no one spoke. The only sound in the room was the hum of computers. The banks of screens flickered in a constantly changing display, showing the life of the house, but in here nothing moved.

"Apparently Kasumi has no sisters," I said at last.

Luce raised an eyebrow. "What's that got to do with anything?"

"Everything." I shook my head. I almost had to admire the woman. It was Machiavellian. "The whole thing was a lie. She set me up."

"Did Jason tell you she had no sisters?" Garth frowned. "He's probably lying."

"I don't think so. It was just a throwaway comment. So if she wasn't here for revenge, what was she doing?"

"But you killed that nurse," Garth said. "You're saying she was just some random bounty hunter trying to kill Ben?"

"No. I think that was Kasumi."

"What the hell are you two talking about?" Luce's dark eyes sparked with annoyance at being kept out of the loop. "You're forgetting I missed all this."

I sighed. "Ben was attacked by a nurse when he was in hospital. Some random human, with no apparent motive. We thought she must have been a secret bounty hunter until Kasumi turned up claiming that that was her sister impersonating the nurse. Said she'd been egged on by Elizabeth and Davison to do it."

"And what happened to this nurse?"

"I killed her."

Luce leaned forward. "What happened to the body when she died?"

I frowned. "Nothing."

"It didn't change appearance?"

"No."

"Then it wasn't a kitsune. When a kitsune dies, whatever form they were wearing dissolves, and they take their true form."

Garth grunted in disgust. "Wish we'd known that before."

A lot of things might have gone differently if we'd had Luce with us from the start. I'd missed her, but I hadn't realised just how valuable her wealth of experience was.

"So it must have been the real nurse," Luce continued, "and the kitsune was possessing her, the way Kasumi controlled Thorne in the throne room. In that case it would have been easy for her to slip free at the moment of death."

I nodded. "I saw something like a yellow mist leave the body when the nurse died. I didn't take much notice at the time. Things got pretty crazy. But I bet that was Kasumi, leaving the body. She probably hid in her hoshi no tama till we'd all gone, and then walked right out of there."

"And then she came to you and claimed you'd just killed her sister? That seems … an odd choice. She was lucky Garth didn't get all over-protective and disembowel her on the spot."

"Would have been happy to," Garth growled. "Still would, in fact."

I shrugged. "She said she didn't blame me, that I'd only acted in self-defence, and that her real beef was with Elizabeth and Davison for putting her sister up to it."

"Some bullshit about the knife and the hand that wields it," said Garth.

If Luce's eyebrows rose any higher they'd disappear into her hair and we'd have to send out a search party. "And you agreed to work with her, thinking you had her sister's blood on your hands?"

I shrugged again, a little more defensively this time. "She was very convincing. But if she has no sisters, it must have been her all along." In my mind's eye I saw the nurse brush past my chair again and knock my bag to the ground. She'd probably kicked my car keys out of sight, the sneaky bitch. "She meant for me to catch her in the act. She knew I'd be back for my keys. She *wanted* me to 'kill' her."

And to think I might have missed out on meeting the delightful Detective Hartley and jumping through all her hoops, if not for Kasumi's little set-up.

"Seems a lot of trouble to go to." Garth looked doubtful. "Why not just knock on the door and offer to work for you?"

"You were there, Garth. You know how it was. We were desperate for allies, but we couldn't trust anyone. Anyone could have been planted on us by Elizabeth—or even you,

Luce. This way she convinced me she was really on my side. Supposedly she had a burning desire for revenge, and I was the best way to achieve it. Convoluted, but it worked." Ballsy, too, I had to give her that.

"So she gave herself a convincing cover story," Luce said. "But what was her real motive? Is she working for Jason?"

I shook my head. "It's bigger than that. She wanted me to trust her, so she saved our arses a couple of times, like when you attacked us in The Rocks. But she was here to kill all of us—Elizabeth, Alicia *and* me. The best way to do that was to help me kill Elizabeth and Alicia, then kill me last. All of it was so she could destroy the succession in this domain, to make room for her real employer."

"You mean one of your other sisters?" Luce asked. "How would she know about them if she only just arrived from Japan?"

"She doesn't. And neither does her employer, which could work in our favour."

"Who's her employer, then?" Garth asked. "Not Jason?"

"No." I sighed. There was Lachie to rescue and Jason to deal with, not to mention Gideon Thorne and my seven surplus sisters. It would be kind of nice to locate my missing boyfriend, too. A lot to accomplish in a few short days. A dragon's work was never done. "The queen of Japan is coming to visit. She thinks she's walking in to take up an empty throne. We're going to show her she's wrong."

THE END

Kate's story comes to its explosive conclusion in *Twiceborn Endgame*. For updates on new releases, plus special deals and other book news, sign up for my newsletter by visiting my website, www.marinafinlayson.com.

Reviews and word of mouth are vital for any author's success. If you enjoyed *The Twiceborn Queen*, please take a moment to leave a short review where you bought it. Just a few words sharing your thoughts on the book would be extremely helpful in spreading the word to other readers (and this author would be immensely grateful!).

ALSO BY MARINA FINLAYSON

MAGIC'S RETURN SERIES
The Fairytale Curse
The Cauldron's Gift

THE PROVING SERIES
Moonborn
Twiceborn
The Twiceborn Queen
Twiceborn Endgame

SHADOWS OF THE IMMORTALS SERIES
Stolen Magic
Murdered Gods
Rivers of Hell
Hidden Goddess

For a full listing of books by Marina Finlayson, please visit the
Books page on her website, www.marinafinlayson.com/books.

ACKNOWLEDGEMENTS

Thanks once again to my beta readers: Mal, Peter, Geoff, Chris and Alana. Your feedback helped make this a better book. Special thanks also are due to the New South Wales Police Force's Public Affairs Branch, who very patiently answered my questions on police procedures. And finally, a big thank you to reader Dee Knott, who suggested the name "Robert 'Bear' Macadam".

ABOUT THE AUTHOR

Marina Finlayson is a reformed wedding organist who now writes fantasy. She is married and shares her Sydney home with three kids, a large collection of dragon statues and one very stupid dog with a death wish.

Her idea of heaven is lying in the bath with a cup of tea and a good book until she goes wrinkly.